GOLD
DIGGER

Also by Frances Fyfield

A QUESTION OF GUILT
SHADOWS ON THE MIRROR
TRIAL BY FIRE
SHADOW PLAY
PERFECTLY PURE AND GOOD
A CLEAR CONSCIENCE
WITHOUT CONSENT
BLIND DATE
STARING AT THE LIGHT
UNDERCURRENTS
THE NATURE OF THE BEAST
SEEKING SANCTUARY
LOOKING DOWN
THE PLAYROOM
HALF LIGHT
SAFER THAN HOUSES
LET'S DANCE
THE ART OF DROWNING
BLOOD FROM STONE
COLD TO THE TOUCH

GOLD
DIGGER

FRANCES FYFIELD

WITNESS
An Imprint of HarperCollinsPublishers

This book was originally published in Great Britain by Sphere, an imprint of Little, Brown Book Group, in 2012.

HarperCollins books may be purchased for educational, business, or sales promotional use. For information please write: Special Markets Department, HarperCollins Publishers, 195 Broadway, New York, NY 10007.

Library of Congress Cataloging-in-Publication Data is available upon request.

ISBN 978-0-06-230547-3

14 15 16 17 18   OV/RRD   10 9 8 7 6 5 4 3 2 1

This book is for two wonderful women,
Hilary Hale and Gill Coleridge.

Without them, it would never have been written.

PART ONE

Scene one

> Picture: *The back of a big, empty house at night, seen from the back through mist and fog: a gloomy scene, with a message about how money doesn't make happiness. Amateur painting, circa 1890. Not really worth keeping except that it gave such a false impression of the inside of the very house that housed it.*

'Come on Thomas, come upstairs and look at the view,' Di said. 'Look at the clouds.'

She hugged him closer.

'I'll keep you warm,' she said. 'Will you come with me? There's this painting I want you to see. Thomas?'

The warmth of him, the glorious warmth was fading by the minute. She was sitting in his lap with her arms around him, cradling his head with its shock of thick white hair, talking into it, nuzzling it like a cat. She stroked his profile, a beak of a nose, the handsome, furrowed forehead suddenly smoothed and by that token, the very lift of his face, she knew he was dead. She had known the imminence of his death from the moment he came in, gave her the flowers and then sat in the chair and closed his bright blue eyes: she had known it for months of illness, and all the same, when it happened, it was incomprehensible. Because he was still warm, and she was realising, slowly, slowly, that most of the warmth came from her.

She told herself not to be silly. He would wake up in a minute, give her the smile that lit him like a light from within and then he would start to teach, talk in rhymes or sing. Such a voice he had, such a lovely voice with a light rhythm, as if there was a song already in it.

'It'll be alright,' she said to him. 'Won't it, love?'

There was no answer. She continued to speak, stroking his hair, still thick, but so much thinner than it had been. She straightened it with her fingers and touched his ears. Cold, but then the lobes of his ears were always cold, even when she breathed close.

'A word in your shell-like, darling,' she said, softly. 'Do you know, you look just like a bird? All beak and chin, that's you, not an ounce to spare. You've been on the wing long enough, you're just tired, you are. You know what? That's good. You've lost your voice, that's all. But you can still hear, so you'll know I'll never say a bad thing about you, ever, because there's nothing bad to say, and I don't tell anyone anything ever. Any secret's good with me. You know me, I'm good for that. Can't talk, can't tell secrets, except about what a good man you are. Mustn't swear, you said, a waste of words, innit? Ok, Thomas? Shall we go upstairs and look at the view?'

He lay, sprawled and twisted, his arm holding her because she had curled herself into him, and he made no response.

She began to cry, soaking his jumper. Then she got up and bound his knees with a blanket to keep him warm, backed away from him, got a drink and moved, lurching around her own house like a crippled ghost.

Scene Two

I remember, she said to him, shouting downstairs in case he could not hear, it was a filthy night with wind and rain, the night I saw you first.

The steel shutters were ugly, but not foolproof. Ill-fitting, not the best made and thus able to be prised open, from the bottom up. Enough space for a small one to get through.

Crazy Di, aged seventeen, although rumour had her younger, was the size of a shrimp and she could do it alright. She was used to it, and used for it in these parts. Not a virgin in any respect at that time, all skin and bone and pliant as a worm, did anything to please – only they had not reckoned on either her conscience or her eyes, or how she would behave when she was inside. It had to be an empty house. Sometimes she would get jittery and come straight back out; other times, she was obliging, like someone out of Oliver Twist, one of Fagin's gang, the Judge said, who would steal to order, whisper in the right code and pass through the small stuff, as directed. *Just get the phone, like the one in the shop. Look round for jewellery and money if there's any, take it, but it's car keys we want. We're really here for the car, as well as anything else going. Car keys, OK? Just those.*

If she did well, (if I did well, the older Di said as she moved round the house) she was cuffed and praised and given stuff. If she got the jitters, she was left by the road. She aimed to please and she stuttered when she spoke. There were gaps in her teeth, and she never minded them laughing at her, those boys and the man who manoeuvred her through the shutters and all the same, for the first time, on that dark night, she knew that it was wrong. She had the morals of a guttersnipe, the eyes of a magpie and intelligence as fierce as fire, only warped for lack of words.

The whole thing was wrong because this time, the house was not empty. It simply looked it from the outside but as soon as she was halfway in, she knew someone was there; she could smell it. She had tried to pull back, but the man in charge urged her on.

I know this house; I've been here before. My mother used to clean here. Don't do it, was what she was trying to say, but the stutter made her incoherent and they stuffed her though the hole anyway and she went in like a rat. They could rely on her for silence and if she screamed inside, let out her weird screech; if she got caught; if she simply failed to come out within ten minutes, they would scarper and Mad Di would never tell. Even if she had the words, it would not have occurred to her.

Car keys, love. Keys for the garage. This old geezer has a vintage.

A what?

Never you mind. Find car keys.

It was dark in here. There was a single light in the vast cellar on the other side of the shutters, a distinctive smell of paraffin, some old heaters to one side and an untidy bunch of kindling wood on the floor. She sidestepped the pile and went on up the stairs, into the house, found herself in a labyrinth facing one corridor that branched into two sets of stairs and felt her way. *The old guy will have gone to London, goes there often.* She was remembering her route with knowledge they did not know she had. They really had no idea what this house was like: she did. It waved and branched and did strange things, it was nothing from the front, because it was the wrong way round with a yard at the back, and if you went up the stairs, you came into a wonderful room facing the sea. The shutters were shut on that room; that was why they thought it was empty; the old wooden shutters were as foolproof as the newer steel shutters to the cellar downstairs were not, so that you could never see a chink between them.

She remembered it well, Di did. She remembered this room. She had adored this room, with the pictures on the walls and the fire: she had sat here listening to the sea. Her fingers fumbled for the light switch in the wall, still in the same place. The same, big old phone on the desk.

The pictures in the room were lit, rather than the room itself. The paintings on the wall were cunningly illuminated, creating individual pools of light and colour. It was all too warm to be empty. She moved over towards the fireplace, not noticing the glow of the hearth, and looked to find the favourite painting. She shivered and squatted down abruptly on the old carpet that she also remembered; all that softness, all those colours. The painting of Madame de Belleroche, if you please, showed the lady lounging in a chair and showing off a hat, a haunting and commanding figure presenting a crooked finger, saying, come here girl, tell me all. It was a loose oil sketch of a beautiful, languid woman who knew how to talk to a child.

Hello, Di said, clearly, gazing at it. *How nice to see you.* She sank further back on to her haunches and stared in admiration. She could have stayed here for ever, looking.

Then a voice came from behind her, drifting from the far end of the room. The voice came from where the man sat in an entirely different pool of light, granted reluctantly from a lamp with a green shade. He had a broad forehead sprouting a mass of thick grey hair, could have been one of those pictures himself because he was worth a portrait with his handsome, symmetrical face, sitting very still behind the desk.

'It would be better if you went,' he said, softly and urgently. 'Please go, as fast as you can. You've got a minute or two, if you're quick. Get out while you can.'

The meaning was clear, even if the fine voice was cracked, she could hear how mellow and urgent the voice was. That voice. The light caught tears on his bruised face and the sheen of a scarf tied tightly around his neck. In the distance, from inside the house, she heard footsteps retreating down the other set of stairs.

(I heard. Not *she* heard. *That was me*. I couldn't move.)

She could not go, could not move; sat where she was, staring at the painting for precious seconds, then at him, until she felt the air move behind her. She glanced back and forth between the painting and him, seeing the stillness of his hands gripping the arms of the chair, the scarf round his neck. A door slammed, far away downstairs. She felt the rising tide of fury, recognising a trap and wanting to kill someone for making such fools of both of them. The wind battered against the windows.

'Go,' he urged her. 'Please go. *Run*. Get away. *Run*.'

She couldn't do it. She glanced back at Madame de Belleroche and her kind, haughty face, and realised her own failure. She had not collected any car keys, and she knew, at the first sound of alarm, that the others had gone. She knew a lot of things at that moment and still she could not move.

She turned towards him and stared. His fingers were drumming on the arms of his chair. There was something wrong with his immovable hands; he could scarcely whisper through the scarf too tight at his throat. They were coming for him, as well as her. The fingers beat a tattoo.

'Run,' he said. 'Run. Don't be killed, *run*. Please, run. Now. You've got the wrong night for staying alive.'

She felt for the knife on her belt and sprang towards him. Di was always handy with a knife. She did not hear the sirens because of the storm.

Later: someone made notes on what happened after that.

Despite immaculate legal representation for Ms D Quigly, aka Mad Di, daughter of absentee father and deceased mother, her sentence was severe. She was no longer a juvenile and according to fact, she had been willing to terrorise an old man out of his car keys. She admitted no remorse and apart from pleading guilty to this and other offences, was uncooperative to the point of being obstructive. The girl was a seasoned thief; she had clearly been prepared to strike and she was dangerous. During the course of her lucky incarceration in the safest place she had ever been, she perfected her considerable reading skills with books she was sent and was a model prisoner emerging a great deal more articulate than when she went in. The sentence would have been even more severe if she had actually inflicted injury, or if her father had ever come forward to acknowledge her existence. No other culprits were ever identified.

Raymond Forrest, lawyer.

No word, or the fact, of the knife, was ever mentioned, nor of the gloves on the desk or the footsteps inside the house, or the slamming door. Or the other person running away, or the freakish foul weather that that blew up such a storm that night that most of the houses on the front were flooded while the angry sea almost submerged the pier. Nor how, after Di was arrested, everyone rushed away towards the emergency, leaving Thomas alone.

A dark and stormy night: the worst in a decade, and nearly ten years ago.

Diana Quigly, now twenty-seven years old, with a dead husband sitting downstairs, suddenly remembered him and worried about him getting cold. She also remembered there was something she wanted to tell him.

'You know what, love, you really mustn't get cold. I'll warm you.'

She stayed in his arms for another hour. He was as thin as a rail, but his hair was so soft and he smelled so sweet, salty and clean.

Finally, she picked up the phone.

Scene Three

Picture: *an empty, yet comforting stretch of green, foam-flecked English sea, with half of the canvas composed of a blue sky and gathering clouds. A small boat proceeds with steady obstinacy towards the harbour it is going to reach. Rock pools in the foreground.* Adrian Daintrey 1938

When the ambulance arrived, following remarkably coherent instructions, she opened the door to them. She seemed perfectly calm, greeting the policeman, who had arrived at the same time, by name. The girl they saw was dishevelled with bad blonde hair and a body as brittle as ice. The initial impression she gave was not good. Too tiny; too fierce, too nonchalant and way too tough for eating.

'He's here,' she said, unnecessarily. The room was small and ignoring the old man in the armchair by a still-live, though waning fire was like failing to see the elephant. There was a side table by the chair, with a half-drunk drink and a cigar smouldering in a saucer next to it. The girl had brandy on her breath.

'Is he your dad?'

The first ambulance man went about his business. The room smelled benignly, of booze and cigar, like an old-fashioned pub before the smoking ban. It was otherwise clean, comfortable, ordered and contained sundry medical equipment. A kitchen led off: it was impossible from here to imagine the dimensions of the house. The room off the street was the size of a maids' parlour, a place where the cook would sit off duty in a period drama, ignoring the grandeur upstairs and the front entrance somewhere else. It appeared as if the Master of the house had died ignominiously in the Servants Quarters. The old man sat in his leather armchair, his hands on the worn arms and his head turned into the leather, as if burying his face in it. He had thick, white hair; his thin legs were crossed and his upper body relaxed.

'What happened?'

'He died, what do you think?'

She was diffident, speaking off stage to someone whose question it was. Jones, the interloper, was there, standing next to a man in the police uniform he had once worn himself.

'Went for his walk, came back, sat in the chair. Stopped breathing,' she said, almost carelessly. 'He's been very ill. I thought he was coming round. Is he really dead?'

They had been shuffling round, testing, moving quietly. An oxygen mask administered to the twisted head, and attempts made to make it breathe.

'Yes. He's dead.'

'Oh, thank God,' she said. 'Thank God.'

There was a moment of shocked silence.

'That his daughter, or what?' someone whispered.

'No, his *wife*.'

'But he must be ...'

The gurney arrived. The girl turned her back and finished

her brandy. The fire in the hearth turned grey and the room turned cold.

There were two of them left when the body had gone. Ex-Sergeant Jones and Mad Di.

'That went well, didn't it?' he said angrily. 'You don't say *thank bloody God*. And what the hell took you so long? Don't you know how it looks? The fire's gone out, you smoked two cigars, you waited two hours before you dialled 999. What kept you? Listen, love, I saw him on the pier and I watched him go. I was there, later, fishing, I thought he was alright.'

She turned a haughty profile.

'I was talking to him,' she said. She smiled a brittle and glassy smile that did not enhance her. He thought she was a woman who would only be beautiful when she was older. At the moment, she looked ugly.

'There'll be a post mortem, Di.'

'Whatever,' she said. 'Do you want a drink?'

'Yes.'

She nodded, moved towards the kitchen and came back with a bottle of champagne. Not right.

'A beer'd do nicely,' he said.

'Of course. What are you doing here, anyway?'

'I followed the ambulance. I was watching, Monica was too. I met Thomas earlier. I saw him go home.'

She swayed back towards the kitchen and he saw the belt, with the pocketknife in a leather sheath, worn at the back, like a hunter.

'Still got the knife, Di? The one your dad taught you to use?'

'What knife?'

He drank and paused and shook his head and looked

around a small room that he knew led on to many larger ones, the huge cellar he remembered from his own school-days, beneath.

'What you gonna do with all this, Di?'

'All what?'

'Christ, Di, you never did help yourself much, did you? Or maybe,' he added, because he was angry, 'maybe you did.'

He was looking at the big nude, noticing it for the first time and thinking that was perhaps the last thing handsome old Thomas saw before dying in his seventieth year. There were hundred of pictures on the walls in every room of this house. A little smudge of a painting above the nude was hanging crooked on a nail nearly out of sight and he could not understand why it was there.

Di stared at the dead fire and lit another cigar. 'Thank bloody God he's out of it. Do you believe in heaven, Uncle Jones?'

'No,' he said. 'Only in hell.'

If only she would cry. He looked at her, half pitying, half disgusted. No one would ever call Di a Lady.

If only she would cry. No one would pity her otherwise.

No one would pity her at all.

She had dug deep for her pot of gold.

CHAPTER ONE

> Picture: *Simply the sea on a calm summer day, regarded from above, as if from a window. There is a pathway by the shore with a single mongrel dog trotting along and a sense of someone outside the frame, watching it.*
> *Tiny, but atmospheric. Circa 1950.*

The Beginning. This was how Thomas remembered it. The last decade of his life had begun with the night of the storm when he had encountered Di Quigly, the thief. The happiest phase of his seventy years was the last seven, after she came back.

If she comes back after her release, Thomas, you must on no account let her in, Raymond Forrest the lawyer said to his client on the phone. *You are highly vulnerable, and yes, I have monitored her progress and investigated her past, but I don't know what she is like.*

Diana Quigly did come back to the house she had attempted to burgle two and a half years before. Inside prison, after two spells on suicide watch, she had stopped beating her head against doors, stabilised and counted not only the hours, but also the days. She did not go to the hostel towards which she was directed: lied that her uncle was expecting her and the lie was accepted. She was assessed as a wild animal tamed, personality disorders undiagnosed, no longer dangerous, perhaps savage when cornered, but safe to bet that her morbid, claustrophobic fear of incarceration would surely keep her on the right side of the law. She was highly literate for a thief as well as numerate and she had domestic skills that should qualify her for some sort of basic employment, such as stacking shelves.

Going back to the house of Thomas Porteous was as great a risk as getting in there in the first place and she was going to do it anyway. Di Quigly had nothing left but instinct and instinct drew her there. This town was her home; the beach was her domain.

To have called on Thomas Porteous after dark would have been rude and entirely against her strange code of manners, but as it was, it was a bright summer's day, the sea as smooth as ruffled velvet and the pier baked in heat. She had once been brown as a nut and now she was as pale as snow and when the sun touched her arms, it burned. She wanted the sea, but whatever else she wanted she did not know. Instinct ruled, and all the same, she felt as awkward as a snail crawling out from under a rock even as she swung her arms, twisted and turned, jumped and ran, making herself breathless with space.

She was twenty years old, small, strong and virtually starving. She ate next to nothing, could vomit at the sight of a biscuit or a burger, the staples of prison diet. Everything was behind the eyes: she relied on memories of places she loved. She had no parameters, no code by which to live, only pictures in her mind and the vision of a house full of paintings.

Di knocked on the back door, accessed by wooden steps over the same steel shutters into the garage and cellar that no longer incorporated a garage. It was an unpropitious entrance for a house which had such a fine, rarely used entrance on the sea side. Thomas answered the summons with alacrity, then stood there, holding the door, not certain, blinking in the sun that hit the back of the house in the afternoon. His eyes cleared and he stood up straight, recognising her, and then his blue eyes twinkled in genuine if suspicious pleasure, turning to real, unfeigned, incautious pleasure. She noticed how straight-backed he was, standing with his hands on his hips, examining her while at the same time his white hair was standing on end and he was acting older than he was, pretending a sort of dishevelment. Looking as if he did not know the time of year it was, let alone the day; looking as if he didn't expect her, while all the time, he had been waiting to see if she would come. It was as if they were both children and she had called round and asked him out to play, rather than he, the householder, greeting the thief who had tried to burgle him over two years before.

'Is it today?' he said. 'What time do you call this? I was wondering if it really was today.'

She looked at her watch, the only thing of her personal possessions she had managed to preserve.

'I think it's today,' she said, pretending to consider it. 'It might not be, though. It might be tomorrow. It *could* be the middle of next week.'

He laughed.

'This is Alice in Wonderland, where Alice meets the Mad Hatter, and he says, come in. So come in, please.'

'Alice wasn't so clever about time, either,' she said.

His eyes twinkled, the joy of a teacher seeing an old pupil he had liked.

Come in, come in. I'll make tea.

They were in the gallery room before she had time to think, as if he had been prepared for her and the kettle already boiled. There was a tray of china cups, a tarnished silver pot, sugar in a delicate bowl.

'I expect you've come to see Madame de Belleroche. Have you come to see Madame de Belleroche? She's been waiting for you, since ever she decided she belongs to you. It was you who saved her after all.'

He was gabbling a little, suspicion returning, the warning of his lawyer echoing in his ears. *If she comes back, don't let her in. She's not a child.*

But I am, Thomas had said.

She noticed the hesitation.

'I haven't come to take anything away,' Di said, handling the cup with care. It felt so different to a plastic beaker. 'I came to say I'm sorry I did it, and I came to say, thank you.'

He was prowling round the room with a teacup in his hand, stopped in surprise.

'Now that really is rich,' he said, 'You thanking me. You shame me.'

'I meant thank you for the books you sent me,' she said, quietly.

'I'm so pleased they arrived,' he said, formally, before beginning to prowl again.

'I'm sorry I couldn't keep them,' she said. 'No one keeps anything in prison. But I did read them. And I cut things out and put them on the wall.'

'So at least you got to look at pictures.'

He looked at her closely, searching for signs of self-pity and resentment, finding none. She was too busy looking round, smiling at Madame de Belleroche, looking, looking, looking, with wide-eyed, hungry wonder.

'Got a question for you,' Thomas said, suddenly. 'There's this new painting my friend Saul found for me,' he began, stopping short of it. 'Well, old but new to me, and I've been longing to know your opinion. I'm not entirely sure what's wrong.'

It was an oil painting in thick paint, showing a small child with tiny fists, sitting in an old, wooden highchair and banging the tray. The face was as angry as the fists and it was a powerful image from a distance, drawing her towards it with a shared joy in the wilfulness of the subject and the noise it made. Di put down the cup and moved towards it, noticing with something like disappointment that the closer she grew, the more lifeless it became. She touched the surface, puzzled by her own reaction, because against all expectation of this hectic, flushed, bumpy-looking baby face, the surface was smooth. She touched it again.

'It's flat,' she said. 'It shouldn't be flat, should it? He used so much paint. I should be able to feel it. Touch it.'

He nodded agreement, suppressing his own excitement.

'Yes, you should. And why do you say "he" for the artist? Why does it have to be a He?'

'Because it usually was,' she said, thinking aloud as she spoke. 'When this was painted. Look at the chair. Look at the baby's clothes. It's a hundred years old, or thereabouts.

19

Those days, lady artists didn't paint babies in chairs, they were too busy feeding them.'

She stared, closely, almost myopically, touching the surface with the tips of her fingers. He looked down on the back of her head, noticing her thin hair, and then he grinned. My word, she'd got it, she'd got it in one. That painting was over-restored, relined, flattening the paint to bland smoothness. He half knew it and she had seen what was wrong. He stepped back, close enough to tap her shoulder, keeping his distance, terribly shy and enormously pleased.

'It's still good, though,' she said. 'Still looks like an angry baby does. But it isn't quite what he wanted to do, was it? He wanted the paint to stand up and cheer, not lie down and die. It's sort of lost its own shadows.'

Thomas wanted to shout 'hurrah!' He noticed that her shoulders beneath the cotton coat were thin and sharp.

'Enough,' he said. 'How thoughtless I am. What can I get you, Ms Quigly? The sun, the moon and the stars? The touch of the sea, salt on that pale skin of yours? A good meal? What do you want to do first? Go for a swim?'

She had paused then, confused and dumbfounded with choices. The thought of being in that vast, salt water beyond the window made her faint with longing, and yet she did not want to move, yet.

'Can we look at some more paintings?' she asked.

'Let's go out first,' he said. 'And look from the outside in. It's a perfect day for a swim.'

Moving downstairs, Di noticed how he never closed the doors, how most of them would not shut properly anyway; how nothing had a lock except the door from the snug room to the cellar. She hated closed doors: she believed that if she was ever placed under lock and key again, she would die. She could not believe this was happening, and yet she knew it was, as natural as it was bizarre. But then, she had no idea of what normal was, nor did he. He led the way, whistling happily.

Outside the house, their footsteps seemed to take the same direction without any discussion as they moved along past the last of the big houses and away from the pier towards the quieter stretch of an already quiet beach where the shingle sloped out of sight of the path and the sea stood proud. Below the slope, the shore flattened out and at low tide, like now, sand peeked through an overcoat of shingle, shells and bleached relics of the sea. Wading into the water was automatic, as if they were pre-programmed to do just that, just now, both drawn to it, inexorably, obeying the call and the dictates of the day. There were few enough days as still and warm as this when the clarion call of the sea was irresistible to those who heard it.

She stripped off her jeans and ran in, the sound of the splash loud in her ears, the sensation one of burning cold, then fresh heat and freedom to scream. Thomas passed her at a fast crawl; she trod water and watched. He was a fine swimmer, as sleek and ageless in the water as a seal and she wanted to say: *don't go far, come back.*

That was what he reminded her of; a seal in water, and a nimble, long-legged bird on land.

He threw a towel round her shoulders when they sat on the bank, he being careful to keep a distance from her and her shivering until the heat of the sun began to penetrate. Then she shrugged off the towel, wanting the sun on her skin, and he handed it back.

'Keep it on, I would,' he said, gently. 'Keep wrapped up for now, or you'll burn.'

The sea, and that single act of solicitude, made her want to weep, and she gripped the towel closer. He had skin like lovely old leather and even then, she wanted to touch it to see if it was real. She looked down at her own legs and began to struggle back into her jeans.

'Milk bottle white, you are,' he said. 'Never seen such white pins. Perfect for an artist's model. Luminous white.'

She expelled the air from her lungs in a big balloon of breath in a moment of happiness so unfamiliar it made her giddy. There were so many variations of white.

'Could I be alabaster white? Chromium white? Titanium white? Or maybe something more like the colour of sand?'

'So many kinds of white,' he said. 'Most of them toxic. Such a struggle to find a non-poisonous white. What was it like In There?'

'Grey,' she said. 'Grey and beige. But I dreamt in colour. I dreamt of paintings and paint.'

'I do that all the time,' Thomas said. 'I need the sea to distract me from it. Give me balance, perspective. Thank God for Nature.'

Di knew no God, but she was briefly in heaven.

'Were you born here?' she asked.

'Yes.'

'Me too.'

He already knew she was. Both of them born within the sound of the sea, albeit decades apart, but with the same response.

'And your children?'

'My daughters? No, they were born in London. Never took to the sea, even in a painting.'

'Poor them,' she said.

That subject closed itself. They drifted back along the beach, retreating higher as the tide came in, both of them with their eyes to the ground, picking things up as they went along, the way he did, most days. Feathers and shells, shells and feathers, nursed in the towel as the sun sank lower and the breeze and the shadow took away the danger from the sun. He noticed how carefully she selected: she was starving hungry but she still had time to choose. Only the best shape, the cleanest white, the least damaged razor shell, the perfect conch, the stone with the hole all the way through, as though she was arranging them into something in her mind: as if they already had another purpose other than to be where they were. The rejects were gently replaced on the ground, waiting for another day. Watching her concentration, he thought she had the instincts of a true Collector, a connoisseur with an innate respect for the perfect as well as that which was less. She found a piece of flint shaped like a bird. No man-made sculpture could rival such a thing. There was a waft of barbecue smoke from a long way away. Her stomach made an ominous growling sound, audible over all the rest, and she clutched her abdomen in apology.

'Food,' he said. 'Food. I have food at home. I can grill some fish and bake some potatoes. Tomatoes.'

Her stomach went into spasm at the very thought of real food, but all the same, they forgot it and talked about paintings. Paintings on the walls, painting behind corners, paintings on the computer screen. Pictures which made her clap her hands. Photographs of children: she wanted to know about his children. Time passed. When they finally ate, she consumed it like a starving waif, and then she was violently sick.

*

23

Raymond Forrest phoned the next day.

'So, did she arrive?'

'Yes, and she's still here. Asleep at the top of the house.'

'Get her out of there. You old fool, Thomas.'

'No, I'm not.'

'She can't stay with you.'

'Yes, I know.'

But the weather changed. Rain in torrents, thudding against windows for two days: the sort of rain that defied movement out of doors and made it easy to stay in. It was August, but all the same Thomas lit a fire in the gallery room. She kept protesting that she should go, but it was weak protest, from a weak body, and she would fall asleep at the drop of a hat.

He worked at the computer in the gallery room. It was still a source of amazement to him, that he could view and buy paintings from all over the world. She hovered, sometimes, watching. *Do you write something every day?* she asked.

Every day, sometimes all day. It's a good thing to do. Here, try it.

She could use the keyboard, clumsily, then easily. Hers was such an open mind, there was nothing she could not learn. And when he was not looking, she talked to the paintings. *My, but you're a fine one*, she said to the Portrait of a Boy on the Stairs. *Don't you love your own hair?* He could tell that her hands itched to rearrange what she saw, make space for more; and he wished she would.

He was glad she had been so ill so soon and he thanked heaven for the rain. It gave him time to observe her and to acknowledge that she had not come back to blackmail him, although she still could. They never talked about the night of the storm; they talked about the house.

He found her in the big room, early on the morning of the fourth day, talking to Madame de Belleroche. *Look, now,* she said to the grand, kind lady in the hat whom she had just dusted with tender loving care. *Do you think,* Di said to her, *that he lets me stay just to see if I'm going to pinch anything? I hope not, but even so, I'd better go before I do. And what about his children? Why don't his children want to come and see* you, *even if they don't want to come and see him? Why don't they? Or is it just me who's the freak? Yes, I am a freak – bet you were, too, looking like that.*

He loved the fact that she talked to the paintings, as if she knew, as he did, that they were alive. Thomas had so quickly grown accustomed to her presence in the house, moving about like quicksilver: it unnerved him how right it felt. As long as it rained, and as long as she was weak, she would stay, but he did not want her to stay for that reason. He wanted the child who talked to paintings, and he wanted her strong.

On this morning it was bright again and the outdoors beckoned. She was wearing the cotton coat she had carried with her when she first arrived and her little bag was by the door. His heart slowed to a standstill. Di sensed his presence, spoke over her shoulder.

'My mother told me about the parties there used to be in this house. Parties for children, when it was a school, and then after that. Your father had parties for children. They were magic, she said.'

'My father was a headmaster who believed in magic,' Thomas said. 'And that was a long time ago.'

'You could do it again.'

The wonderful, glorious possibility of that, of filling this house with children, entered his mind for a minute, took hold and then began to fade.

'No, I don't think so.'

She shook her head. 'Pity, Mr Porteous, Thomas. Perhaps it's just me, but if I was magicked by this house and all the paintings in it, so would other kids, other people be. There's nothing different about me. If I could have kept on coming to a place like this more often than the few times I did, I'd have known there was another world outside my bastard own. So, I just thought if more people could see all this, love all this, for free, there might be a few less thieves. Kids need magic. People need paintings, don't they? Even if they don't know they do, they do.'

He sat down, impossibly excited this time. How did she know what he had always wanted? She was frowning, looking like a monkey, frustrated by her own lack of coherence.

'It's time I went, Thomas. Thank you for bringing me back to life. But I'd better go. It's not fair on you. You can't be seen to be harbouring jailbait like me. But, yeah, thanks.'

He made up his mind. Bugger Raymond, bugger anyone else. He'd rather be an old fool than take the risk of ignoring his instinct. There was guilt in the equation, too. She had already honoured his secrets. She seemed to have forgotten what else she had seen on the night of the storm, forgotten the cellar through which she came, and she seemed to want nothing but to exist and learn.

'You can stay as long as you like.'

She shook her head. 'You'd be branded a nutcase, Thomas. They'd reckon you'd gone mad.'

'I'm branded already,' Thomas said. 'I'm the freak, not you.'

'That makes two of us, then,' she said.

'We'll make it a job,' he said. 'You can be housekeeper. You can be my eyes. And if you're the housekeeper, maybe we can have the party. And if you're here, maybe my daughters will bring the children ... and, who knows?'

She was laughing at his excitement, feeling the infection of it, knowing it was hopeless. He stopped, breathless, smiling the smile that made him look like a boy. The man had such a capacity for joy, it was infectious, made everything possible.

'You're a Collector,' he said. 'That's what you are. A natural born collector. Look, stay for a few weeks. See how it goes.'

She paused, trembling. He waited, holding his breath. Then she spun round.

'Will you teach me, Thomas? Please, teach me.' She banged her fist on his desk, making a startling sound. 'I want to learn. I know what I love, but I don't know WHY. I've gotta learn. But shit, if I could help make your children come back, that'd be something, wouldn't it? Oh yeah. But I've gotta work, and you've gotta tell me stuff, 'cos I know nothing. And you know nothing about me.'

'Yes, I do,' he said. 'You have eyes, you have a conscience, and you're a Collector. You talk to paintings, as collectors do. I need help, and quite apart from anything else, I like you very much. That's all I need to know.'

She turned on her heel and addressed the painting at the far end of the room, pointing at it. It was another loose sketch of a courtly man in evening dress, raising a glass towards Madame de Belleroche.

'Did you hear that?' she demanded of him. 'Like *me?* Do you know what, no one's ever said that to me before. You know this man here? He really is a freak.'

'Recognise you, then,' he said. 'Like a true colour. A lake colour, made of dye, lets the other colours shine through.'

She stopped short. She wanted to cry, but Madame de Belleroche would not have approved of that.

'Let's go out,' he said, understanding it. 'Look at it from the outside in, again. Shall we go up to the bay?'

Di looked at him with shining eyes.

'The sanctuary? Oh, yes, yes, yes. I know the names of the birds, I do. I like the sticky little waders with the flat feet. Only you mustn't scare them, you gotta be quiet. It's their place, no one's but theirs, you gotta have respect.'

'I never did know their names,' Thomas said.

'Well, I do. I'll tell you. Hey? Something you don't know? Works two ways this teaching business, I can tell you.' She was grabbing her coat, and then she remembered and her face fell.

'Someone'll see us, Thomas. Someone will see.'

'Does that matter?'

'It should, it should to you. I'm the slag and the thief, and my mum's dead and my Dad's bad and I'm not what you call popular in this town.'

'And I'm the old freak,' he said. 'I'm the Pervert. The child abuser.'

She laughed out loud.

'Bollocks,' she said. 'Is that what people say? Oh screw it, then. We can go skinny dipping off the pier. And go bollock naked up the High Street. Go into Monica's and get our hair done in the nude.'

'A day of frivolity, then,' he said. 'And tomorrow, we learn.'

It was on the tip of his tongue then, to tell her. To go back over the night of the storm and whatever else had happened in his house that night, but that would be later. Instead they spied upon the birds in the bay, and made pies in the sky, she said.

From the pier, Jones watched them go.

They played like the children they were.

And then, they worked.

CHAPTER TWO

Picture: *A shop window with condensation on the inside of the glass, light streaming out into a narrow street. Busy figures half visible inside. A barbershop sign. After Edward Hopper, Artist unknown. Part of a series of shops and streets painted in the 1930s.*

It was months before anyone other than Jones noticed that Di Quigly was back, although it would be fair to say that few of them had noticed she was gone. The Quiglys had always been on the edge and well nigh invisible: scarcely anyone knew them. It was only the shopkeepers who remembered Di and her nifty fingers, and even they were slow to make the connection, even Monica.

On a grey October morning, Monica's unisex hairstylist opened early.

Delia was the oldest client at ninety-five, and spoke in a grumbling monotone. She still walked a dog, and it was she who had seen Di and Thomas Porteous coming out of the big house that she remembered as a school. Someone else had seen them at the station, getting on a train.

'Well, well, well. Thomas Porteous,' Delia said. 'Well, it wasn't a pretty story, but there aren't many of those. It's a story with holes in it, like a string bag, and where do you get a string bag, these days?'

Monica was putting rollers in Delia's hair. Tuesday was discount for the over sixties, including Delia, who thought she should get it for free.

Monica discarded a yellow roller too old for further use and picked another.

'That house,' continued Delia. 'It was a dame school, see? Primary school for the parish, started by some rich do-gooder. Got closed in the sixties. Old William Porteous and his missus ran it and lived over the shop if you see what I mean, and he was mad about education, education, education. After it shut, he got to own it, no one knows why. Maybe they gave it to him rather than knock it down, and people don't like that. Why should he get a free house? Anyway, he kept opening it up for kids. Had those marvellous parties, until they got stopped.'

Monica slowed down with the curlers.

'So? Why? What's wrong with having parties for kids?'

'No licence, or some such. Might have been funny things going on, see what I mean?' She tapped her nose. 'Someone said so, reckon old William Porteous loved them kids a bit too much and not in the right way. Anyway, Young Thomas was a war baby, toddled off to London as soon as he could, like anyone with half a brain did. Came back to visit with that bitch of a wife and kids after he got married and then later, when he wasn't. Settled here after his mum and dad died and left it to him, which was quite a surprise 'cos no one knew they actually owned it. And Thomas got rich, what with all his inventions. Not just a teacher by then. *She* must have been sick as a parrot, that wife, Christina, that was her. You don't leave the man *before* he gets real money. That's stupid. Should've waited.'

Sorting out fact from fiction was always a problem. Monica was fifty to Delia's nigh-on endless age and Monica had a vested interest in local knowledge, tending to believe in the senior memories. She tightened the last roller over the last strand of hair hard enough to make Delia screech and then loosened her grip, because Delia was a highly satisfactory customer, always ready to fill in historical gaps – whether the information was accurate or not hardly mattered. The hairdryer came down. Delia pushed it up and continued talking. It was a week since anyone listened and she was going to go on as long as she could.

'They reckon he was a bit dodgy, old William Porteous. Parties for children at his age, I ask you. As for young Thomas, well maybe he was, too.'

'It was only his wife said so,' Monica mumured.

'That Christina? Thomas's ex? Came in here, didn't she? Snooty cow. Well, she would have known, wouldn't she? Two daughters, she would have known. Come to think of it, she was the one who spread the rumours about old William too. Maybe she was wrong about that, but she must have been right about Thomas liking his daughters too much. I mean, look at it. He seems to like that Di Quigly and she's no more than a kid. At his age . . .'

'She's only the home help, Delia,' Monica said.

'My arse,' Delia said.

Monica smiled her sweetest smile and closed the lid on her,

thanking the fates that Delia was halfway blind and would never notice when Jones came in. She would find something for Jones to mend in her house, Delia would, and he was too kind to refuse. He was due any minute for the monthly trim of his hair and he always came in when business was slack. Monica and he were old friends, with old histories. Delia dozed and Jones shuffled in, still shabbily manly after all these years, but never the same without his uniform. Monica smoothed her hair and checked in the mirror. All that stared back was a middle-aged face and a salon in desperate need of a makeover. It was all so tired but never mind because Jones had news, and news was gold.

'So have you been up there, then? Have you? Have you seen her?' she asked him, trying to sound as if she did not care either way.

'Yup. Got a nice cup of tea in the best room, best china, too. Heart-to-heart talk with Mr P. No sign of her, at first, keeping out the way, but I tell you, the place was as clean as a pin, so I reckon someone's been hard at work. Then Di came, and then she went out. She's a bit wary of me.'

'Why's that, I wonder? You her mother's cousin, and all. You've always looked out for her.'

'Come off it, Monica. Her dead mother's cousin and the one who arrested her? She don't want to fucking know me now.'

She combed his hair, looked at his pink face in the mirror. He was always halfway to boiling point, Jones; every second word a 'fuck' and he no longer noticed he did it.

'Must have been one of the last jobs you did before you were sacked. Arrest little Di, you big man, you.'

'Only sacked in a manner of speaking, Monica. Prematurely retired.'

'Bet you miss it still, don't you? All that power.'

'Like a hole in the fucking head, I do. What power? I got more time for fishing.'

Delia turned under the dryer, fixed Jones with an empty glare and dozed on.

'Fancy Thomas Porteous giving Di a job,' Monica said. 'After what she did.'

She could feel his temper rising under her fingers. He was always so protective, and yet so critical at the same time.

'I reckon he owes her something. Her mum used to clean up there. And what Di did was all she was forced to do. Her fucking dad may as well have sold her to a pimp. Fucking Quig.'

She put down the comb and stuck her hands on her hips.

'Di knifed him once, Jones. She knifed her own dad. I'm not having you talk about Quig like that.'

'She was ten years old and he wouldn't let them take her mother to hospital. Besides, it was him who taught her how to use the fucking knife.'

'So *she* says,' Monica scoffed. 'There's always another story.'

'Like the one he told you?' Jones shouted. 'Di never told a tale against anybody, never did, won't now. Couldn't ever get herself off the hook. Fuckit, I'm out of here.'

'Without your haircut? Come back!'

The door clanged behind him and Monica cursed. Delia stirred. Then the door opened again. Jones was there with a scowl.

'Fancy a drink later?'

Monica nodded.

She was a silly woman and a good one, even if she didn't know it, Jones thought, and anyway not half as much a fool as himself. Shouldn't have got riled so easy at the mere mention of Quig and the way he knew Monica thought about him. Jones walked faster, scratching his head, wondering if it was really his hair that irritated, or if it was Di, or the word 'sacked'. Monica thought she knew everything, and she fucking didn't. They competed for information like a couple of spies.

Sacked, my eye: it was only halfway true and yet it rankled. He may have been disgraced for the many infringements that led to his suspension and early retirement, but Jones alone knew that he was still regarded by his police peers as an invaluable source of information. So what if his loyalty to the town and its inhabitants had conflicted with his loyalty to his masters; so what if he tipped off local suspects before others had the chance to arrest them? So what if he enabled his favourite pubs to flout licensing laws? So what if he spiked the odd dawn raid, failed to report the whereabouts of certain persons who came from the same streets as himself? Jones could turn a blinder eye than Nelson and sometimes a sharper one, but he was crooked in the right way and still trusted. Jones had never taken money for favours and the place needed a dedicated fisherman to watch over it and turn out to help if things got busy. There were difficulties enough in controlling this subversive, under-policed town from afar without relying on Jones. News was a phone call away and information was two-way traffic. Jones knew where the reputations were bogus on both sides of the fence and was the unofficial outpost of law and order, and long would it last. The chip on his shoulder was a mile high, but he loved the place and fretted about it – particularly about the people he liked and with a special soft spot for the kids; the ones who never had a chance, like Di Quigly. Also the old ones, including Thomas Porteous, for his quiet courtesy and his love of the sea and the fact that he walked on the pier, drawn to it on a daily basis. Jones thought of Di's father by way of contrast. Di's fucking Dad, aka Quig. One of the few Jones had actually wanted to put away and never managed it. He was rehearsing in his mind a memo he had once written about Quig for his superiors, trying to make light of it.

Quigly.B. Ex army, traumatised and altered by combat somewhere. Country boy, shit for brains, but plenty of cunning. Devoted to and abusive of wife and daughter. Addicted to violence; dirty fighter, found release by specialising in pest control. Cleared gardens of pigeons and squirrels, barns of rats, attics of bats and farms of vermin, before moving on to larger specimens. (Cheaper to get Quig to shoot and bury the old dog or cow than it was to call the vet.) Beloved by farmers for solving problems caused by inconvenient corpses. Moved on to the more lucrative business of disposal of humans, of which breed he never killed, but he always knew how to get rid of bodies afterwards: dead baby, granny or gangster, made no difference. Out to sea or into landfill; Quig could find a way, wherever he was. Quig's in the business of concealing human carrion, worldwide: also blackmail. He can't come home now, can he?

And yet he does, sometimes. *You're making that up, right?* No one had believed him. Quig had been gone for years. Bequeathed his only daughter to a gang of thieves, stood by and watched. Quig, who would always be homesick and afraid of his daughter for what she knew about him. Sounded like a good story. If only Quig really never came back, but he did; Jones knew he did. He snuck back when he could; he was there on the night of the storm, and he would be back again and Monica just might give him shelter. If only Di was not his daughter with such a genetic inheritance, and if only she was not working for gentle Thomas Porteous, that enigmatic man, rumoured to be a pervert. The man whose wife, Christina, had kept coming back to haunt him until she fell off a cross-channel ferry and drowned, according to records Jones had assisted in compiling. A man whose daughters hated him for that and everything else.

The pier hove into sight and Jones felt his spirits lift like a seagull in flight. He felt it was his duty to warn Thomas against Di Quigly, because she was her father's daughter with bad blood in the veins and a scavenger parent, and at the same time, he thought that he also ought to warn her off whatever she had in mind, whatever that was: couldn't be good. Jones had a penchant for thieves, especially those who refused to inform on each other, but they were still thieves. *My intentions are entirely honourable,* Thomas had said to him earlier, anxious to reassure as if Jones was a real uncle. No telling what Di's intentions were towards him; Jones couldn't guess those.

Fuckit: no one would listen. They were both damaged goods. Thomas would be all right; Thomas was rich and the rich lived in another territory where they took care of themselves. As long as it didn't go any further: as long as Di and Thomas didn't get basic, like have sex. Naa, surely not. The man was an old gent, and little Di had no tits. But, did Thomas know about Quig? And what did Di know about Thomas with his penchant for little girls?

Surely not, Saul Blythe thought. Surely not. Thomas has been effortlessly celibate for as long as I've known him: the passion goes into the collection, and so it should. And he shouldn't need another protégé; he has Me.

Saul never made an orthodox entry, loathed being announced and sidled in whichever way he could. Why knock on the door when you could manoeuvre the lock and gain the advantage of an unobtrusive entrance even when expected? He was standing on the stairs leading up to the gallery room, admiring the way the assembled paintings had been rearranged and listening to the merry sound of talk, drifting down. The sound was almost unearthly for its unfamiliarity. For all the glory of the contents, some of which Saul had enabled Thomas to acquire, and despite the sheer amount of vibrant life in the paintings on the walls, the house had become a sombre place in the last three years.

Someone had brought it alive.

'Writing something every day doesn't have to mean an essay. You excel yourself, Miss Shakespeare, but could you do it in rhyme next time?'

'No time, Teacher – I've got another job, remember, but I got another bit here, and that rhymes, alright? *Twixt Beatrice, Gayle and Edward/ There's more love than you think/ But never a bloody word of it/ Is ever distilled in ink. Please write or phone, or email, do/ Because the sea is missing you.* Shit poetry, but.'

'That should do it,' he said, 'But not yet, perhaps. What else did you write when I wasn't looking?'

'I planned what I would like to eat at a party if I was a grandchild. Stick to short sentences, you said, so I put: Lots.'

That was when Thomas laughed, *as if it was funny*, Saul thought a little sourly, subsumed with a kind of envy. There were two doors to the room, just as there was to almost every room in this house. He entered, stage left, behind them, always relying on that little element of surprise that was his stock in trade. He carried the pictures he had brought with him.

'Hello,' he drawled.

They were not touching, although they sprang apart as if they were, the two of them at the desk on either side, sharing a screen as if taking bites at the same fruit. Thomas leapt to his feet.

'Saul, you old bugger. How many days late this time? Di, this is Saul; Saul this is Ms Diana Quigly. I've spoken about you to one another.'

He had. She smiled at him, uncertainly. What a little mess she was, looking like a mongrel dog fresh from rescue and all in mangy black and smelling of bleach, in contrast to Thomas who was pressed and trimmed. Saul looked round, suppressed a gasp. The room was subtly transformed – the same as it was, but different. Light gleamed off dull polish: the colours of the oak floor, the carpets seemed to be enhanced, somehow, like the skin of the paintings on the wall, no longer as crooked or as haphazard as they were, but not entirely aligned either, simply shown to better advantage.

''Allo, Saul,' she said, wiping her hands on the back of her trousers. 'I'll leave you to it, shall I? Would you like a drink?'

Then she was gone.

'What has she done to you?' Saul murmured, sinking into a chair, gesturing to the room at large. They never did much by way of small talk.

'Ah, that,' Thomas said, without a shred of guilt or embarrassment in his voice, smiling at him affectionately. 'I fear she's reinforced my mission in life. I was always a teacher, and now I'm a pupil, too. I know the names of all the birds in the bay.'

'She's a thief, Thomas.'

'There's little to choose between thief and collector, Saul. Similar instincts, perhaps, so somebody said, and you should know. A reconstructed thief, let's say. To whom I owe a great debt.'

'What debt?'

'Never mind, and anyway it was you who always encouraged me to follow instinct, and that's what I'm doing. And condemning someone for being a thief, as if theft was a permanent vocation, is less than kind, coming from you. You're a born burglar, and you were trying to cheat me the first time you met me.'

Saul grinned, ruefully. Trying to sell an inferior painting to Mr Thomas Porteous on the naïve assumption that he was a nouveau riche, middle-aged idiot trying to buy himself a bit of class had been a big mistake, pointed out to him with infinite good manners in an encounter which had changed his life. Now he acted as agent, the additional hunter–gatherer for a virtual recluse as hell-bent as he was himself on finding the best and preserving it honestly. Finding great paintings, large or small, in mint condition, preferably untouched. They were in this together, however rarely Saul appeared and in whatever guise. He did not want a third party in on it, especially a female: he did not want his Collector to be distracted, and yet he could see the necessity. Thomas had been losing the will to live and now he had it in spades.

'That's a lovely scarf you have,' Di said, coming back with a selection of drinks on a polished tray. 'Mr Porteous says you're partial to gin.'

Saul raised his eyebrows. She sounded so like a parody of an uppity parlour maid, he failed to realise that she found him terrifying.

'Saul's bought some pictures on approval,' Thomas said smoothly. 'Shall we look at them together?'

'Mostly drawings,' Saul said, 'And a couple of oil sketches. I think our collection is short on English drawings. There's scope for plenty more, space to have a room full.'

'Oh yes,' Di said, nodding so hard her head looked loose. She had delivered the drinks and sat on the edge of her chair as if waiting for a treat. Saul turned to her, with obvious condescension.

'And what exactly would you collect if you could?' he asked her.

She sat with her hands pinned between her knees. Saul disliked girls who did this, as well as girls who were garrulous, and she was both, as if she had just discovered speech, but then he didn't like girls, full stop. Gauche was the word that sprang to mind; Saul didn't like it.

'Don't know,' she said. The hands were imploring, gesturing like windmills, irritating and endearing, prefacing a torrent of speech. 'Yes, I do. I probably like sketches, best. Sketches for oil paintings, when the artist is halfway there, trying it out. When it isn't fully clothed and ready to go out, when it's sometimes, like more perfect than the finished thing. Like Constable's sketches, I like them far more than the polished paintings. I'd have lots of sketches here, something to show how things get made, even sketches that show when the painter should have stopped, and said, that's enough.'

The speech got faster and faster until she stopped, hesitating in embarrassment, pausing to think and then rushing on.

'I suppose I like the rejects. I'd like to have been there, in the studio, picking up the stuff left on the floor. Sometimes the best version gets thrown away.'

Saul raised an eyebrow.

'How on earth have you managed to see Constable's sketches?'

She was flustered.

'In a book. And we went to the museum, in London.'

'Are you particularly fond of Constable?' Saul asked. She shook her head, emphatically.

'No, no more than anyone else, I haven't got favourites, but I do like his sketches and the portraits. Personal things.'

'Well,' Saul said, looking at Thomas with a gleam in his eye. 'I've got something for a Constable fan.'

He reached into the large bag he had placed by his seat and withdrew a small panel of wood. Thomas took it from him, moved over to the desk to look at it under the light. Di could not resist looking at it over his shoulder. Saul noticed that they almost touched, but not quite, wondered which of them it was who resisted it.

The panel was obscured by dark varnish with a greenish tinge, allowing the emergence from behind the surface of a figure of a girl in a dull, brown dress sitting in a chair that might have been upholstered in red beneath the murk. She was intent on reading the book she held, ignoring the light from the window on her left. There were visible highlights of white on her forehead, on the collar of her dress and on the edges of the pages of the book. Thomas turned the panel over, breathing deeply. There was a name scratched on the back. *John Constable RA.*

'Oh, clever Saul. John Constable, the younger. The son who could paint like his father. A picture after my own heart. Great minds think alike, Saul.'

He turned the panel back. Di reached out and touched the surface of the paint, tentatively. She had sensitive fingers and bitten nails, Saul noticed.

'Oh,' she said. 'Oh, oh, oh, oh.'

Saul smiled his sedulous smile, revealing his perfect white teeth.

'Wouldn't you like to clean it up?' he said. 'I mean, that's what you do, isn't it? Clean?'

She looked at him without hostility. She either did not notice his sarcastic condescension, or chose to ignore it. She was gripped by the moment. She nodded.

'Just a bit,' she said. 'Not much.'

'You could try,' Saul said. 'Mainly nicotine, I think. A most benign sort of filth, almost a preservative. If you're going to pollute a painting with anything, smoke around it. Acts as a barrier.'

Thomas sat back and lit a cigar.

'A bit of mild washing liquid on an almost dry cloth won't do any damage,' Saul said.

She smiled at him, completely unoffended by his tone, made a swift bow and bore the panel away.

They sat up late, Thomas and Saul. Diplomatically, Di did not come back.

'Might she stay up until midnight, admiring that thing?' Saul asked.

'Easily.'

'Will she damage it?'

'Never. But she will work out what it's made of. And she'll treasure it more because it isn't valuable. She doesn't do values, not financial values anyway. Tonal values, another matter.'

'Quite a find then, your little thief. Are you sure she isn't just echoing you? Liking sketches, liking the lesser as much as the greater? Not giving a hoot about who painted it as long as it's good?'

Thomas considered. He looked younger than when Saul had seen him last, as if he were shedding years rather than acquiring months. His dear daughters would not be pleased to hear that.

'She is no one's echo, she is herself. She dislikes things as virulently as she loves them. We don't always agree. Please don't call her a thief.'

'Alright, I won't, but I know how she came here first. To steal.'

'You don't know, Saul. She came here long before that.'

Saul raised his hands in surrender.

'You wouldn't respect me if I didn't warn you, Thomas. This place may be a temporary refuge for now, but she's still a thief. Maybe she's worming her way into your affections,' he emphasised the word *worming*, 'with a view to isolating you?'

Thomas lit another cigar. These little cigars were an unadulterated pleasure that Di had come to share. *You could buy a lot with one of these in prison*, she said.

'On the contrary,' Thomas said. 'She finds the idea of split families abhorrent. She's sorry for them having a mother who died. The idea is to have a party for the grandchildren. The sort of party that used to be given here. She's planning it.'

Saul whistled through his perfect white teeth and adjusted the crease in his trousers, meticulously.

'Oh, Thomas love, is that really a good idea?'

'I hope so, because I would so like it to happen. We have rather frozen luncheon meetings in London where the boys are terribly well behaved. Even the duty visits here stopped after Christina ... disappeared.'

'After Christina drowned,' Saul said. 'After she drowned

45

on her way to France, on a detour that might have ended up with her coming to visit you, scrounging again. I keep in touch, as you asked. At one remove. And I don't think getting them to come here is a good idea.' *They will simply come to put a value on everything, make them greedier than ever.*

'It's the children,' Thomas said, sadly. 'Their children. I would like them to see me for what I am. A silly old man who wears silly hats and does magic tricks, that's how I'd like to be remembered. I want them to have fun. They don't seem to have much of that. Patrick loved it here. Patrick needs nurture.'

Saul did not say, your two daughters wish you were ten years older than you are so that you would die sooner. You criticised a man's children only at your own peril. They are desperate, and Edward, the husband of one of them, is more odious and dominant than the two together. And the existence of a housekeeper/protégée, unless such a person was an ancient crone, would not improve things at all, but Thomas would do what Thomas would do. He had a terrible naïveté about his daughters, forgetting that most of their genetic identity had come from their mother who had been, in Saul's eyes, insanely possessive and envious. She was the one who took her daughters away to a richer man when they were both under ten, when Thomas was not rich at all: she was the one who denied him access and spread the self-justifying legend of his sinister propensities as well the legend of being abandoned herself. The one who reinvented her own persona again and again, self-deluding, jealous bitch and a lousy artist to boot.

Saul's opinion of the fairer sex carried a distinct prejudice: his affections were confined to men, apart from his sister, but even taking all that into account, Christina had been dangerously manipulative and prone to violence. And there was Thomas, the innocent, who still hoped his daughters would change into people who shared his values. It was not going to happen. Their minds were addled and worst of all, they had no taste.

'If anything happens to me whilst Di is still here, you won't let her get locked up again, will you? It would kill her.'

Thomas said it suddenly, as if it was something he had only just understood. It came out of the blue and in a moment of petulant suspicion, Saul wished that something would simply eradicate Di, like rubbing out a line of a pencil drawing. Then he reprimanded himself, because after all, he did not want Thomas to return to his life of quiet desperation. He wanted him happy.

'A Paragon, she is, this Diana,' he said. 'So tell me, what are her real virtues?'

He was thinking that perhaps Thomas wanted the same from the girl as he did from the paintings he collected. He wanted them raw, untouched, unrestored, authentic and with a protective layer of sheer dirt.

'Di? She sees things. She never stops looking. She's intelligent, she's obsessive and she's kind.'

It left out the whole issue of the intense mutual attraction which they were both denying, and all the same Saul was impressed, although it did not do as an answer.

'And her family? What do they think?'

Thomas hesitated, reluctant to discuss what was secret.

'The only real relative is her father, someone she holds in revulsion, and a man once infamous in these parts, but no longer resident. No longer here. Tell me about mine, Saul. How are they really?'

Beyond hope, Saul thought, but did not say. *Edward, your*

*elder daughter's husband, is teaching himself about art in order to
turn your collection into money as soon as allowed.*

'They're well,' he said.

He stretched his feet towards the fire and wondered what
spring would bring. And when, if ever, these two would
notice what was happening to them. They were melding, like
ivy on a wall.

Later that month, or was it the next, when the wind rose and
the draughts whistled, Di got herself locked into the laundry
room on the first floor. It had one door only, with a catchy
lock, and when she couldn't get out, she screamed and hurled
herself against the walls so hard she was covered in bruises.
When Thomas found her, he held her tight until she made
him let her go. Later still, when she saw him weeping at his
desk, she went in to him and held him. They sat and talked
about how, when the house was open to all, there would be
no locks on any doors, and no barriers against touching precious things. It would not be that kind of house.

And they talked about the night of the storm. And the
parties there used to be, and would be again.

Chapter Three

Scene. *Family Portrait of two daughters, then in their twenties, one slender and elegant, the other plump with flyaway hair, their three sons sitting between them. A garish portrait in acrylic paint, in which all the sitters, bar one, look unwilling. The smallest child is absorbed in some activity: the other two fidget.*

Painted by Christina Porteous, amateur artist. A painting for hiding in the attic.

It was the spring of the year after Diana Quigly returned to the house of Thomas Porteous, Collector of pictures and Inventor of games.

Gayle and Beatrice, the two daughters of Thomas, now in their late thirties, sat on the same sofa where they had sat to indulge their mother's desire to capture them in paint some years before. Patrick was the only child this time, sitting on the floor near his mother's feet. Gayle nudged him aside with her foot and he scuttled across the room out of the way of her exasperation. Edward, Patrick's father, Gayle's husband, sat facing the women as if chairing a meeting. He was, without doubt, the head of the family.

'He wants us to bring the children down for a party,' Gayle said in her calm voice. 'To leave them at the door for tea with him and a chaperone, amuse ourselves, and come back later for supper. How desperately inconvenient. Why should we?'

'To keep him sweet,' Edward said.

'To mourn our mother,' Beatrice said in her sing-song voice, which irritated Edward. 'To remind him what he owes us. To make him feel like shit.'

'To spy out the land,' Edward said. 'To see what else he's acquired with *your* money.'

'*Our* money,' Gayle said sweetly, looking him straight in the eye.

'I like parties,' Patrick muttered from the floor, and then kept quiet. Edward and Gayle kept him close. He was small for his age, looking more like five than eight. Gayle was lost in thought, remembering the house by the sea she had visited as a child, and latterly only with reluctance, taking Patrick at her own mother's insistence. There was a niggling, older memory of a party with fancy dress, something that eluded her. Patrick loving the place when he could scarcely walk, when he and his cousins, Alan and Edmund, were towed to visit Grandad.

'We don't have to go and see him,' Beatrice said. 'We can just continue to have lunch in London every now and then, let him give us presents. We don't need to keep him sweet. His conscience should do that. He's going to look after us once he's dead. He made his will long since, Raymond Forrest said. We don't need to risk the children. I can't bear them to be near him.'

'There's no risk to the children,' Edward said, angrily. 'They're boys, not little girls, and he's an old man. We should go. Besides, I need to look at the house. Do a little revaluation.'

'I wonder what he means by a chaperone,' Gayle said. 'I wonder what he means by a party. I wonder what he's trying to resurrect and who he's trying to impress.'

'I wish he was dead,' Beatrice said. Patrick put his hands over his ears and rocked gently. He was an insignificant presence, always engaged in small, constant movement as if his fingers itched, however still he seemed. They appeared to assume that since he was generally so silent, he could not hear, either. He wanted to go to a party by the sea: Grandpa knew they never went to parties, and the fact that his parents might refuse the invitation filled him with despair.

'He killed our mother,' Beatrice intoned. 'Abandoned us and killed her.' She was usually over-dramatic, designed for martyrdom and always, it seemed to Edward, about to burst forth in a stream of malice disguised as a hymn of moral outrage.

The portrait of them all was in Gayle's home. For the moment, they were gathered in a small studio flat in Clerkenwell, a pied-à-terre owned by their father and frequented, in clandestine fashion, by their mother, Christina, before her disappearance. It was here that the evidence was found to unravel what was in Edward's eyes her timely death. Receipts for prepaid tickets for a cross-channel ferry to which she was bound in pursuit of yet another lover or another kind of fortune, or maybe, cheap booze. Jumping or falling over the side was the best thing she could have done to save him from her constant rants on the subject of life's injustices and the perfidy of his father-in-law, who had ruined her life and her potential, blah, blah, blah. Gayle smiled at her husband, in a slight warning to hold his tongue and refrain from telling Beatrice that it was no wonder her husband had left her in her own herbal soup. She smelled of patchouli, dressed in sackcloth and her two sons were each twice the size of his only one.

'We'll go,' Gayle announced, forestalling her self-righteous sister. 'To keep the peace, we'll go.'

'No peace for the wicked,' Beatrice sang. 'I suppose he'll invite other children, to meet ours. He wants to show us something. He wants to show us up. He's courting us.'

'He's courting our children,' Gayle said.

It was almost summer when they delivered the children for the party with the chaperone. Patrick would remember it forever, but then Patrick was the eldest and knew his grandfather in a way no one else did. Patrick had been here before, like his superior cousins who scarcely remembered and never noticed anything anyway.

It was wicked, that party. There was a tent of shiny turquoise material in the centre of the big room, reaching from floor to ceiling, flickering lights on the walls and inside the tent, a tea party laid out on a low table covered with a white cloth. There were pink and yellow cakes and crisps and sweets and other things. The table was surrounded by cushions and resplendent on the biggest of these, facing the draped entrance to the tent, sat a large green frog, eating a sandwich. He had friendly eyes, this frog, and a nice voice.

'Delicious!' the Frog said. 'Will you come and join me for tea once you're dressed? Only in Fairyland, we like to dress specially for tea.'

He took off his soft frog helmet and put on a red fez, and

there was Grandpa in a green coat with long white hair sticking out of his hat and over his collar and he was accompanied by a small witch with wild hair, who encouraged them towards a mountain of soft, rich clothes, including rings, beads, crowns, tiaras for the three girls, crowns and helmets for the boys. They put them on over what they wore, emerging from the spangled heap as princesses with rings on fingers and princes with hats on heads. *That one's better*, said the pretty little witch, *try that*, and he did. Then they sat with the King Frog, who still wore his fez and his green cloak, who told them stories and sang them songs until they were singing, too. They ate and sang and sang and ate, and did races round the room where everyone managed to win and saw themselves reflected in their finery in a mirror on the wall, and yelled and laughed and laughed. Then Grandad did his magic tricks, which made them quiet for a while, and then they played another game where they had to turn away and draw each others' faces on paper the witch gave them, fold up the paper and put it in a pot, and each of them pull one out and guess whose face it was. And then the witch got them playing again. Then the Auntie of the three girls who was called Monica came to collect them, and she laughed, too, and took them home still in their adorning garments which they were told by the witch they must keep, and yet the Auntie lingered, watching the King Frog waving goodbye from his seat and telling them, *don't ever be sad* and they said, *no, never*.

Then it crashed: the whole thing crashed.

Beatrice came back early to collect her sons, just as the little girls stumbled downstairs in assorted garments and pushed across her path on the stairs. She saw three *common* little girls pulling coats over petticoats, blowing bubbles and waving feathers, drunk with fatigue, being led away by a woman who smelled of heavy perfume with a fierce face and overdone hair who was lighting a cigarette as she went. The woman nodded and smiled through crimson lips. Beatrice had an abhorrence of smoke and lipstick. When Beatrice entered the room, she saw a scene of depravity and reacted with horror. Not only were there scruffy little girls who had clearly undressed, there were her boys, flopped on the floor, wearing silly clothes, filthy and exhausted. They were playing dead. She pulled at them, hissed at them, come away, come away now and shouted for Gayle, who followed her. Gayle came in behind and saw an almighty mess, a scene of carnage, loud colours, fabric trampled into the floor, and a pretty girl dressed in a tattered cloak, who was breathless from running round and who bowed towards her. There was rouge on the girl's cheeks and black lines round her mischievous eyes. She looked like a precocious and knowing child. Mess was anathema to Gayle: she hated mess: it was tantamount to losing control and Gayle never lost control.

''Allo,' Di said. 'You aren't taking him away yet, are you? The others are playing at being dead.'

Patrick was clutching at her tattered cloak and looking at her adoringly. He had a pencil stuck behind his ear; his spectacles looked as if someone had knocked them sideways and his mouth was smeared with chocolate.

'I did drawing, Mummy. I did . . . ' He stopped.

'We got supper a bit later,' the pretty Witch said. 'Once we've cleaned up a bit, eh, Patrick?'

She wiped his chocolatey face with the hem of the cloak. Gayle touched her own white linen jacket and shuddered.

'I think not,' she said in her calm, deep voice, looking her up and down and down and up, until Patrick detached his hand from the material of the cloak and let it fall. 'What on earth do you think you're doing? They're filthy. My child is filthy.' *And as happy as I have ever seen him.*

'I was wearing them out, I thought,' Di said, cheerfully. 'You can't go yet. Come on in. We've had a lot of fun and your dad's dying to see you.'

'Dying? How sad.' Beatrice murmured, not quite inaudibly, glancing across the room to the tent. 'Look at what you've done, Father. You've got them drunk. Poisoned them. They're behaving like drunks.'

'Not *drunk*,' Di said, stung. 'But we did get a bit excited. I thought that was the whole idea.'

Alan, the youngest cousin, took his cue from his mother, stood up and began to sniffle. Edmund began to whine.

'Who are you?' Beatrice hissed at Di.

'I'm the housekeeper.'

'Really?'

Beatrice pulled her two towards the exit and Gayle followed. The room emptied. Patrick saw his grandfather sitting with his head in his hands; remembered trying to go back and kiss him and waving at him instead, with a brief wave back. He remembered Di calling out to them all, *Oh please come back, there's food.* He was aware of his own father's presence in the house somewhere; wanted to shout some sort of protest, but did not. He simply waved goodbye and the witch blew him a kiss.

The room fell into a terrible silence for a whole minute. The early evening sunlight shone through the window. There was a whole adult meal prepared downstairs for later. Salmon with capers, supper for a family; potatoes waiting to be cooked, wine to be drunk.

Into the stunned silence, Edward, Gayle's husband, came

into the gallery room through the second door, looking as if he had lost his way, which indeed he had. Despite the warmth of the day, he was wearing a bulky coat, with something held beneath it. He began to back out, and couldn't quite do it, grinned foolishly, trapped.

'Good evening, Edward,' Thomas said. 'How nice to see you.'

'Nice to see you, too. I was just ... er, looking around. Sorry about the fuss. I was just staying out of the fray, keeping in the background, that's me. Don't worry, they'll calm down. It's Beatrice, you see. Always a bit hysterical. I'll see if I can fetch them back, shall I? Can't promise, though. Women. Always getting the wrong end of the stick.'

Thomas smiled at him.

'No, of course you can't promise. I quite understand. It would be nice if you could try, though, bring them back, or come back yourself.'

'Right, will do. See you later.'

Edward sidled out of the room, pulling his coat around him. Di watched him, her mouth opening and closing. He seemed to be able to feel her staring at him, and at the door he surreptitiously slid his hand inside the coat, extracted a silver box he had purloined from a room upstairs and placed it on the side table.

'Sorry,' he said. 'Seemed to have picked that up by mistake. Bye.'

Di looked towards Thomas, her mouth forming words.

'Don't,' he said to her, softly. 'Don't say anything.'

After Edward's hurried footsteps had echoed away, Di followed. There was a trail of sweets left by Alan and Edmund who had stuffed their pockets to overflowing. Beatrice had knocked over a figurine in the hall, leaving it broken in her headlong rush to leave. A small piece of crystal next to it was gone, along with the cash in the red jug, kept for emergencies and anyone who came collecting at the door. Oddly, someone had taken the flowers. Di came back, slowly. Thomas seemed to have guessed what she had found. He took off his hat, threw it in the air, let it fall, looked at her and shrugged.

'They can't help it,' he said. 'They always take or break. Like their mother.'

Di wanted to cry.

'They'll come back, won't they? They'll come back for supper?'

'Oh yes,' he said. 'They'll come back.'

The drawings of faces were scattered all over the floor. Di began to pick them up slowly. She handed them to him. He looked at them slowly, as if drawing comfort from them, and yet she knew he was inconsolable. So much had been invested in this day.

'We made them play,' Thomas murmured. 'At least we made them play. I can't bear it when children aren't allowed to play. Christina wouldn't let them play.'

'They'll come back,' Di said.

She thought of the food she had lovingly prepared for later, the wine in the cooler, how she planned to leave daughters and father together, take the children for a walk and show them the sea perhaps, come back and find them talking, like the families of her imagination did. What stupid imaginings she had, as if she ever had any power to make things better. Why would anyone ever trust her?

Thomas put his arms round her and stroked her hair. It had grown long and thick in her year's residence.

'Was it me? Was it me who spoiled it?'

'Oh, no,' he said. 'It wasn't you.'

They did not come back. The rest of the day fell into darkness and disappointment. Thomas tried, but could not help his own, utter despondency. The turquoise tent disappeared, the floors were cleared; the room returned to the grand room still full of the magic of the paintings, the light in them, the music they brought. She left him to write. He wrote to Saul.

You are quite right. When I die, they will descend like locusts. There will be no collection left. They will spread everything to the winds. They will kill everything I love. The collection will die.

Saul emailed back. *You must make sure it doesn't. You owe the world more than you owe your children.*

After dark, she crept up behind him. His hands were quiet. She could see his face mirrored inexactly in the screen of his computer, next to her own, blurred, brown complexion. She could feel the vibrations of his sadness from a mile away, it was if it was in her own blood, and she could not bear it. His hands and feet were icy cold, and the skin on his neck was hot and she wrapped her arms around he. Soft and brittle, she was, featherdown and steel. And he, old polished leather with a layer of salt and bright, bright, blue eyes, holding on to her so hard, he almost hurt.

Thomas in his gallery room, having an attack of sheer panic, déjà vu, fear, so acute it paralysed the hands that wrote something every day. She read the words on the screen.

Tell her about the alterations made to the basement. Explain what happened.

Di leant over him and typed with one hand.

I know.

His hands began to move again. The shaking stopped. She

waited, holding his shoulders with her strong hands and this time she did not let him go.

The next morning, they walked on the beach in a different way, still holding each other. An invisible jet plane flew above them, leaving a fussy white plume behind itself as far as the eye could see, scarring the sky with a line of ragged lace, making them stop and stare, shielding their eyes. They stood and stared like imbeciles, wondered out loud where that jet would go after leaving its mark, and not wanting to be anywhere else. It was the perfect, abstract picture with the blinding colour no one would believe.

I'd like to collect the clouds, Di said. *And flints.*

Will you marry me? Thomas said.

She laughed, and held on to his arm.

'Some pictures are best unframed,' she said.

Raymond Forrest, the lawyer, called in the late summer. There was a sign on the door. *Gone swimming.*

CHAPTER FOUR

Well, Monica said. 'Well, well, well. I must say, they give a fine party. And it was nice of him to ask my nieces, even if he did it through you. They liked it. Been telling each other stories ever since, which was more than they did before. And Di's good with kids, I'll say that for her, but then she is one, isn't she?'

Jones sat in Monica's barber's chair, heavy-hearted. He thought of watching from the pier with his binoculars fixed on the front door, seeing the daughters of Thomas Porteous stuffing their wailing children into two cars and driving away as if the hounds of hell were after them and that shifty fucker, Edward, running down the front steps last. That was a month ago.

'Something went wrong, though,' he said.

'Something was always wrong,' Monica said, 'with those girls of his. Maybe their mother.'

'How would you know?'

'Because I know a woman who worked for old Douglas,

that lawyer Thomas used for the divorce. Retired now, but she was the typist and she comes in here. Remembers every bloody thing she ever typed.'

'Go on,' Jones said.

'Thomas really wanted custody of his girls, and because Christina was the deserting one, and not very stable, he might have got it, and that's when she started saying he wasn't natural towards them, touched them wrong, he was a pervert. Like his father was. Faintest hint of that and Thomas couldn't win, and he didn't.'

'That simple?'

'Look, think about it. If a man is put down as a monster by his own wife, you gotta believe it. Only later, when Thomas gets rich, she needs to change her tune. She wants to take it all back and parade her kids and then *their* kids to get back in favour and have at the money, 'cos by this time she's alone and they're all broke. Simple? Not quite.'

There was the *snip, snip, snip* of her sharp scissors, a sound Jones liked, although it reminded him of something sinister.

'How come they're broke?'

Monica did not like being asked a question she couldn't answer, but she was happy to guess.

''Cos they ain't bought up to work, like their mother wasn't? Posh schools and no training? 'Cos they got through life maintained by Daddy and think it's going to last for ever? 'Cos someone's told them they're going to be rich some day? 'Cos they were brought up lazy? Maybe 'cos they were brought up thinking of themselves as victims. I don't know. Someone owes them. I haven't got the end of the story, only the beginning. Porteous got another lawyer.'

So much Jones already knew.

Snip, snip, snip.

'You're all done,' Monica said.

She brushed the stray hair from his neck with a soft brush and took off the black nylon gown that made him look almost judicial. He looked sad enough to kiss. No doubt about it, he missed the job.

'So you reckon no one ever believed Thomas tried to touch up his own kids?'

'I never said that,' Monica said. 'No smoke without fire, old Douglas said.'

'No wonder Thomas fucking went to someone else, then,' Jones said. 'Hope it's a good one he's got now, because he's going to need it. He's only wanting to get married.'

Monica gasped. 'Di?'

'Who else? The fucking Queen of Sheba?'

'She wouldn't,' Monica said. 'She wouldn't. Oh my word.'

She paused, scissors in the air, half smiling. Jones turned away, not liking that smile, not liking it at all, because he thought he knew what Monica might be thinking. It might just be crossing her mind that if Thomas P married Di Q, it might just bring her father back.

'She wouldn't,' she said. 'She wouldn't have the nerve. She wouldn't do that to him. Look at the size of her. Makes everything they said about him look true.'

'She isn't a child,' Jones said.

She wouldn't. Di wouldn't. She told Thomas, again and again, *some things are best left unframed. You can't marry the burglar. And don't you see what it would do? It could bring in all the demons.*

No it won't; it'll keep them at bay. Come on, Di; make an honest man of me.

You are an honest man.

No, not entirely.

And then, she did. It took another year.

Painting: *The woman at her toilette, with an old man in the background, coming through an open door.*

English, late 19th Century. A woman in a white night gown, sitting before her dressing table, surveying herself in preparation for an event. She looks at herself. Her figure is upright and youthful: the copious hair is young and yet the reflection of her face in the mirror she holds is old.

Attributed to . . . Walter Sickert.

The figure of the man moved towards the young woman. She smiled him at him.

'I like you in white,' he said. 'Can you wear that?'

She shook her head.

'I think I'll go as I am.'

She stood up and stripped off the white garment, to show a small, naked, body that had grown from that of a girl to a woman. Thomas sat down on the spindly dressing-table chair she had vacated, clutching his chest, mimicking a heart attack and fanning himself.

'Oh my, I'm too old for this. The stress, the stress. You've got to wear clothes otherwise you'll get a chill and I shall be incoherent. Am I too old for this?'

'Think of Picasso,' she said. 'And you're much better looking than him.'

Thomas wasn't remotely old to her. He simply was what he was and she adored him. She was struggling into a tight dress, and stood with one arm in it, one arm out, striking a comical pose, yanking it down over her knees, getting stuck in the thing, peeking at him through a sleeve, looking at his velvet jacket.

'I wonder what's it like to be elegant?' she asked him.

'I wouldn't know,' he said.

Thomas was remarkably inept with his own clothes today. Vintage velvet jacket and unmatched trousers, a lovely clashing ensemble which had virtue in her eyes, simply because it was what he wanted to wear and it showed off the fine colour of his skin and the whiteness of his hair. She came and sat next to him.

'Will they turn up?' she asked. 'Please, let them turn up and see you so handsome.'

'*If* my daughters turn up,' he said. 'They may behave badly. Announce just cause and impediment.'

She seized his hand and kissed it.

'But it was right to ask them,' she insisted.

'Even after they threatened to put me in the madhouse?'

It was a ragged red dress she had on, but sublimely comfortable. At the end of her third summer, her skin really was the colour of sand.

'Thomas, my dearest and only love, I want to know. I want to know that you aren't doing this to spite them, because if you are, it isn't a good enough reason. I don't *need* a ring.'

He stroked her head. 'But I do,' he said. 'I want to do this for the future. To keep us safe. To acknowledge you for being what you are. To make us partners in name. Let no man cast us asunder. And above all, because I'm so ...' he struggled for words '... so very *proud* of you.'

'Shush,' she said, always embarrassed by compliments.

'And because, do you know what, I have always wanted to be a *happily* married man.'

She took his face between her hands and kissed him. Then she pulled him upright, straightened his clothes and regarded him with frank admiration. So handsome in his crazy garb; she curtsied to him.

'You can run away afterwards,' he said, solemnly, tucking her arm into his. 'When I turn into a Frog.'

'My Prince,' she said. 'Shall we walk, or shall we take the pumpkin?'

She was thinking, *if you knew how much I love you, you might be the one to run away.*

'Not a good day's work,' Jones said later to another onlooker of his acquaintance, both of them waiting outside the Town Hall that morning. The onlooker spat on the ground.

Jones looked anxiously at the gathering crowd. News like this got about: there were curious faces, predictable remarks, such as, *I can see what's in it for her, what's in it for him?* But there was distraction. It was early afternoon and warm, a group of drunks newly released from the pub reeling into the space, guests from another wedding earlier in the day, a warring family spoiling for a fight, just there by accident. Jones's attention was distracted by a figure on the other side of the street and he moved quickly.

Thomas and Diana emerged into the light, blinking at the unexpected gathering. The man Jones saw had one arm outstretched towards her as if begging, as she moved into sunlight. She was blinded by the light, squinting, looking heavenwards to focus, confused by the presence of people. Jones stopped the man with a punch: he stumbled down the step into the drunken group and from then on, the fight started from nowhere and swayed across the street, as if someone had ignited the blue touch paper and failed to retire.

The witnesses to the marriage, someone remembered, namely that foppish man, and the other, earnest creature who looked as if he was sent from central casting to be a lawyer, flanked the wedded couple and shepherded them away. No one could say if the pair looked happy or doomed: the focus was on the fight.

'My, my,' Beatrice said. 'Cinderella goes to the brawl.'

Gayle and Patrick stood to the side, too late to attend the wedding, because by some odd mistake, Raymond Forrest had given them the wrong time.

'No matter we couldn't stop it,' Gayle said in her calm voice. 'Nothing as tawdry as this could ever last. Come away.'

King Frog has got married to the witch, Patrick said to himself. *Good.*

'Well, that went well,' Saul Blythe said to Raymond Forrest as they travelled back together on the train later in the day.

'As well as can be expected,' Raymond Forrest said, stiffly.

The two men were not mutually sympathetic. It was the first time they had met and even in the enforced intimacy of a shared table on an empty, London-bound train, they could not quite be frank with each other. One was a creative collector with a dubious morality, the other a solid man of duty. While Raymond was concerned to protect his client's assets and scarcely noticed his client's environment, it was that environment and all the paintings in it which was Saul's sole concern. The landscape passed by in a journey already familiar to the couple whose strange marriage they had witnessed. Di loved the train, she had told Raymond Forrest, but then it seemed to him she loved everything without much discrimination at all, and would inevitably love the spending of his client's money, a prospect he regarded with grave suspicion. He was wondering if Diana Porteous knew the extent of her husband's assets, and decided she probably didn't – yet – whereas this man on the other side of the table most certainly did.

Saul could almost see Raymond's mind whirring with polite queries and a certain, sterile curiosity.

'One would hope,' Raymond said, 'that people would leave them alone for a while.'

'I fear they will,' Saul said. 'Can't see local society rushing to embrace them. But tell me,' he said, leaning forward over the table so far and so confidentially that Raymond recoiled, 'how did the girls take the news of the nuptials? I gather you were deputed to give them the happy tidings and invite them to the wedding.'

'Yes. Always the messenger boy. Are you acquainted with them, Mr Blythe?'

'Yes, slightly.' The lie tripped off his tongue. Saul was beginning to know them rather well.

Discretion returned, along with pomposity. Raymond shook his head.

'There was mention of moral degeneracy. Beatrice in particular considered her father's decision to marry as an obscene insult to their mother. I was able to reassure them, in accordance with my instructions, that their expectations of him were assured, and he would do his duty by them. In other words, their inheritance remains whatever it was before.'

Saul wanted to laugh and instead assumed an expression of equal gravity.

Family duty; a concept Saul could not understand. He

simply did not comprehend the duties created by blood.
Duties towards things of beauty were surely greater.

'But he's done his *duty*,' Saul said. 'They got into adult-
hood on his money. After that, it was up to them, wasn't it?'

'You might assume so, but that isn't quite how it works, in
my experience,' Raymond said. 'Children of rich fathers will
always feel entitled. Especially if they are already aggrieved.
Especially if they blame him for the mess of their lives.'

'But they did attend the wedding,' Saul said. 'Even if they
were too late to bear witness.'

Raymond nodded with the glimmer of a smile.

'That was my fault, I fear. And then there was that con-
venient fight. Otherwise, I fear that Beatrice might have
attacked the bride. She feels . . . strongly.'

'And Gayle?'

'Mrs Edward Morton is a civilised woman. I do not know
what she thinks.'

The old fool admires her, Saul thought. *Try again.*

'So they feel secure about getting the money when the
time comes?' He was asking for confirmation of what he
knew.

Raymond nodded. 'They have been told there is no change.
Thomas thought that was best. If they were to think otherwise,
they would plague the pair of them. Edward would be sent to
bully him. Beatrice would pretend to love him.'

'Well,' Saul said heartily. 'That's all in the distance. Thomas
is as fit as a flea. They've got years and years.'

They did not have years and years. They had three. And Saul
was right: they were left alone. It was not that young Mrs
Porteous and youthful old Thomas Porteous were shunned in
the time that followed: it was simply that they were not

embraced. They fitted nowhere, belonged in no social pocket, complied to no known formula in the town where they had been born. The doors were always open Chez Porteous; anyone who came in search of a donation was never turned away, but the odd couple seemed to need for so little by way of society, and were always so busy, they were almost insulting in their self-sufficiency. They travelled, left and came back with ease. Maybe the quiet happiness, or the appearance of it, was repellent, all by itself. Maybe envy played a part. Anyway, they were left alone. They were seen staggering back from the beach with pieces of flint.

And the house breathed in and out and bloomed and blossomed and the paintings on the walls grew in number, size, variety. Wisteria grew in the back yard, birds nested. Di Porteous was better dressed and had her hair done. Thomas kept a daily journal, *so that you will know,* he said, *how happy you have made me.*

He did it till the day he died. They did not have years and years. They had two of health and one of illness. Cancer of the oesophagus, and still, the children did not come; they did not see the point. The adult children, that is. Patrick came, though, as soon as he was old enough to catch the train: he came in secret, and went back in secret. He came because he wanted to.

And Thomas Porteous kept his vibrant will to live almost to the end. He died when he had done what he thought he needed to do.

The evening after Thomas Porteous died, the fireworks started popping all the way along the beach. November 5th, Guy Fawkes day, with a mist.

Like fireworks on the radio, she remembered him saying last year.

Like somebody digesting food, he said. *Listen to them.*

Noises on shingle, heard from this vast, unobtrusive house where she lived, explosions in the mist sounding like a series of farts. Di looked from the gallery window and went back to the desk, which was full of neatly stacked files, lists of indexes, lists of contingencies printed from the screen and, most explicit of all, the words typed out in his steady hand.

You make it your business to acquire beautiful things, to keep them from the rapacious who would destroy them. You acquire them so they can go on living and delight and inform others. Then you give them away, with love, so that they can become something else to somebody else. You pass them on. You're a Collector, Diana my Huntress, and Collectors must keep things safe. Remember to record what you think before you forget, for thus is learning. I love you so much …

She looked at the words. *Love things, pass them on, let them go. Keep them first.*

Then she heard the sound of breaking glass and went downstairs. Someone had hurled a stone from the beach against the leaded window of the disused front door. A small pane broken; a portent of what was to come. Only a small window, only a small life, not hers, somebody else's.

I am the Collector now. I carry the flame. You are only ever the custodian. The trustee.

She was waiting for him to come back, listening for the sound of him.

Wait for the friends, he wrote. *And beware the enemies. You carry the Flame.*

You are the best thing that ever happened to me.

And you to me, she wrote.

*

The greatest mystery in the entire world, someone said, is the true state of a marriage. She only knew that the brief years of hers, which had passed with such reckless, joyful speed, would never be enough, and now there was no one alive who knew her. But Thomas had; Thomas did.

Recognition of a true colour. No one knew the colour of her, except him.

It was a dangerous way to be.

Nobody knew her, and the last that anyone would think was how much she loved him. She was ashamed of that last afternoon. Perhaps she should have let him speak.

Jones thought she had killed him.

She went down to the basement, to the point where she had first come in, almost ten years ago. Curled herself into a ball in the warm dark.

Come back, Thomas: please come back.

Thought of what might be happening elsewhere. Raymond Forrest giving the daughters the news. Surely there would be room for grief. Regret that they had not come, even when she begged them to. Surely there would be regret that they had not seen him, known him. Surely they would soften and see the point of their father.

She could not cry.

Later, Raymond Forrest wrote notes on the occasion when he had witnessed the response of Thomas's children to the news of his death and his legacies. Like Thomas, he enjoyed writing notes.

There were a few small drawings on the wall of this little pied-à-terre. Childish scribbles: Thomas loved drawings by children. A selection of porcelain objects on shelves, a room full of light and knick-knacks, darkened by the presence of three adults standing crouched around a laptop on a bare table, with the child, Patrick, sitting to one side on the floor, scribbling in his sketch book.

Don't shoot the messenger. Raymond was sick of being the messenger, and yet he knew it was his role. He had heard one of them, Edward, remarking that Forrest looked like a large mole, which he did and he knew it, but he did not like him for that observation. To his eyes, they looked like hungry rats, Gayle the elder, Edward her husband, Beatrice with her snake-like eyes, dressed in smelly wool, all of them ready for the reading of the will from a screen.

We met in the London abode of my late client, Raymond noted. *Same place as before, cosy little studio place, where Thomas came on shopping trips and Di rearranged. No oil paintings, a few drawings and these ceramics, which look a little fragile, especially in this company. These are fragile people. Gayle, elegant, Edward, stocky, Beatrice, the loose cannon. They have planned for this occasion . . . oh dear.*

There was a sharp intake of breath, he wrote. *Then they all hissed, like wasps humming in a nest, until Gayle raised a hand in a command to be quiet.*

Edward looked as if he might have shouted, but refrained in response to his wife's gesture. As the mere messenger, Raymond would not have minded them shouting; anything would be better than this ominous silence. He noticed how the boy – how old was he now? Eleven? Twelve? – put his hands over his ears.

'So, no mention of us,' Gayle murmured. 'Absolutely no mention at all. Some mistake, surely? Our father, the children's grandfather, and he doesn't mention any of us at all.'

'I'm terribly sorry,' Raymond said, and for a moment he was. He admired Gayle, and to disenfranchise your own children completely was a terrible thing to do.

'However,' he added. 'It really was his last will and testament. And he was in sound mind when he wrote it.'

'Was he really?' Gayle murmured, moving towards him, maintaining her mesmerising eye contact throughout before moving away. 'Of course, you had no choice. You drafted what he wanted. You had no choice.'

'He drafted everything, I merely received,' Raymond corrected, appreciative of her understanding, while Beatrice hissed in the background. He always managed to encourage the perception that he was on everyone's side, expressing sympathy for events beyond his control and they believed him.

'That *bitch*,' Beatrice hissed. 'That BITCH has got it all.'

'Hush,' Gayle said.

'Diana has been heroic,' Raymond said quietly. 'It hasn't been easy.'

'Bitch,' said Beatrice. 'Perverted bitch.'

'Be quiet,' Gayle said. 'That isn't fair. Would you give her condolences, Raymond?'

Gayle smiled at Raymond, entirely in control of her emotions, and he knew he was afraid of her without knowing the reason why, while being grateful to her for keeping the peace.

'Formidable girl,' Gayle murmured. 'Truly formidable. She took him on, coped wonderfully well. Is there anything she fears? Poor soul.'

She turned to Raymond, trustingly. 'Tell me,' she said, looking into his eyes. 'Anything at all? We must try and help her through this terrible time. She did nurse our father after all. Artificial feeding and everything. Kept in touch. Must have been hell.'

And where were you? Raymond began to stutter under the impact of her gaze.

'Yes, I think it was. Yes, of course she has fears, everyone does. She's claustrophobic, I think: it was hard, being shut in—oh well, never mind.'

He had said too much.

'That might explain why she needs so much space to live in,' Gayle said smoothly. 'We do want to help. To comfort, to understand. Poor Di, didn't she have a terrible childhood? Didn't she go to prison, once?'

'We've had her THOROUGHLY INVESTIGATED,' Edward shouted. He was slightly drunk at that stage, although not as drunk as he would be. He could hardly control his fury. All these years, he had been studying, valuing, for *this*. Raymond smiled, uncomfortably, disliking himself for spilling the smallest bean. Edward laughed, not quite in tune, not an amusing sound.

'You know what you are, Forrest? You're a bastard. You're the messenger boy. You've got us all believing that Thomas was going to leave it to us, while all the time you knew he wasn't.'

'I didn't say that. I said he would do his duty.'

'And YOU think, YOU,' stabbing Raymond's chest, 'YOU think we know nothing. But we do, you know, we bloody do. Like we know what an evil bitch she is. We've got her dad, we've got him watching.'

The ravings of a disappointed lunatic.

'Hush,' Gayle said. She got up and moved Raymond towards the door.

'Thank you, Raymond, for being so trustworthy. Keep in touch and tell us anything we can do.'

The door closed behind him. Silence followed. Patrick continued to draw, Beatrice to hiss.

'Well, there's the clue as to what to do first,' she said. 'We get the claustrophobic little bitch sent straight back to prison. Like her dad said, that'll kill her.'

'Hush,' Gayle said again, turning to her husband.

'She killed him,' Beatrice said. 'She killed him.'

'I've got a plan,' Edward said.

Patrick put his hands over his ears.

PART TWO

CHAPTER FIVE

The wedding was a distant memory when, four days after the date of Thomas's death, Raymond Forrest walked down the pier, circumnavigated the café at the end, retraced his steps to the road and turned left purposefully. The sea murmured to his right, traffic ran parallel to his steps; shops and the town centre were somewhere beyond. He had never been particularly interested in the place, but thought it was time he explored it.

An English seaside town, with all the hallmarks of decay, was an unlikely place for an almost-millionaire inventor to live, unless said rich old man was as eccentric and as splendidly single-minded as Thomas Porteous. Raymond made himself walk faster against the wind. He was prematurely elderly himself for sheer lack of exercise, so his own dear wife told him, and he was thinking that it was a great advantage in a man with a mission to have a younger spouse, something he applauded in Thomas, but not, maybe, a marriage with such a colossal age gap. Raymond and his wife were a mere decade apart, both middle-aged, so at least they sang from a similar hymn sheet and had some national history in common. Surely there could not have been similar reference points between Thomas Porteous and his incredibly young wife, Diana, as named in the will. They could not have known the same songs, or even the same rhythms. Impossible, with almost two generations between them, even allowing for one being preternaturally youthful for his years and she being unnaturally old for hers. And yet she was the inheritor, and Thomas always knew what he was doing. Or so it had seemed. He should have lived for ever, because no doubt about it, Thomas had been happy; they had been as happy as a pair of singing birds, even if some of the songs had been sad.

Striding on his short legs, Raymond Forrest looked forward to the meeting. He paused, because he was early, a bad habit, although a valuable one for an eavesdropper. There was a moment of regret that he had not been here more often in the last month, listening to the words between the lines, when Thomas, however ill and speech-afflicted, had still seemed immortal and even relatively healthy. Cancer of the oesophagus had decimated his life, but he could still walk and communicate although with increasing frustration. Perhaps Raymond himself might have influenced the current plans Thomas was rehearsing with that deeply suspicious agent of his, Saul, if he had been here more often, and he might have warned his client that it did not do to be too complicated or rely on anyone who was not a lawyer. Thomas had been formulating plans for all sorts of contingencies in the event of his own demise and it was better for Raymond not to know every detail. *Just prove the will, Ray, do your bit.* Ever the messenger boy.

Pausing for breath, he reflected that nothing he might have said would have made the slightest difference. At least he had been there often enough to bear witness to the man's mental health. Extremely robust, he would say in any court of law. Agile, even. The man wanted everything left to his absurdly young wife and he was absolutely determined about that. *Keep things away from the rapacious and the destructive:* those were his instructions. He meant, of course, his children, Thomas's children by his first wife, Christina. Di did not come into the category of the treacherous, yet. Perhaps her treachery would be in indirect proportion to the colossal trust Thomas had placed in her.

Raymond puffed a cigarette, as he often did before a meeting, in anticipation of it not being allowed indoors. Then he remembered that it was Di he was appointed to see, and there were no such rules in a house too large, convoluted and downright draughty to allow the lingering of toxins. Smoking was mandatory in Thomas's palace, anyway: it was the first thing he had done when released from hospital, encouraged by his wife. *Too late for self-denial,* he said.

Raymond walked on, remembering also in his approach that the grand front entrance to this grand old house was not the point of entry. Access was via the door in the side street at the back, the one the children would use when the building had been a primary school, full of stately rooms as well as some mean ones. Most rooms were full of pictures, paintings, drawings, sketches, but that was the man's hobby, and what he and Di held in common was an obsessive love of art and the acquisition thereof. They responded with the same intensity to visual things, and that transcended all the differences there might have been. Raymond frowned. This child, Di, was about to be thrown if not to the wolves, certainly among them and she was far younger than his own daughter.

He reached the house, via the narrow street at the back. A fence faced him with a small door in it, leading on to a back yard full of pots and iron steps up to the raised back door. There was a steel grilled entrance to the basement that could also be reached from the inside. Raymond knocked and went in without waiting for an invitation.

This was the room where Thomas had died. The room he had occupied most during the last six months of his so-called recovery from a cruel operation. The equipment for tubular feeding was packed away into a corner awaiting collection. Di had overseen all that, anything rather than have him stay in hospital – and that decision, too, would be open to scrutiny. Widow Diana was certainly under suspicion, and yet it seemed from their telephone conversations that she was blissfully unaware of it.

Don't ever let her go to prison, again, Raymond; that's the one thing that'll kill her.

There was a different picture on the wall above the fireplace. It was of a plump nude, lying comfortably on a mattress.

'He called that his last Duchess,' Di said, coming through from the kitchen. 'Lovely, isn't she?'

'Yes. She looks content.'

The scale of the thing was large for the room, dominating it. A calm face gazed at him over a generous bosom.

'She's nothing like me,' Di said, looking at the painting. 'But she's more like I'd like to look. Less skin and bone, always wanted to be fatter.'

Raymond patted his own, ample stomach. 'Believe me, it doesn't have much to recommend it. Slows you down.'

'Perhaps that's why I need the weight, then. Cup of tea? I'm glad to see you.'

He found that touching, bowed his head in acknowledgement. He had been anxious about this meeting, but yes, he had looked forward to it. Di was an enigma, a keeper of secrets: she looked at everyone with a frank and unnerving suspicion until she made her own judgements, and only then did she smile at you, and when she did, he felt peculiarly blessed as if he had earned praise. A strange way to feel about a convict he had once monitored on Thomas's behalf, and all the same, she outmanoeuvred him. Intimidated him, was the way he might have described it and that worried him too, because it was odd to feel that way towards a person with whom he also felt entirely safe. *She's the cat who walks alone,* Thomas said. Raymond had not expected to find her devastated four days after the death of her husband, and she was not. She was woven from tough material, but how tough, he really did not want to investigate. She was certainly a fiercely protective little protége of her man and his memory, but she was not sentimental. Perhaps caring for the sick knocked that out of her.

'Why did you move that particular painting down here?' he asked.

'She belongs here, and we loved her. She cheered him up, me too. He always liked a painting he could talk to.'

Many paintings had been purchased in the last years. There had been a veritable orgy of discreet buying. The children had hated that.

'Saul found it, you know Saul? I wish he were here. He's somewhere. He's doing one of his disappearing acts.'

There was a note of panic in her voice, quickly suppressed.

A fair weather friend, that Saul, Raymond thought. He

sipped the tea and decided to be brisk. One of the eccentricities of collectors was the way they could talk about paintings and ephemera for hours, before getting down to business, even in an emergency. They were like that, to death and beyond.

'Look, Di,' he said. 'You're in trouble. I know Thomas is dead, and that's the worst thing,' and as he said it, he did not really know if it was the worst thing for her and wondered wistfully if he would ever know. All he knew is that he had never known Thomas Porteous to be as contented or as deviously determined as he had been in Di's company. They chattered like starlings, behaved like puppies, patently obviously slept in the same bed. He did not wish to think of that aspect, which he found distasteful. But they talked, by God they talked, and walked. And went swimming. They did simple things that pleased them as much as spending money. On household management, Di was thrifty, he remembered. Thomas practically had to force her to buy clothes.

'The children are certainly going to contest the new will. After all, it appears to have been executed so soon before he died. *I* know it was drafted long ago, and they were kept in the dark, but they'll fight to the end and beyond and fight dirty, no doubt. The balance of his mind was disturbed, etc, etc. He was suborned by an opportunist, criminal girl, who seduced him into marriage, etcetera, etcetera ...'

His voice trailed away, then hurried along with the bad news. The trouble with this death was that although Thomas had lived beyond medical prognosis due to the care he received, it was still unexpected.

'... who then took him out of hospital, prematurely, took over his care, fought with everyone for the right to look after him, and thus ensured his premature death. At a point when he had difficulty communicating and was entirely dependent, he was starved to death, denied official entry when he did die, and in the meantime, his hand was forced to a *new* will, which should therefore, be overruled. That's the sort of thing, anyway. There has to be a post mortem, of course. So everything waits for that. You know I spoke to them, and Gayle sent condolences, but oh dear, I can't believe anything, because Edward phoned me afterwards, you see; he was rather drunk and it was extremely revealing. They do wish you ill, my dear. And they do know the circumstances of his death.'

He did not want to tell her how bad his interview with what he called 'the girls' and Edward had been. He sat back, exhausted by his own recitation. She bowed her head, allowing him to look down on her wasted hair. It had grown thin during the last months, balding at the back. She looked up and smiled sadly.

'As bad as that? Well, it isn't true, you know. It'll be ironic if they construct a case against me on the basis of what I've told them.'

'*I* know it isn't true,' Raymond said, 'because I had many conversations with Thomas. And I know he didn't want anyone else around him but you. It might have been easier now if you had insisted otherwise.'

She nodded.

'Yes, I can see that, if only to have a witness. But to suggest I kept people away is not right. Thomas went out every day: he could walk and he looked well; no one knew how ill he was and he didn't want them to know. There might have been more offers of help otherwise. What people saw was a man who could walk to the pier and back and smile at people. He had his pride, Thomas. You knew that he spent hours a day attached to a feeding tube because he told you. His daughters knew because I told them; I made sure they knew what was happening, and so did you. I reported to them regularly, and I pleaded with them to come and see him. They wouldn't or couldn't.'

'It would indeed be ironic, if they use what you have told them against you. But I do suspect they have other sources of information, and they have certainly investigated you. Are there records of what you told them?'

She shook her head, baffled. 'No, mostly phone messages. Beatrice was unpleasant. She told me I'd made my filthy bed and I should lie on it. I only spoke to Gayle or Edward after that. I think Gayle thought she still had plenty of time to visit, only she didn't have time. As for taking him out of hospital, they wanted it, I wanted it, he wanted it. He was desperate to come home. I didn't refuse aftercare, but the nurses didn't understand the feeding equipment. All they could suggest when there was a problem was going back into hospital, and Thomas said it was like going to prison and no one goes to prison on my watch. We were better working things out for ourselves. I thought Gayle understood.'

'You don't have to justify it to me,' he said.

'Yes, I do,' she said, remarkably calm and non-indignant. 'And as for me forcing Thomas to make a different will, that's crazy. No one could force Thomas to do something he didn't think right to do.'

'Maybe it would have been better not to have misled them,' he wondered aloud, guilty about his part in that. 'Only they weren't misled, exactly, they were allowed to *assume*.'

'To assume whatever they assumed before. Thomas thought that was safer.'

'And I agreed about that. Was there *any* happiness in the last few weeks, Di?'

He had a memory of arriving here the last time, in September, early again, and finding them both helpless with laughter, arguing the merits of a piece of flint and what it resembled. A woman or a bear, he couldn't remember.

She nodded her head, vigorously. Hair drifted away.

'Oh yes, there were plenty of good times, until he realised his sight was going. Thomas lived through his eyes, you see. Until he realised it wasn't going to get better. Until he knew he shouldn't swim any more. When he thought he was a burden to *me*. The hot summer tortured him: he was writing more than speaking, oh yes, he could still write . . . oh shit.' She turned away.

'Is that when he went into planning overdrive?'

'Serious, long term planning – he started that long ago, you know that. Plans to preserve the collection and extend it. The will is all about that. As for contingency plans, well – he was hatching those with Saul in the last three months. Plans based on their knowledge of his children. You all know them better than I do. I was glad of the planning, it gave him a purpose.'

Raymond stared at the nude. 'With great respect, and with all these contingency plans, I doubt if even Thomas could imagine how vicious it might get. He was a great judge of people, of course, but anybody can underestimate.'

'I don't know about that,' she said. 'I can only trust whom he trusted. What I have to carry is *his* trust, Raymond, his trust in me to do what he wanted. But all the same, it doesn't seem right to leave his children with nothing, however cruel they've been. If there's a way to rectify that, that's what I'd want to do, for the sake of *their* children.'

Especially Patrick. Brave little Patrick, who bunked off school and caught the train, and came to see Grandpa in secret. *Don't mention that.*

'Why should you care about his children?' Raymond asked, listening to her voice.

'Because *he* did. Because I want to change their minds? Because maybe, being the way they are isn't entirely their fault. And because, in a way, I feel sorry for them. Thomas was the most marvellous man in the world. To have a father like that, and not to know him, strikes me as not just sad, it's bloody tragic. They must feel it.'

She got up and marched round the room with her arms crossed across her chest.

'*But,* preserving this house and this collection comes first. Because it *is* for his children in a way, but not just for them. It's for lots of people and their children, and their children. It's for everybody in the end and that's what the money's for. There's only so much of it, after all. Of course they can share it, but only like everyone else.'

Raymond was noticing how Di had a wonderful panoply of accents, ranging from something local to posh, slipping and sliding in between, a voice that went from the modulated to the strident. She was a natural mimic, which was, he thought uncomfortably, a great attribute for a confidence trickster. *You can trust her absolutely,* Thomas had said.

Raymond wanted to, he definitely did, but the truth of it was, he could never be entirely sure. He did not know quite what she was. For the moment, he couldn't care either way, sitting here in the warmth, feeling the comfort. It would not be a bad place to die and the manner of it was appropriate, too. The man did as he wanted to the last moment, went for his walk, admired the scenery through misted eyes, came home and died. He died when he still had some of his own vigour and dignity, nursed and nurtured beyond his natural span of life after a hideous operation that should never have been conducted. That was the transparent version and most of the time, Raymond believed it to be true. And yet there was another interpretation, one he knew would be voiced, and that was that Di had kept her husband alive and captive until it suited her convenience to end it.

She was looking at him wryly.

'If anyone's going to make out I killed him, they'd have to think twice.'

'I'm afraid you might have laid yourself open to that suggestion, Di.'

'I did think of it,' she said, surprising him. 'And you know what? I was too much of a coward to do it. I thought if I did it, I'd go to prison. Someone would lock me up. If it wasn't for that, I might have found a way to let him die sooner. I shall always feel guilty about that, because his last week was hell and I could have spared him that, at least. It would have been kinder.'

Raymond was shocked. How would she have done that? He could imagine it. Thomas was weak and highly susceptible to infection; the simplest way would be to contaminate the food supply. The elaborate intravenous feeding machine was still under cover in the corner of the snug, waiting collection and squatting like a toad under cover. The evidence might still be here. Thomas was utterly dependent on her for whatever he consumed. Raymond told himself not to be ridiculous. She had only thought of it, she said. But if she had thought of it, others would have thought of it, too. And it was perfectly clear to him that Thomas's daughters had more sources of information than Di could have guessed.

A lawyer to his bones, his affections subsumed by his objectivity, Raymond hated the shocked silence that followed. Di was fully aware of his surprise and his ambivalence. She seemed to have retreated to a world of her own. Thomas said she did that sometimes. *Time in prison does that, makes them infantile or hideously mature. Contemplative or angry. She's claustrophobic; we can never have the doors closed.*

Raymond had a sudden regret that he had let certain facts slip to Gayle. Given her the clue as to how to undermine the enemy, as if she did not know already.

He prompted Di, with a polite cough.

'There is a possibility,' he said carefully, 'that you're already a suspect. I fear I cannot tell you what the children might do with the facts at their disposal. Or what enquiries they might have initiated to date. They seem to have ... sources of information. They might accuse ... There was the ... delay.'

'It wasn't my finest hour,' Di said, flatly. 'I was relieved. I told Jones.'

'Jones?'

'Never mind. Anyway, I can't imagine the children would ever think I hurried up Thomas's death. Gayle thanked me for taking care of him. And come on, nobody's that bad. I mean, they don't like me, but it isn't personal.'

They hate you and it's highly personal.

'We *could* try to compromise,' he suggested. 'Offer them a portion of the estate, something like that. Offer to settle it, before it gets nasty.'

She considered.

'Yes, for sure, but not if it means breaking up the collection he wants me to continue and not if it means selling this house; Thomas had plans for this house, we both did. He said he never really thought it belonged to him, and I don't think it belongs to me. He said if we gave them a half or a quarter, you may as well burn it all. He also said they've got to learn to live. But yes, in principle, and only on certain conditions.'

Raymond left that aspect alone.

'There'll be an inquest, postponed. He hadn't been seen by a doctor for two weeks.'

'Not for lack of effort,' she said. 'Either he wouldn't or the doctor couldn't. Have you ever tried? I had to fight for everything. Should I compromise? I reckon that was the last thing he wanted me to do, but I would if it could be done in a way he'd approve. If it would keep the collection safe and me to continue it. And keep his reputation, perhaps that most of all. I want Thomas to be famous, one day. That would be the condition, they honour his reputation instead of slurring it, and they let their children come and visit, if they want.'

He thought about it, looking at the cheerful fire in the hearth which gave him courage and drained all memory of the November cold outside, reminded him of the days when he had loved a good fight. The conversation with Edward had indeed been illuminating. Raymond was refraining from telling his client exactly how much both Di and her deceased husband were hated by his kin. And how little the preservation of a blasted collection of paintings for posterity mattered to someone in need of money to which they felt entitled. He shook himself. There was fight in him still, and he still relished the idea of a fight. Besides, there was no way this lot would settle for less than everything.

'Consider it, certainly, and I shall, too, because it's going to be a rough ride if you hang on. The law's one thing and fact's another. They'll tear his memory to shreds to prove entitlement and they'll accuse him of everything to gain sympathy. They're entrenched; they have the moral high ground. I'm not sure if they would compromise. They want it all, and they'd rather destroy it than you have it.'

They'd like Di dead and buried, Thomas had said. *They would cut off their own noses to spite their own faces. They are their mother's children, Goneril and Regan. And Edward is a thief.*

'But it isn't mine to give them,' Di said. 'I simply hold it in trust. And they've wasted so much already. So did their mother.'

'Ah yes, the earlier Mrs Porteous.'

The real Mrs Porteous, Raymond reflected, who took her children away and accepted an irrevocable financial settlement she later regretted. A bitter, violent, attractive woman, who might have been a young man's dream and the nightmare of his middle age. Mrs P who kept on coming back.

'Those who have, want more,' Raymond said. He hesitated, wondering how much of his own experience in these matters to explain without being condescending, pessimistic or alarming. 'There is a level of hatred in some families which goes beyond the rational. These daughters believe that their mother was the victim of great cruelty, as they were themselves. They believe Thomas was responsible for her unhappiness and for the failure of their lives. Such hatred knows no boundaries. None at all.'

He could tell she couldn't quite get it. Collectors could be so naïve. They couldn't quite believe that other people simply didn't care about *things*.

'I don't hate anyone,' Di said. 'I can't. Gayle and Beatrice were half Thomas's flesh and blood. That means, whatever they've said and done, they can't be totally bad.'

Was she really naïve, or was she pretending? There was a clock on the wall with an audible tick. The day marched on.

'Whatever happens, whatever comes next, you and I have to do an inventory of the possessions. The London flat, too. Where shall we start? In the attics or the basement?'

The attic floor vibrated with the wind. Heat rose up the two open stairways, dissipating as it went. There were three casement windows in a long narrow room, spanning the whole of the house, and the other light came from the windows at either end. The room looked upon nothing other than sea and sky. The ceiling was low enough for a man as short as Raymond to walk through the centre but not around the edges; taller Thomas would have stooped in here. The casement windows were floor level and the ceilings sloped to join them. The floor was wide boards of mellowed pine, creaking gently with every step. It was the room with the fewest paintings, confined to the side walls, since even Thomas could not find a way to hang a painting on a sloping attic wall. Small, cameo paintings in here on those end walls, miniatures and tiny works of art on one side, and on the other, a large painting of flowers. Three pristine beds and minimal furniture in this room, bathroom off. It would have been a dormitory, once.

Descending the alternative stairs, he found three large, higher-ceiling rooms. Doors interconnected the rooms and there were also doors into a corridor; all the rooms were made to move through, and move round; it was if every room in this house had two doors. He was already lost, had stopped looking at the pictures and was thinking instead of how well it would have worked as a public space. These rooms had no particular dedication: study rooms, bedrooms, elegant whatever they were, always with one door in and one door out.

Raymond could not understand why the corridor curved, but curve it did.

The next floor down housed the gallery. It was formed, mainly, of two huge rooms, again with doors, more interconnecting doors between them as well as those leading on from the corridor. Raymond could see one room as the headmaster's office, perhaps, with its grander accoutrements, the other as a classroom. They merged together when the doors were flung open. Brilliant rooms with long windows, full of grey light. The gallery room, the heart of the place. Thomas's old partner's desk was in the finer end, complete with computer and files of neatly assembled paperwork. It was a library room, shelved in oak down one wall, while the rest of the walls were covered in pictures. Thomas's ancient office chair was a Victorian model, precursor of the modern equivalent in terms of comfort, but with twice the authority. There were fireplaces at each end; he could imagine them blazing. Today there was a distinct chill in the air, a different temperature to the rooms above and below. Despite the magnificent view of the sea outside and the pictures within, Raymond could understand why Thomas had abandoned this place of command for the snug downstairs at the back, at least for the winter.

'You know what Thomas wants, of course,' Di said. 'It's to be a gallery, museum, for everyone, but especially for children who wouldn't otherwise ever *see* real paintings.'

Raymond could see it: for the first time, he could see it.

'And is that what you want?'

'Yes,' she said. 'And sometime along the line, his daughters are going to see it, too, and be proud of him.'

Fat chance, Raymond thought. *They think it all belongs to them anyway. They think it's theirs. They will* snatch. The word stuck in his mind, a mean word, *snatch,* reminding him of a sneak thief who came up behind and punched, hard.

'We did a complete inventory of the existing paintings,' Di said, handing him a copy from the desk. 'You don't need to do it again, just check it. The valuations are pure guesswork, except for the recent stuff. I'm in the process of writing descriptions, my own record, writing sketches of paintings, if that makes sense, so I remember them. Saul's making a proper catalogue. I wish I knew where he was.'

Raymond nodded. The inventory would be correct, insofar as it went, with whatever omissions the client chose. If Thomas had not already hidden things, he would be markedly different to any other client Raymond had had. Likewise, he was sure there would be immaculate accounts, fit for the severest scrutiny. Thomas knew his tax law. He had planned for death long before it came over the horizon, planned it for years to make sure that Di got governance of the lot, the tax man got the least and the children nothing at all. There was simply not enough to do everything. The pot of money was deep, but not bottomless.

Raymond consulted his favourite painting above the fireplace on the left in the gallery room. A swagger portrait of a man about town, circa 1880, the man dressed in evening clothes and cloak, lounging in a chair, one hand in his lap and the other resting on a cane. There was a red flower overflowing from the lapel of his jacket, the only colour in the piece. A man in his prime without a care in the world, looking across at the painting of a lady at the other end. Raymond wondered if there was any theme in the Porteous collection, such as were all the portraits celebrations of youth and beauty, or were the landscapes and interiors pieces of wish fulfilment, places where Thomas would have liked to have been? Had he been creating another, alternative world with his seemingly random eye and his voracious, acquisitive appetite for line and colour? Were these his alternative family, his dreams, to replace what he had either driven away or lost? And his father, the headmaster, before him? Raymond plodded on, thinking what a pedant he was, with his composite roles of lawyer and liaison, walked down the last set of stairs, lost. Whatever the theme was, he had certainly not collected as an investment: the theme, if there had ever been one, was blurred now. He had relied on Di's eyes. And she might have killed him.

She whisked him round like a tour guide and then they were back where they had been. Back in the snug room, with the comfortable nude, illuminated by the fire that granted a kind of benediction. Di produced food with the automatic efficiency of someone long practised in the art of the picnic and he forgot his reservations about that. Good bread, cheese, tangy green leaves. 'You have to eat before you go,' she said. He was surprised by the simple sophistication of it, not only because he had never supposed this faded town to provide anything of the kind, but also because he had assumed that she would be incapable of assembling it. Then he remembered triumphant Thomas, when he, Raymond, had advised him against the marriage. *She can cook, dear boy . . . doesn't that persuade you of her immaculate taste? She has eyes, Ray, in the back of her head as well as the front. I'm a lucky man and I owe her my life.* A man either besotted or convinced.

'So,' Di said, pushing food in his direction rather than eating it herself, then lighting a cigar, which suited her, 'how bad is it going to get?'

She got up to rattle the fire, shoving on another log, sparking it back to longer life. The fire had been dead by the time she called the ambulance. It took hours for this fire to die. She had done nothing to revive or warm her wedded husband; she had let the fire go out. That would be remembered. *All she had to do was contaminate the food.*

He cleared his throat and reached forward for her to light his cigarette. There was nothing seductive about her action, but it was still intimate. She was all sharp angles, shrill, comforting, charming and graceless, all at the same time. Distracting.

'Well,' he said, more cheerfully than he felt, wishing she had more of a sense of the dangerous pathways ahead, wanting to spare her and yet wanting to shake her with his own sense of dread. 'The house is beautiful and you should do what he wanted to do, to the letter. It would be helpful if you were the model of good behaviour in the meantime. A demure and grieving widow, perhaps. A connoisseur, leading a gentle life. That kind of thing. No loud noises.'

She shook her head, smiling.

'The inventory? Haven't we forgotten to look in the basement?'

She clapped a hand to her brow. 'So we have, I forgot, but you know there's nothing much in there. Too damp, too cold, too . . . this time of year. The sea comes through from underneath, you see, sometimes.'

There were stone steps leading down from the heavy door inside the snug room. Raymond did not want to go but knew he must, for the sake of duty as well as curiosity. He hated the dark and longed for the light upstairs. She was fooling him, leaving this until last, but then again, maybe she wasn't. The lights were fused, she said; she had taken a torch which swept round the vaulted ceilings of what was once a wine cellar, with arched alcoves in glorious patterns of brick in pale, russet stone. There were wine racks and rubbish, boxes and baskets, cardboard containers, tidily stacked, and to his inner ear, a faint shuffling sound, as if of someone breathing. The floor at the furthest end away from the inside steps sloped upwards towards the steel shutters leading into the yard.

'You can hear the sea down here,' Di said. 'And there were mice and rats and things, but I think they've gone now.'

Again, half lost in admiration of the room itself, Raymond asked a question.

'The late Mrs Porteous . . . did she know this house well?'

The torch wavered alarmingly in the large space. Even a claustrophobic could function here.

'Thomas said so. She would have known it when his parents lived here and they came to visit. She hated it and hated bringing the children, but admired it, too, when it was never as valuable as it is now. She had no idea then that Thomas would inherit it. Yes, she must have known it, but probably not well. I only know what Thomas told me. There's been changes since.'

He was accepting stray pieces of unverifiable information in the dark and he wondered why he had asked. He knew Christina Porteous had visited Thomas in this house before her death, to plead for money: he was unsure if Di knew, or how much she knew of that unstable, poisonous woman. Raymond needed no encouragement to go back upstairs as fast as his legs could carry him. He hated mice and the very thought of rats unnerved him so he went back upstairs, sat back and accepted coffee, again experiencing the strange sense of comfort she offered. Excellent coffee, as it happened. He was particular about that, took a sip and shuddered with the thrill of it, sipping it like an old lady who had never tasted the taste before, and looked at his watch. A train would go at fifteen minutes past the hour and he had time for the next, if he went now, resisting the comfort and the urge to stay. He heaved himself to his feet, sat down again, remembering there was more to discuss.

'Look Di, you've got to make your own last will and testament, and make it soon. Thomas said so. I've got a draft, setting up a trust. I know it might seem ridiculous at your age, but it's got to be done. He was very keen about that.'

'Yes. He knew very well that if anything happened to me, and I died without making a will, my father would claim as my only relative. So, yes, it better be done soon, and publicly. So that he has less of an incentive than he already does to kill me.'

She said it so calmly, he almost choked.

'Your father? You'd better explain this to me, Di. Thomas never did.'

'Perhaps because he didn't want to shock you,' Di said, calmly. 'Or force you to consider the violent propensities of his wife's parent.' Sometimes her speech had the modulations of Thomas and his dedication to precision, so that she sounded like an echo of a scholarly brain.

'I have a father who is rather a bad man,' Di said, matter of factly. 'A sort of undertaker, outside of the law. About whom I know rather too much for his comfort. Still alive, as far as I know. The last thing he ever said to me was to wish me dead. He's lived away for a long, long while, haven't seen him for years. A decade, at least. So, no worries, hey? And anyway, he's not a murderer and Thomas thought of everything.'

The speech has lost its careful intonation.

'Good Lord,' Raymond said, faintly, thinking to himself that maybe this was a little over the top, not to say creative and stress-related. It had already occurred to him that Di was in danger, for the simple reason that the hiring of an assassin was a far cheaper expedient than the expensive business of contesting a will. He had known those who had contemplated it, but it did not happen in polite society. Edward would have thought of it: Edward had contacts, but not that kind. And now there was this other string. A homicidally inclined father, dear God, what overdramatic nonsense. It made him suspect her all over again. What was it Edward had said about Di's father? Something and nothing. It was all too much.

'The will,' he said. 'I'll get on with it, shall I? Because in any event, Di, you're a bit of a hostage to fortune without one.'

He meant, even if your father exists, and is not a phantom of your own making.

'Yes,' she said, like someone shaking herself awake. 'Yes, but I would like to bury my husband first. I can't make a will until Thomas is buried. And I wish Saul would come.'

Saul, Saul, always Saul, who knew about paintings and might have much to gain. Raymond felt an unreasonable flash of jealousy. Saul, the Dealer, the Interface, a man with whom Thomas had hatched contingency plans before he died, not shared with his lawyer who ran errands.

'I expect he'll arrive,' Raymond said, brusquely. 'I'd better go, Di. Just keep a low profile, will you? They may send their own envoy. I'm liaison, but if they try a direct approach, let me know. They'll certainly try the back door as well as the front. They have access to the London flat, they always have. We need an inventory there, too. Are you planning to check it out, or do you want me to do that?'

'No, I'll go, I need to. Safe journey. I'd let you out through the front door, only it's stuck.'

Mice and rats in the basement, Raymond remembered on the train. Something rattling around among all the boxes; things covered with canvas, no smell of damp, never mind. His stomach was full and his mind was empty. Di would win, and they would have a good fight, if only she played fair and looked demure. If only there was not another lover and she didn't blow it all sky-high. *If* she didn't fill the house with undesirables; *if* she hadn't killed him. En route home, he remembered with guilt the haste of his departure, his willingness to believe that she would be fine, wondered quite how lonely she must be, how tough she seemed and how soft she might be. He had failed to remark on the boarded-up window, awaiting repair, failed to embrace her and wish her well and entirely forgotten the inventory. What kind of man was this father? Why wasn't she more afraid?

Maybe she was not afraid, because as Thomas had said, *she has no malice in her, she doesn't understand it. I don't know why, but that's her blind spot.*

Diana Porteous was certainly afraid; temporarily fearless, because the worst had happened and Thomas had been taken away from his house. One thing she had learned long since: that the person who looked afraid was always the first target. Man kicked the animal who cowered. Her father taught her that. She counted her fears and put them in order.

Fear of locked doors and confined spaces ... and alongside that, for the moment, the great fear that she would not be capable of fulfilling the enormous trust that had been placed in her. That she would not Honour Him. That she would not be able to show him how much she loved him.

After Raymond had gone, Di went back downstairs to the

cellar, turning the lights on as she went, not apologising to herself for lying about the fuse. There was more to the cellar than Raymond could ever have seen, deep alcoves at the back with raised floors, snug places like berths in a ship and between them, a door to a further room. The door was rusted shut and there was a chest of drawers in front of it, raised on blocks against the now dry floor. The chest held blankets. Di peered into the first alcove, finding some small traces of occupation, not recent. She left the chocolate and the bottles of water on top of the chest of drawers. To feed the mice, or the cat, of course. To feed anyone who needed shelter here. It was a place of last resort, always had been, always would be, whatever else was here.

She went back upstairs to the best room in the house. Turned on the computer automatically. They had written to one another, Thomas and she, even when they were in the same room. The day had turned dark and the interminable rain began again. There would have been more visitors after his death, surely, if it were not for the rain. No use to blame the rain, she blamed no one. She lit the fire, sat in Thomas's chair and dreamed.

No one had come to see her, because no one trusted her and she trusted no one even though she was known in the town; she had gone about, to Monica in the hairdresser's. Monica knew how her hair had thinned. Di tried to predict what Gayle, Beatrice and Edward would do.

How easy it would be to undermine her if they knew how.

Not late. Keep on writing.

Goodnight, Madame de Belleroche. When can I grieve?

Not yet.

There was a banging at the door.

*

Raymond Forrest was on the ugly station platform, waiting for the high-speed train, watching it slink into the station. Then he heard footsteps and saw a rumpled man running towards him.

'Listen,' the man was yelling. 'Fucking listen, will you? Come back, they're going to fucking arrest her. It'll kill her. I saw the car from the pier, someone told me.'

'What? Can't hear you.'

The shabby man was shouting over the peep, peep, peep of the opening train doors, and he was pointing at the mobile phone he carried in one hand, as if it was the fountain of all wisdom and explained what he was saying. He was red and sweating. He clutched Raymond's coat sleeve; Raymond brushed him off. The man's hands dropped to his sides, defeated. The train breathed its desire to depart. Raymond stepped inside as the doors closed. A case of mistaken identity, surely.

Jones stood on the platform. *Fucking lawyers, fucking bastards, hate the cunts.* Then he ran out to the taxi office. Got back to Di's house, just as they got going. Just in time. Fucking bastards.

He remembered a screaming child he had rescued from a cellar.

And Di, behind bars.

CHAPTER SIX

Jones had the picture in his mind from many years before.

A dirty girl, huddled in the corner of a cell, with her fingers stuck in her ears against the noise. The prevailing colour is dirty yellow. Nobody arrives.

He went round the back. The car was still there. He was shouting before he burst in, even though shouting made everything worse. His fucking police contact had given him the right information about the fucking search warrant, but the wrong time. They were supposed to come tomorrow with the warrant, give him time to warn her. Not like this, with him watching from the pier with his binoculars, seeing the lawyer walk away and thinking he'd go and tell her then, until he saw the police car nosing round, unsure of the address, and he knew what they were after, and then he'd run in the wrong direction, panting up to the station to fetch back the Brief who'd have the right words, wasting time. He hated fucking lawyers.

The back of the old schoolhouse was milling with police,

all of them kids and none of them old enough to be mates of his. Someone should have had the sense to ask him first, like the older ones would have done. No one used to question anyone in this town without consulting Jones. Di was as white as a sheet, standing there, holding on to a chair and looking like shit. Two uniforms stood by the door, shuffling. It was true, then, what Jones had heard on his mobile phone. Diana Porteous was not only under suspicion, she was being taken in. Fuckit. That little claustrophobic beast was being put in the frame again.

Who, fucking who? Surely it wasn't him, telling them that she had waited for two hours? No, no, it would have been that young one who was there, and the doctor they called and the fact that it was obvious he was cooling and the fact that she looked like shit, but who the fuck had put the sting on her now?

'Who the fuck are you?' Jones bellowed, full of his own forgotten authority.

'Got a warrant to search for evidence. Information received of suspicious death in this house.'

'What? You fucking joking, boy, what information? Not at liberty to say are you? The fuck you aren't. So an old man died here last week, is all. You search every house where someone dies with their name already on God's waiting list, you'll be busy in this town, I tell you.'

A search warrant, not an arrest warrant. What does it cover? Kitchen equipment, foodstuffs ... are you serious? Why? You're going to take her away without a warrant for her arrest and leave these bastards to search the house without even knowing what the hell they're looking for?

'Mrs Porteous has agreed to assist us with our Enquiries. She's agreed to go with us.'

'Has she?'

Di nodded. Jones looked at her, listening for the sound of a cell door closing; a sound they both knew, just as she knew what she was like, ten years ago, once inside that cell, twisting and screaming, bashing herself against walls until they put on the straightjacket and then she was utterly silent. The memory scorched him. She looked at him.

'Was it you called them, Jones? Was it you?'

'No, on my fucking life it wasn't.'

She nodded. She was cold and polite and yet shimmering with sweat. Silence fell in the room.

'You don't have to go, Di, you're not under arrest,' Jones said. *Not Yet.*

'I have to show willing,' she said, with a grim little smile. She was distant and unreachable, pausing before asking. 'Will you stay and watch? They want to check out anything I might have used for poison. They may as well find out what there is.'

She laughed, a horrible, frightened laugh. 'Make sure they do it right.'

'You don't have to go.'

What did she mean, they may as well find it? Find what?

'I do. It's a test,' she said. 'A test.'

'Talk to them, Di,' he yelled after her. 'Use your fucking voice. You ask the fucking questions.'

She went, quietly, tucked inside the car like an ugly toy.

'Give me that,' Jones said, snatching the search warrant out of the hands of a young policeman who was an open-mouthed rookie, not used to this nor a place like this and definitely in need of a leader. He read it quickly. Christ Almighty, it was a fuck-up; look at it, no one but a half wit would have issued a warrant as bad as this, in such a stupid hurry, it was crazy. It confined them to the kitchen and its environs, as if obsessed by food. Jones kept them there, pointing at the words on the printout; otherwise they would have been all over the house. *No, you can't go upstairs, nor down; it doesn't cover that. No, you fucking can't, stop that or there'll be trouble* and by a miracle, and because they were rudderless, they obeyed him. It was dark by the time they had gone, taking away selected pots, pans, the feeding equipment, all Thomas's survival machinery, part of the scullery and fuck all else. Enough left for her to carry on. He learned that this sorry crew had only been pulled off an aborted job and sent on this to give them something to do, thank heaven for small fucking mercies.

Fuckit. Jones waited and phoned. He sat in the hallway by the redundant front door and waited, working it out. *If someone really has it in for Di, they've given info and some fucker's believed it. They weren't supposed to come until morning, at least, but these idiots needed a job. Supposing someone was supposed to come along and plant some evidence they were supposed to find? Oh shut up Jones, fucking paranoid git.*

And still, he waited. He sat in the hall and waited. Used his phone for updates, waited. His contacts had gone home. He thought of Di and Thomas, the way they were. She thought no one else knew, but he did. She looked after him good; he had to say that and if she killed him it was for pity, but why did she wait? And why, he asked himself, am *I* waiting in the pitch dark? Thomas's kids, they hate her. (Christ, they even tried to hire me.) And Quig's around, I can feel it, and supposing this lot got together? As if. You are one fucking paranoid git, Jones; you really fucking are. You've been dreaming of bloody Quig.

He waited. And then, suddenly in the silence of the

house, there was a rustling from outside the front door and there, framed against the stained glass, a figure, trying to get in. A shadowy substance leaning, turning the handle, pushing. Jones could see him, forcing his way inside, trying to plant his evidence, his little bit of filth, a little bit of dirt. That would be the plan. A little suggestion that Di had not taken care, that was all it needed. Put a bit of filth in the kitchen, plant a few germs, a single turd. What would some-one plant that would incriminate her? Condoms, deadly nightshade, anything would do. Anything to suggest negli-gence; anything to suggest she had a vested interest in hastening the death, even the presence of another man. What would he have planted? Salmonella or porn? Or maybe the man was calling to see Di herself. And if he were Quig, he'd bring a rat; that's what he'd bring; he'd bring vermin, dead or alive.

Someone was trying to fiddle with the disused front door and it had to be someone with out of date information, because no one had used that door in years.

Jones flung himself against the door and put his mouth to the glass, so that his lips were pressed against it. 'Give us a kiss, you bastard! Kissy, kissy,' he yelled. 'Fuck off, you cunt. Don't even think of it. It's too late. You're too fucking late. They've taken it all away. Is that you, Quig, is that you?'

The figure disappeared into the November mist like a ghost, as if he had never been. Maybe he hadn't, maybe it was nothing but paranoia and yesterday's hangover from dreaming of Quig. Jones stood back, trembling. Shook himself like a dog, tidied up, left a note, saying *call me*, hoping she would, and thinking she wouldn't. Di wouldn't thank him for being here. She really would not want Uncle Jones and he wished she did. He prayed for her, spoke to her.

Shout at them, Di. They ain't got nothing. Warrant's fucked, and I'll be raising Cain if you aren't back in the morning.

The interview room was larger than a cell, and she could smell the cells on the way towards it. They left her waiting, behind a locked door. She was waiting while listening to the offstage sounds, breathing deeply, thinking of Thomas's diary files, of something he had written over a year ago. *Today,* he wrote, *we went to the bay to see the geese in flight. I've had to get Her Laziness out of bed to go at first light and she does need her sleep, whereas I need less, but I have never seen a creature so revived by a cup of tea. Crosspatch turns human, and so do I.*

She thought of that day, and other days. She felt in the pocket of her old coat and found the outline of shells: how many hours had they spent, inspecting shells. She felt sand in her fingers, closed her mind and put herself back by the sea. The panic receded.

The interview proceeded. Two men and an older woman, who looked doubtful. Di did not meet their eyes, nor they hers.

I'm not in a cell, the door is open and I have to breathe deeply. There is no reason to be silent. Help with enquiries. Talk; be aggressive, even though the prevailing colour is a sort of sick, mustard yellow. Think of a painting ... that one of the Poor House, the same coloured walls. Don't let them smell the fear. Talk. She hid her clenched hands under a scarred desk, and said anything that came into her head.

'My, my,' she said. 'You could do with a coat of paint in here as well as a few pictures. Maybe some nice, peaceful scenes with water, like they have in hospital waiting rooms. Even a bit of graffiti.'

'Mrs Porteous, you're helping us with our enquiries.'

'A few watercolours, a tapestry, something bright. Curtains.'

'Your late husband.'

'A tablecloth,' she gabbled. 'That would do. My husband died, you know. Four days ago, or is it five? What kept you so long? You could do with some pictures in here.'

She looked at the contours of the corners, looked at the ceiling, looked at anything but them. She turned the room into a picture of itself, hummed manically. What was the line from the poem Thomas taught her: *It is fear, little hunter, only fear.*

'Mrs Porteous. It's for us to ask the questions.'

He was a portly man, sweating a bit in this overwarm room. She remembered sitting in a room like this, wearing a paper suit, after they had taken away her clothes. She took off her coat; then she took off the sweater beneath, slowly while they looked at her in alarm, paralysed, not moving to stop her, wondering if she was going to strip. She sat back.

'Well, ask the questions then. Is this about the post mortem?'

'Post mortem hasn't happened yet. It's not about that.'

Di shut her eyes against a sudden overpowering jolt of sheer, physical agony; a vision of his thin, wiry body lying in darkness all these days. She put her hands over her mouth. 'I thought they did it at once. I thought ... '

'Doesn't always work like that,' the woman said, leaning forward, seeing the distress. 'There's a queue, this time of year.'

Di thought of the days they came home with feathers and shells. Ate scrambled eggs. Grief came in like a wave, coming in and going on a slipstream of sheer, redemptive anger.

'Why am I here, then?'

'We have information—'

'What information? What real, concrete information?'

They looked sideways. She was tapping her foot on the floor.

'Information that indicates you isolated your husband, neglected him, forbade his children to visit, and this alone makes his death suspicious, since you had sole care of him. Perhaps you can understand, Mrs Porteous, that we have to investigate.'

Tap, tap, tap; her foot on the floor unnerving them.

'No, I don't get it. If no one's done the post mortem yet, there's nothing to ask. What information can there be, except rumour? You really do need to do this room, you know. Pink, blue, anything but this.'

'Not at liberty to say,' the man said.

She looked around. It was the constant grime she had hated, the omnipresent grease, surfaces always slightly slippery to the touch. Impenetrable walls, invoking helplessness in the innocent as well as the guilty, and at the moment, she did not know which she was. Oh yes, she had loved him, and oh yes, she had wanted him to die. Because *he* wanted it. She closed her eyes. Reached for the old coat, to stick her hand in the pocket and feel the sand. Did it only take half an hour for the geese to fly by this time last year, or was it three? This time last year.

Di opened her eyes and glared at them.

'No one forbade his children to visit. Quite the opposite. Is that what they say? Are they the source of the information?'

There was another uncomfortable silence. She put the sweater back on, then the coat.

'They wouldn't visit. Shame on you,' she said. 'You've kept

me here for three hours, for nothing. Someone's put you up to this. I'm going now.'

She rose and no one stopped her, or observed that she could scarcely walk while wanting, desperately, to run. She was slow and determined, rigidly controlled, scenting the air outside like an animal. The older woman walked her out. Di could smell that peculiar cell smell of bleach, urine and desperation.

'Ok, we jumped the gun,' the woman said, grudgingly. 'Bloody men, know what I mean. I told them . . . hey, whatever happened to your hair?'

Di fixed her eyes on the exit. The shaking would start again when she got outside. She turned to the woman.

'I get it fixed tomorrow. What about yours? Who made the report?'

'Can't tell you. Someone jumped the gun, that's all.' She leaned towards Di. 'All I can tell you is, it wasn't Jones.'

When she got out of the taxi with the key in her hand, she saw that Jones had left the lights on. She read the note and did not phone him. The kitchen looked much the same; the snug, tidier and barer. They had taken Thomas's processed food and feeding equipment, left the same, sanitised oven. The idiots. The shaking began again, and then subsided, because she had won, she had taken control, for a while, passed a test. She drank the brandy, carefully, smoked a cigar, sat at the computer. Tomorrow, she would do exactly what she had planned to do. Smarten up, get out of here. Go to London.

Don't deviate. Be passionate and dispassionate, Di. Remember who you are. Remember who was proud of you. Write down what happened. Write something every day.

Sleep now. Think of summer. Control the breathing. Put the fears in order of priority. An image of her father rose to mind, along with the conviction that he was close by. She supplanted him with another image; the geese over the bay this time of year. That was the way it worked. You displaced ugliness by thinking of something effortlessly beautiful, like a piece of flint. She would go tomorrow. So much to do, tomorrow.

Where was Saul?

A dark, winter morning.

Morning was a different creature to night; easier to rationalise in the morning and even this poor daylight made everything simpler. She had been taught to analyse what she saw with such joy; she was growing an ice chip in her heart, forming a lens through which to see. It was only Thomas's opinion of her that counted. It did not matter that she was neither liked nor loved in a town she loved dearly, and perversely loved even more, now. So much so that she was dreading leaving it, postponing the moment of movement by sitting in his chair, looking at the screen.

She was reading an article she had found online.

Collectors, the screen informed her, *must not be confused with the art-lover, or the person who is simply interested in art. The urge to possess, bring together objects, is inseparable from the taste for the unusual and the flair for discovery. As soon as man developed a sense of beauty and the ability to choose, he felt the fascination of coming under the spell of coveted objects.*

Collectors have been treated as the victims of a disease, with four main symptoms: the possessive instinct, the necessity for spontaneous activity, the desire to surpass oneself and the need for social standing. The collector is by definition inseparable from

a love of risk or battle. Supremely unsociable by nature, he has
no self confidence apart from his conquests, which recall the
moments when he has, to some extent, mastered his fate. He may
even feel obliged to keep his collection from the sullying gaze of
alien eyes.

With few exceptions, the screen said, the great collectors
are self-made men, who began life shining other peoples'
shoes. They may have wanted to establish a personalised,
grander past. Master their own fate.

'Rubbish,' Di said to the screen. Her irritation with this
googled script of cod analysis from a learned source made
her uneasy. First because although she was addicted to keyboard and screen, she could never quite trust the text as
much as she would if she had seen it in a book. Pictures were
another matter; text was less convincing, somehow.

Another reason for the irritation was because some of this
psychological treatise was so true, while the rest was patently
false. Whatever kind of collector Thomas had been, he was
not like that and neither was she. They were not ego driven,
they were rescuers, celebrators of neglected beauty, seekers
and restorers, and the last thing Thomas had wanted was
status. Di Porteous was trying to discover what she was. A
small thief, turned by circumstance into something else, or
better than that. Someone who would always need to learn
something, every day.

She lit a cigar. OK, OK, the author on the screen was
right. Collectors could be persons in search of an identity;
collecting was a highly effective way of sidetracking loneli-
ness. A substitute for a family, even. Boys collected cards
and coins; girls collected ribbons and nuts and bolts and
other people hoarded thimbles. Collectors had their own,
alternative sanity, an excess of passion, rather than the

opposite and even if it began with disappointment in real life as others knew it, it also came from a longing to take pride, another version of the creative instinct, and, in this day and age, it enabled a man to be a hunter–gatherer without wielding a spear.

I need this disease, Thomas, she said. *It was our mission in life, but is it really still mine? I want this illness. I want the passion I found through you to stay with me.* She logged on to another website and scrolled through the images to find the scarce-known gem of an English artist who Thomas had seen in that last week before his final walk.

Alfred Studd, a tiny oil panel, with a title, *A gust of wind, circa 1914.* A woman in a pink gown, holding on to her hat on Brighton Beach. A small, vulnerable figure, dressed in her Sunday best, struggling with the indignity of the wind which made her gown billow around her knees and threatened her balance, looking as if she wanted to smile, but the struggle to maintain her poise made it impossible as the wind rendered her naked. Someone out of the picture was laughing at her. The colours glowed, the brush strokes were delicate and confident; pink gown, probably wrong for the weather, grey skies, a hint of turbulent sky and sea foam. Di caught her breath, touched the screen as if she could feel the texture of it and sighed. There was a place for her here, and Di was out of her seat and moving towards the door to find her. Yes, she was a Collector. She was not Thomas's protége, put upon earth to fulfil his mission. It was in the blood. She had the dreaded disease.

She went back to the screen. Google map; she found her own town, where she was now, and examined that first, a way to orientate herself before going any further. She never went anywhere without a map. Maps were important.

Find the place, then, look at it from above. The town came into view, straggling out along the curving coast and clinging to it, spreading back reluctantly until it melted into fields, with the railway line snaking away, leading to the greater world. Her town, seen as a picture, examined as such. A town that needed this house and all that was in it. *This town needs this house.*

Di chose her route. She would go to the High Street first, ten minutes' walk away, then the train station which would take her to London and the studio flat; she would make an inventory and make it as safe as Thomas would have wanted, although it had never been inviolate. Maybe she could mourn him there, away from the sound of the sea. Thomas had lived there when he was young.

Half an hour later, she was outside the hairdresser's, a place where she was almost at home. It was the place that made it clear that while small-town dwellers thought they knew everything about everybody, they only ever knew a fraction and sometimes, nothing at all. There was no one alive who could be said to have known Diana Porteous, but there were several people who thought they did and Monica was one of them. Monica had known Di's mum and dad, not that they ever discussed it. Di had taken to going to Monica's, irregularly, since she was married, because she liked it. She never talked in Monica's, only listened.

The town ran to two hairdressing salons, one beautician, a nail clinic and other small, useful shops. As a level street, it was popular with one-legged persons in motorised buggies, persons on crutches and mothers with prams. On Saturday nights, it was drunk.

Reaching Monica's Hair Salon on this Monday morning, Di could see that the window had been cracked again, along with a couple of others. It followed from that that the brick through her own window last week was equally impersonally delivered, although her house was outside the drinking zone. The salon door was wide enough for a zimmer frame and, once inside, the smell of perfumed chemicals outdid the scent of dog and damp overcoats by the door which, when opened, let out a glorious warmth. Coming inside here was like entering a ship, to sail away for a while.

Monica's diplomatic side was often defeated by naked curiosity, especially when she did not think that sympathy was called for. She placed delicate hands on her thin hips as the door shut behind Di. There were three other customers.

'Hallo, what's the cat dragged in? He's dead, then, is he? About time, though, wasn'it? Shame, though, lovely man. No time for crying, though. That'll come later. You'll have things to do, won't you?'

You could assess a woman's mind by the state of her hair and Monica knew that. She was a graduate in widowhood experience. Grief was not always immediate, or at all, although Di's hair was certainly stricken. Thomas had been welcome here, too.

'Going to London, are we? Thought so, you've got that bag.'

Di carried a small antique suitcase whenever they embarked on a day away; that much had been observed, along with the fact that she had acquired nice new clothes since she became a Mrs, lucky her. Monica had once been sweet on Di's dad: Jones had been sweet on her mother. Not mentioned now, not ever. The salon still needed a makeover and Monica was feeling sour.

'Terrible, your hair. Been dropping out, has it? Don't worry, it'll grow back when you've got him buried and people stop talking. Won't be church service, will it? Take a while, I expect. Right, what do you want me to do?'

Make me beautiful. Make me grow. Give me height. Anything that stops me looking scared.

'Last time he came in here,' Monica said in Di's ear whilst patting the gown around her shoulders, 'he asked me to cut his hair really short. I wouldn't do it. He wanted to save you the trouble of washing it. Lovely hair, lovely man. You can cry if you want. No one'll notice. You got plenty of time. You need the works. A colour?'

'Whatever you think.'

'Right,' Monica said, offended.

Di sank awkwardly into the comfort.

'You keeping the old barn, then?' Monica asked. 'Thought that'd be on the market sometime soon. Must be worth a fortune.'

'No. Not yet awhile.'

'He's never left you *everything*, has he?'

Di was silent. Monica's sharp eyes calculated the odds on persisting, decided not. This hair was a mess, like a mangy dog. Give it some colour to disguise it. The customer rarely knew best.

'There was a man in here yesterday,' she said. 'Asking all about you, well not so much about you, more about the house. I reckon an out of town estate agent, we get them now we're going upmarket. I didn't tell him you were living there alone. They'll be over you like flies. Now love, you can tell me, have you really copped the lot?'

A hush, as Di's hair was massaged into a lather of unlikely colour. Di said nothing, flushed pink. There was the sound of a magazine being dropped.

'That means you did, then,' Monica said. 'Until someone

takes it away. There'll be plenty ready to do that. Anyway, hasn't the girl done well? Hasn't the girl done well,' she yelled round the salon, so loudly that the pictures shook on the walls.

The silence was palpable. No envy in the tone, only wonder, and a sort of congratulation that a little scrubber like Di could do so well and yet there was a touch of malice in the perfumed air. Di Quigly had won the lottery and no one loves a winner. *Earned it on her back.*

Monica pouted and paused. The noise resumed.

'Didn't mean it, love,' Monica said, leading her to the basin. 'You were always good with the waifs and strays.' She leaned down and whispered. 'Did I hear right that the police were round yours, yesterday?'

'Yes,' Di said. 'Came and went.'

Monica nodded, satisfied to be proved right. At least she'd got three words out of her. It was impossible to relax. Di kept her face still and did what she did to distract herself, thought of a painting, and replaced one image with another, so as not to think that it might have been someone in here who had sent the police to her door. They did not understand, but Di Quigly had never expected understanding; ever since her father first shot the birds, and the finding of it once, in the way she had, was not going to qualify her to find it again. Being misunderstood was a fact of life. She fingered the map in her pocket. Cartwright Street, the studio flat: perhaps he was waiting there, ready to open the door.

They couldn't be so bad. *His* children couldn't be so bad. Gayle had thanked her for nursing her father. Patrick had come, although in secret. They would come round, they could work something out, they would come to understand. It can't have been them who sent the police.

*

Eleven in the morning, only, the same grey day advancing towards a lighter afternoon. Where would she be, how would she be and who would she be, come the spring? There would be the battle of winter darkness. Once in the safety of the train, she made up her face in the lavatory to correspond with the hair. She had been sabotaged; the hair was a mass of spikes with an unnatural sheen. The speed of the train was awesome. Thomas had approached train journeys with the joy of a child, as if each journey was a novelty to be accompanied by a picnic; she remembered that. Out at St Pancras, still in love with the speed of the train and resenting it too, because she arrived too fast to allow time to adjust. She hunted in the case for the print of the painting she wanted to touch and then for the map. The studio flat where she was bound was where Thomas had been a student and he had never relinquished it. Christina had been allowed to use it in her nomadic phases and despite that, it was still Thomas's bolthole, the base for city forays and the seeing of exhibitions. It had been his home when he was still shining other men's shoes before he became a dedicated teacher who also invented games. Perhaps he would be there: perhaps it was all a mistake. Perhaps he had simply gone back in time.

She could see how it must have been, a floor above a long defunct pub, a garret of three small rooms, accessed by an old door in the alley between. How he loved small doors, obscure entrances into large rooms, and how she did, too. The studio was a haven of peace and light and a place to hide, as well as collect. Hence the inventory. She went up the dark stairs from the narrow door, lighter hearted, wanting to see it again, imagine him in it. She heard them before she saw them.

Gayle, Beatrice, Edward. Patrick, sweet Patrick.

The door was not locked. There was a small, mirrored vestibule inside the entrance. Di could see them, reflected in it, visible in the mirror through the half-open door. She flattened herself against the wall, saw her own profile, witnessed a thin girl in a loose red coat, black leather trousers and artificial hair, looking like a tasteless tramp; a girl in another person's clothes.

There was stick thin, elegant Gayle and plump husband Edward in his good suit; no colour in them at all, except for Patrick, the boy, who sat on the floor with his sketchbook and pink face. Di put down the suitcase, quietly.

The studio room was in the process of being dismantled. The walls had been cleared of all the small things that had found their way here, the comforting drawings and pictures, the little bits and pieces worth pence. The walls gaped with the marks of plucked-out hooks and the booty was gathered into untidy piles. The ceramics, which had always been there long before her time, and which she had arranged along the window ledges, the mismatched cups and plates were also gathered in. There were three boxes, one already sealed. The smallest, nostalgic part of the collection Thomas Porteous had spent half a lifetime creating, was being bundled ready for removal. They had come prepared.

Edward was speaking. The women listened to him.

'We can come back for this later,' he said. 'It's all rubbish, anyway.'

Patrick leaned sideways and picked up a ceramic green frog which lay forgotten on the floor. He put it to his ear, listened, put it in his pocket and then put his hands over his ears.

'Better than nothing. Do you suppose they'll keep her in?' Gayle said.

'I hope so,' Edward said, in his loud and resonant voice. 'But they might not have enough to keep her. Enough said. A young, convicted thief in charge of the medicine chest. They'll keep on looking. She'll never be free of suspicion.'

'It might at least drive her bonkers,' Beatrice said, carelessly. 'Best thing to do, keep on hounding her till she loses it. Who knows what they'll find? Ha, ha.'

'But it isn't what Saul says we should do,' Gayle said. 'And nor is this.'

'Saul's not the only one with ideas,' Edward said, in his resonant voice.

'The bitch,' Beatrice said in her singsong voice. 'Thinking she can have what's ours. The skinny little bitch.'

Di saw the back of Gayle's head, shaking disapprovingly.

'You have such a small vocabulary, dear,' Gayle said wearily.

'She's a thieving con and he was a paedophile,' Beatrice chanted. 'Likes little girls and boys. Did you tell them that bit, Edward?'

'Do hush,' Gayle said, pointing at the child indifferently.

The voices descended into mumbles. Beatrice was dressed in homespun folds that wafted around her as she moved, clumsily. The odd thing was broken as they packed: there were shards of glass on the floor, as if they did not particularly want what they took, only wanted to take it.

Edward yawned. 'Leave most of it, make it look like someone broke in.'

Contempt shimmered in the air, like a mist.

Di listened. Watched. Frozen. They hated her; they hated him.

The boy, Patrick, looked up, gaped round with his myopic stare, pushed his spectacles further up his nose, gazed towards the half-open door and saw Di, pressed against the wall. He began to grin, then wiped it away with the back of his hand immediately, shook his head, warningly. Then he screamed, *yeugh,* in a single, barking shout and drummed his heels on the floor. They gathered around him with their backs to the door, shushing him as if he was a baby. Gayle slapped him.

'Oh really!' Beatrice said.

In the confusion, Di picked up her suitcase and crept away.

She had been utterly wrong. She had been quite mad to imagine that the genes they had inherited from their father would somehow emerge. They were not his children; they were Christina's. And Christina had wanted him dead.

CHAPTER SEVEN

Diana Porteous sat in a small park near the station, sitting on the pedestal of a sundial, which bore the inscription 1809, and even in extremis, she noticed that. She felt cold to her bones, stripped bare. Thomas's children had keys to his flat and they could not wait to desecrate. They would break up his things and put her in prison, even though she had nursed their father and he had loved her and she had been stupid enough to think that would make a difference.

Abuser, paedophile. Christina told them that was what I was, and they believed it. They were six and nine when she took them away. She gave them their memories, their fantasies and their sense of entitlement. She kept coming back to haunt me. I never wanted them to know how mad she was and I still don't. They aren't my daughters, Di, not any more.

Thomas had told her that.

They would not come and see him. They lied: they informed: they wanted their father's wife to be mad. She hated them; she hated them with fierce intensity. They would

125

have torn her to pieces if Patrick had not warned her. She could not stay here.

There was only a numb desire to get home to a dark house and the sound of the sea. She had not been ready for this: she had not been prepared for the reality of greedy hatred. Thomas's children were what they were, and Edward was worse than either of them. Not nature, nurture. Raymond Forrest was right; she was wilfully naïve, clinging to naïve belief.

The mid-afternoon train was the slow one that stopped at every station and marked the real distance between here and there. Thomas had wanted her to be at home in London. He wanted her to feel at one with the slender Europeans of Bond Street, demanding priority at Sothebys and Armani and Ralph Lauren. He wanted her to have the chance to be some-one else entirely if she wanted it. She smiled at the thought of that. The smile was fixed.

Was it so strange that no one, not Monica, or even Raymond Forrest, nor Thomas's daughters or anyone she had encountered in the days since his death, had ever con-sidered that she might actually be grieving? That she might actually be afflicted by his death? As well as rendered inco-herently miserable and angry. They were right; they were capable of driving her mad. And Saul: Saul had been with *them*, but then she knew that, didn't she? It was part of a plan, but it still hurt.

She also knew that she had not exactly helped herself. She had been abrupt in response to enquiries, economical with information, saying *yes, thank you, the notice will be in the paper,* simply because she was incapable of functioning otherwise. Except with Raymond, to whom she had lied a little, the artic-ulacy she had learned from years of talking to Thomas turned into half-formed syllables. She might well have driven away the truly sympathetic, had they arrived. No flowers, no offers of food, no disingenuous gestures. No one saying, *are you lost?* No one beginning to entertain any other assumption that a young woman saddled with an old, sick man was merely waiting for the opportunity to dance on his grave.

She was reconciled to not being known, to being misunderstood, to being treated with indifference, but actual, vivid hatred from his children was another matter. Hatred was a different beast from mere contempt; accusations were different to mere innuendos. *Abuser, pervert;* the words were obscenities. Sitting on a half-empty train going home to an empty house and all the vast responsibilities and instructions he had left, she had never felt lonelier.

Saul had a plan. Had a plan. On whose side was he? Where was he?

She pressed the tears back into her eyes because once she started, they might never stop. Then she opened her eyes wide and blew her nose. Halfway home. *You carry the flame, Di. Have pity, but not self pity.* She got out the map, and looked at the view as well as the other faces, distracted herself by imagining them painted in oil.

Voices impinged, one plaintive, one resigned.

'Look, love, this ain't the right ticket. It's just any old ticket you've picked out of a bin. Or you've nicked it. It's only valid for a senior citizen. So have you got a valid ticket or not?'

Di turned and saw the girl cringing in her upholstered seat.

'It's the ticket I got.'

'You ain't got a valid ticket and you've been locked in the lav since London. You can buy a ticket. Show us your money.'

127

'Haven't got any money.'

'Right then. Off, next stop. Let's have your name and address.'

'Haven't got an address, go on, give us a break.'

The girl was blustering, the bluster wearing thin, bravado giving way to desperation. She was what? Sixteen or so, with a bruise on her forehead, half covered with a thin fringe.

'You can't put me off the shitting train in the middle of nowhere,' she said. 'You can't.'

'Yes, I can.'

Di looked at the darkening afternoon sky, checked on her route map for the next stop. The middle of nowhere.

'Rules, love, Can't pay, can't travel. The police'll be waiting for you.'

The girl stood up, panicking, ready for flight, realising there was nowhere to go. The few other passengers hid behind books and newspapers. Di saw a small, plump girl, with thick hair, pierced ears, black sweatshirt and leggings not warm enough for the outdoors and too tight for her frame. Scuffed shoes and a plastic bag round one wrist, acting as handbag. Kohl-blacked eyes, smudged with disappointment. A brave stud in her red nose. She was clutching a dirty tissue and making a keening noise, put her hand across her mouth to stop it. The sky outside grew darker and the train slowed. The girl looked like jailbait, she had that terror: she had been in prison, Di knew it. Di stood up with her thin, spiked hair and leather trousers, looking hard and aggressive.

'I'll pay,' Di said, looking the inspector in the eye. 'Wherever she wants to go.'

'No,' the girl said. 'No I don't want that.'

'I'll said I'll pay,' Di said.

*

They sat opposite one another for the rest of the journey, the girl looking down at the ticket on the table between them, screwing up the tissue between her fingers. Maybe older than sixteen, Di thought. Unprepossessing, Saul would have said. Di got out her google map of her own town, last stop on the line. They were both getting out at the same place, but it seemed as if the girl was guessing her destination, a name conjured up out of her head. Perhaps the name of the destination on the ticket she had pinched was the only guide to where she was going. Di watched herself being watched.

'I didn't nick it,' the girl said. 'Only I had to get out of there, anyway. I was hanging round the station, and this old guy dropped it. Should have guessed it wouldn't be right. I wouldn't have dipped an old guy.'

'But you might a young one,' Di said. 'And you've been caught.'

The girl nodded.

Di turned the map round so that the girl could see it. She squinted at the page, trying to focus, finally getting it. Her brow cleared. 'I like maps,' she said.

'This is the station where we get out,' Di said, marking it with her pencil. 'And this is where I live,' she said, drawing another cross. 'I know where I'm going. What about you?'

The girl was silent, panic seeping into her expression. Di took out her purse, peeled off a couple of twenties and a ten and placed them on the table.

'Take it,' she said, 'There's a good B&B where they don't ask questions. It's here,' again she pointed at the map, before folding it and handing it over. 'And remember where I live. If you forget, someone'll tell you.'

'Why?' the girl said, bewildered, unfolding the map, staring at the money. 'Why would you?'

Because someone hit you. Because you have such lovely thick hair. Because you've been inside. Because I can save someone from a few hours in a cell.

'Because somebody has to, Peg,' Di said.

The girl pulled her hair down further over the bruise and gasped. 'How did you know my name?'

'You've got it on the necklace round your neck.'

The train pulled into the station. Peg was out of there and running over the bridge to the exit, as if she was being chased or as if Di was going to take back the map and the money. In the middle of the bridge, facing the car park and the lights of the town, she turned and waved. Di waved back. She had not wanted thanks; she preferred straightforward rudeness. It was she who should be grateful for the added distraction, for the tiny little endorsement of self that came from an act like that: even though it was never enough. *That girl's like me – I was once her. I've got to be hard, but I've got to remember who I am. And one of these days, Thomas, I might even be able to laugh at myself again.*

Di walked back through the town and turned right at the front, away from the pier and down the road, following Raymond Forrest's footsteps, seeing it through the eyes of a stranger. How did he see it? Scrubby little dump, with an ugly pier, lit with deceptive jollity, but coming up in the world. Houses, stage left, seaside stage right, the bigger houses taking over from the small, keeping themselves apart from one another. She passed the defunct paddling pool and the decorative public lavatories, the makings of a mini golf course, a stretch of green with the old Bandstand in the middle. Memories ran deep in town, greater tragedies than hers.

Memories to the right, the sea to the left, hissing away on the steep-backed shingle, promising continuity. *Hiss, shhhhush, shush, crash, take a deep breath and start again,* speaking to her. *I go on and on, unlike you. I don't hate you, but I may destroy you. It's all the same to me. Hiss, hiss, crash, shush, shush, shush. Anytime, I can come over this bank and take out your great big house. I could flood your cellar in a minute.*

Di turned away from the concrete path and walked out over the shingle. Her footsteps were noisy and she only went as far as the first slope, spied the first waves, grasping at the bank and drawing back as if they did not like it, trying again and again, not greedy tonight. Not driven by the wind to gnaw at the foundations, infiltrate cellars, flood basements, tell the grand house owner that they really owned nothing. Live by the sea at your own risk. In summer, Di swam here and let the tide take her. Thomas also. He swam every day that he could. She had dragged him back, twice. That was the way he had wanted to die and she had not let him.

Tonight, she could see the temptation and the luxury of drowning; of just not going on. The wind teased, rather than tore, reminded rather than hectored. She crunched back over the shingle and went via the back road into her house, went upstairs, looking for him, the way she had always done, wanting to tell him about the day. If he was out, he would leave a note, a drawing, a sketch, a clue and if he was not immediately visible or audible, she would call for him, take one room after the next, until she found him. And, latterly, if the place was empty, she went back out to the sea. Started again.

She did the same this time. Scoured the house, looking for him, and almost set out for the sea again, before she remembered he was not there and there was no need to look. Still, she went through all but the attic rooms before she realised and then she was back in the kitchen quarters, sitting in his chair in front of an unlit fire, eating an apple, thinking of the picture of the Lady in Pink, thinking of the girl, Peg, Peggy, hoping that she had found somewhere safe. She could read a map: she had promise.

Phone messages, some simpering. Mr so-and-so will call you back tomorrow. Email messages, you expressed interest in ... Where was that treacherous Saul? Where was anyone who loved Thomas?

Di went slowly towards bed. She tidied the kitchen parlour with almost obsessive attention to every detail, packed food bought in the station supermarket. The searchers had left enough equipment for cooking. Hygiene was paramount when Thomas was ill and artificially fed; she doubted she would ever break the habit and anyway, she had been raised with standards of aggressive cleanliness. The blood was always cleared off the walls in the Quigly home by a gentle mother who loved to read. Di rearranged the shelf above the sink that housed a row of little birds, fashioned from various metals, a silver robin, a starling, a wren, a blackbird made of iron and a sparrow made of tin. More loved objects, almost as loved as the real birds in the back yard which came every day to feed in winter and the birds in the bay. She left the room reluctantly and made her way down the corridor and up the fine flight of stairs, turning lights on and off as she went, looking once more into the gallery room, lit like a stage.

Thomas, darling Thomas, did you ever hurt anyone on pur-pose? Was it by accident that you earned such hatred? What did you do to her that made her want to destroy you? I know your version of events, but is it true? Is someone trying to make me question you? Well, I won't. I know who you are.

The master bedroom, a bateau bed, like a boat with a polished prow, a place of simple comfort, next to an old-fashioned bathroom where she washed away the taint of the day in the enormous bath with claw feet. The same bath with the shower where she had washed his long hair. Then at last she slid naked into bed, wanting to sleep, craving it, the first real sleep in a long time, surely she would sleep when now, at least, she had seen the nature of the enemy. *Some* of the enemies, and there were more. There was her father. She wanted the oblivion of sleep to free her from fear and fury and let the fury win. She would sleep and dream of finding allies in the morning, because that was what she needed. It would take more than solid Raymond Forrest to win this war and save the memory of Thomas Porteous from being dragged into slime and that mattered most of all. Thomas being revered for what he was and what he wanted to do.

She fell into sleep abruptly, halfway through the making of a list, thoughts veering to the Lady in Pink, the map, the girl called Peg who was on the brink of something, thinking also of the fortifying of the house, lulled by the familiar sounds of it settling for the night. She was aching for the most familiar sound of all. She had been staring at the picture on the opposite wall, a crowd of daffodils. The sound she had missed most was the sound of deep sleep and quiet breathing.

She could hear it now, imagined she could, only it was unquiet breathing.

Someone else was breathing in this house. It was more than the sound of the sea.

The noise came from overhead. Then it turned into the creak of a floorboard, a groan, and then, sobbing.

She lay still, pulled the blanket over her head, denied it and willed it away until she could no longer believe it was not Thomas, still breathing, somewhere close.

Chapter Eight

A restful room, with moss green walls and no pictures. Night time. There were mismatched tables and chairs, a blue window seat with a view of the sea.

'I shouldn't have done it, you know,' Monica said. 'Her hair came out all wrong and she was all the wrong colours, already, but I was that annoyed with her for not talking, my hand slipped. Although I have to say, it went with the leather trousers and all that. She doesn't suit red, never did.'

'Dressed to kill,' Jones said.

'Well, she wasn't in mourning, that's for sure. I mean, really, she looked like an anorexic barmaid with attitude. As if she meant to look brazen. There were half of us in the shop wanting to hug her, the rest wanting to know what'd gone on, and she doesn't say a word. Black leather trousers. Off to London, with that silly old suitcase. I mean she looked like a footballer's wife down on her luck. She doesn't help herself, really she doesn't – doesn't exactly reach out, does she?'

'There's not been too many people reaching in,' Jones said.

He sipped his whisky. Monica and he were sitting in the snug on the second floor of the Bell, right on the seafront, near the pier with a view of it made gloomy by the salt- and dirt-encrusted windows. The sea mist had risen and gone away. It was after closing time and they had been there long enough for the outside world to become uninviting.

'If only she'd *said*.'

'Said what?'

'Said how it is. How she feels,' Monica said.

'She doesn't do that. Never bloody did. Close as a clam. It's me should have asked more.'

Monica pulled at an earring, looked at her watch and decided on one more drink. The late night arrangement in the Bell consisted of the landlord rolling to bed and leaving the out-of-hours customers to fend for themselves. Jones and Monica were the only ones remaining, smoking like chimneys in public premises that for all intents and purposes looked shut. Only a short walk home; if it happened that they should coincide later, at his or hers, no one would notice, although neither of them cared who knew about such an occasional, private arrangement. The town was full of such. Only Monica wasn't going to invite him in tonight and she hadn't for a while. She was hiding something and listening too closely. He should have noticed that sooner, shouldn't he? Monica came back fairly steadily and resumed her seat with a degree of dignity. Two middle-aged old soaks, a long way from being fully soaked, yet, close, but becoming adept at keeping secrets and avoiding hidden subjects in a way they never had before. Now they lied by evasion and told the truth with equal ease, always avoiding that other agenda of Di's dad.

'C'mon,' she nudged. 'Tell me what's going to happen next?'

He considered the question.

'I'm going to the lav.'

She punched his broad shoulder. 'I didn't mean here and *now*, I mean with *Di*. Will they come and take her away again?'

She knew about that already, or he wouldn't have told her. Didn't want to speculate about how she knew.

'Madam,' he said, touching his nose. 'I am no longer a member of the Constabulary. How the hell should I know?'

'Come off it, Jones. You still got people who do.'

'Only just. And no, I don't think so.'

Shouldn't have told her. Shouldn't have boasted about the contacts and how he knew that the Porteous children were raising Cain and pulling strings and all that shit. Fuck. Whatever slipped his tongue to Monica got passed on some- where else and he had a sick feeling he knew where. He hadn't told her how he had waited on at the house, but he bet she knew that too.

'I only know those kids of Thomas have got their fucking teeth in. He left everything to her, and they want it. And maybe someone else is helping drip the poison, don't sup- pose you know who, do you?'

Monica shrugged. 'Course not. It'll be his bloody kids. They must be sick as parrots, but what did they expect? They never went near him after he came out of hospital, nor much before that, for that matter. Brought *their* kids and fled screaming from the party. And as for Di, well, you've never been sure of her yourself, have you?'

No, he hadn't. Still wasn't, but he was always going to defend her, and this affection he and Monica had all depended on not falling out. He leant forward and patted her hand. Didn't trust her and didn't want to lose her. Quig was the problem, unless he really was fucking paranoid.

'I don't *know* fuck. Di's got bigger problems. And the cops are going to come back, for sure. All I do know is that maybe we all should have done more, you know. Can't have been easy.'

'What's so hard about waiting for a rich man to die?' Monica scoffed.

'She didn't just wait, Mon. She stopped it happening. She hauled him out of the water twice last summer, I saw it. Whatever her reasons, she didn't want that man to die until he was good and ready.'

'Or she was ready to collect.'

He stared at her, aghast at her callousness, and hid it with a shaking of the head, clinked his glass against hers, and started on a joke. *Have you heard the one about* . . . and forgot the punch line. He thought, sickeningly, of the figure at the door of Di's house, pressed against the glass. The hat.

'You'd think old Quig might get in touch,' he said, as if it was simply an observation. 'Like he might like to know that his daughter's fucking widowed.'

They didn't talk about the wedding.

'I wouldn't know about that, Jones love. You're getting maudlin. Best go home, hey?'

'Can I come with you?'

He was teasing her, knowing what she would say.

'Another time, love. I'm bushed.'

Jones got up and swallowed his drink, started pacing around the little room, lighting another fag and feeling queasy. He wanted to go up to Di's place, now. Small town, they knew everything and knew nothing. He grinned at Monica as if to say, no hard feelings.

'Couldn't have done anyway, Doll. Got fishing to do. I've left my rod on the pier with a nice young bird looking after it.'

She smiled back. There was never any winning with a fisherman. They always had to have the last word.

Jones had been fishing earlier in the evening, coming and going. He wasn't lying or talking big. There *had* been a girl there, hunkered down with nowhere to go. Told him she was fucking resting, did he mind? He gave her some chocolate before leaving his rod and telling her to get inside soon, love, it's fucking cold. The pier was open all night tonight: he might even catch a fish. His conscience was heavy, but his steps grew ever more certain as soon as he saw the lights. The pier was his haven, his space, his vantage point, his extra lung. It was always like that. He was a free and powerful man there; the pier ennobled those who loved it. No fancy wrought iron, no elegant railings and definitely no amusements. Solid concrete, with a closed caff at the sea end and a bunker by the gates on the landward side, the pier wasn't for fun; it was for fishing. Others said it was so ugly it existed purely for the convenience of the suicidal. Jones knew the three watchmen who worked the shifts and took turns to bed down in the bunker by the gates, so the pier was always open to him. Jones's idea of heaven would be to live on the pier because it was home. He found his rod where he had left it, stroked it fondly. Not a bite, but that was not the point.

The pier was officially open all night, four nights a week, depending on the seasons and the fishing competitions. Fishing folk brought foul-weather clothes and stayed the course, sheltering in the open concrete shelters that hardly deserved the name. To stay out there all hours, catching fish in a gale, was the highest achievement most of them knew and they rejoiced in it privately. They weren't a club but a confederacy, not of close friends but distant allies, co-existing in silent, apparently indifferent harmony like card players concentrating on their own moves. No hierarchies except between the skilled and the unskilled, no enmity either and no social barriers. Harry, Jack, and Stefan would share a smidgeon of disgust for the incompetent newcomer who would not ask for help and got in the way, while Harry might envy the equipment owned by Abdul, but that was it. What Jones liked was the blessing of their sheer indifference: no one cared who the fuck you were. They would let you sleep. You could die quietly here.

Then there was, of course, the other reason why he loved and needed the pier. From here, he could see the whole sprawling frontage of the town for a mile in either direction and when he was here, he used his powerful binoculars as much as his rod. He knew when lights came on and lights came off; knew the colour of the doors of the houses and the shadows of the alleyways in between. *So dull on the front these days*, one of the old fishermen said. *When my grandad came here, every second house on the south side was a pub or a brothel, that was the rough end; you could hear the screams from here. So ordinary now.* Not to Jones it wasn't.

There was that same girl huddled asleep in the shelter near his rod, and Jones paused to pity her. He had given her the blanket from his bag, and the chocolate, and that was all. You couldn't touch runaways these days; you had to keep your distance and watch, like he had with Di. He smoked a cigarette, ignored the girl and trained his eyes on Di's house. There were lights in the top windows. Nothing to worry about, then.

Someone hit him from behind. He staggered, keeping hold of the binoculars, and crumpled slowly. The girl leapt up, shouting, ran into him and broke his fall.

In her dream, Di was in the water with Thomas, hauling him to shore and fighting for breath. She could swim like a fish, even against the tide which she knew better than he. She knew what he intended, and she yelled at him, *Not yet*, she said, *please not yet. You've got things to do.*

All the sounds of the house had become background to that loud, laboured breathing, turning to sobbing, an undisguisable sound coming from close by. She sat up and listened, touched the surface of the pillow, then the bedside table, feeling with her long fingers for anything tangible to prove she was alive, turned on the light and saw the picture on the wall to the left.

Man with dog and child. Blue sky and sea. Prominently placed waste paper bin, dog cocking leg against it, old couple on bench all looking forward, him looking at them. A conversation about to start. Stubby figures against a great big sky. Her own description of it, written yesterday. *The sort of picture that makes you listen to it*, she had typed, *like putting a shell to your ear.*

Big sky, big sea. It wasn't the sound of the waves she could hear, nor was it Thomas, but someone weeping and coughing next door.

The master bedroom was next to the gallery. She put on her dressing gown, put the knife in the pocket, plucked a scarf from those decorating the bedpost and a blanket from the chair and moved towards the next room. The gallery room glowed only with the light from the windows. At the furthest end away, there was a fine old settee and a man lay

141

on it. He was dressed from top to toe like a stage burglar, black lycra, black surfing shoes, his face a pale contrast of chalky white. He was wheezing *ah, ah hah, a hah hah,* trying to smother his own noise. She stood over him, taking in his slenderness, the handkerchief clutched in his hand. Then she flung the blanket over his body and knelt on his chest. His eyes opened as she placed the scarf against his neck, pinioning his chest with her knees, throttling him with silk. A sweet, salty smell came from him. Blankets were good for catching birds without hurting them. She had even caught a rat that way. She released the scarf, slightly.

He spoke.

'I was only fishing,' he said. And then the coughing started. A racking cough, enough to make him buck and rear, flail his arms and legs, thrashing like a landed fish. She touched his white face and felt the hectic heat of a fevered body, relented, took away the scarf. He raised his arms and shoved her off. The coughing resumed until he lay back exhausted. She sat on the floor next to him, assessing weight, size, appearance.

'You're a bastard, Saul,' she said.

'So I am. I do apologise.'

It was a disarming thing to say and she was not disarmed.

'Such an intrusion,' he said. 'Such a terrible intrusion at a time of grief. Only I couldn't resist it. Not such an opportunity to see things in secret, so I found my way in and then I couldn't find my way out, got sick, something like that. And all I find is lovely stuff, collected with love. He was a real collector, wasn't he? The real, real thing. You're one, too. I was overcome with sorrow. So much crap out there, and so much real.'

'You're a shit, Saul. Where have you been? Why didn't you even try to speak to me?'

He closed his eyes. She flicked her fingers against his pale cheek, painfully.

'Nearly a week since Thomas died and not a word. You shit.'

He shook his head, opened one eye.

'Dear, dear. I thought Thomas had cured you of bad language. Where do you think I've been? I've been consorting with the enemy, as instructed. I have been in their houses and in their minds. I have been reading their correspondence and listening to them. Playing bluff and setting snares. As well as waiting for you to learn about hatred and greed. Are you going to call the police? You may as well. I'll go quietly.'

She looked at him closely in the bright light. His face was gaunt with bright blue eyes and a large mouth. His body was thin, his legs like sticks and the voice was exaggeratedly well bred. Saul was Saul, the chameleon, and it was a relief to see him, the relief tempered with acute suspicion until she remembered the sobbing. Saul had been sobbing for Thomas.

'Ah well, let's get it over with,' he said. 'Just call them.'

'As if.'

She shook her head, hiding the beginnings of a smile. Then she tucked the blanket round him so tightly he could not move.

'I've seen you looking better, Saul,' she said. 'So why didn't you knock on the door?'

'Insatiable curiosity,' he said. 'Absolutely insatiable, demanding instant gratification. I had to see for myself that you were keeping faith. That you hadn't removed anything. Besides, old habits die hard. I hate to be announced. Anyway, you were out, gone to London, taken that case.'

'Saul,' she said, 'You insult me any more and I am very likely to disfigure you. I have a knife.'

She placed a hand on his groin. Colour flooded his face; he struggled to free his arms and began to cough again.

'Leave my gonads alone, Di. They might be useful. In case I need to sleep with the enemy, which is, in a manner of speaking, exactly what I have been doing. And believe me, it isn't comfortable. And if I'd spoken to you, I wouldn't have been able to keep up the act. Oh, screw you, Thomas, you old darling, why did you have to die?'

The weeping began again.

Jones woke in the third shelter on the left on the north side of the pier. The back of his head hurt like hell and he raised his hand to feel it. No blood, a lump the size of an egg. He held his forefinger in front of his face and touched the tip of his nose, like he was testing a drunk. The next test was to see if he could walk in a straight line and he got up to try. Not so good. He could stand. The binoculars were still round his neck. He leaned against the concrete balustrade of the pier and put them to his eyes but they were too heavy to hold. Dawn was waiting somewhere, but not near enough. Di's house still blazed with light. Someone was dragging at his arm. He turned, focused on a kid with a badge round her neck so big he could read it, *Peg*, looking at him with big anxious eyes.

'You all right?' she asked. 'You've been asleep.'

He looked at her blankly.

'Don't remember, do you? You gave me some chocolate, earlier on. I came on here to sleep. Then you went away and came back. I looked after your rod ... Then someone hit you and you fell on me.'

'Christ,' Jones said. 'And you fucking stayed around? You mad or what?'

She shrugged. 'Someone had to. Nobody else noticed. They wouldn't, would they?'

'No, not on here they wouldn't. They mind their own business on here.'

The lights of Di's house twinkled in the distance, like a welcoming beacon in the lightening sky.

'Fucking nightmare, this place,' the girl said. 'Nowhere to get a cup of tea.'

The deserted pier was no longer a friendly place. Jones started to walk, unsteadily, but purposefully towards the open gates of the exit. The door to the watchman's bunker was firmly shut. His memory was fitful; came on the pier, set up rod, talked to someone, what time? Went for drink, came back. Perhaps someone thought he was coming on to this kid, no, no one would ever think that, because whatever else he was, Jones would never do that, he was passionate about kids, but not that way. People saw stuff that wasn't there to be seen, anything would do if you wanted an excuse to hit him and Jesus H Christ, he was weary and hungry, and this kid seemed to be going the same way. They wavered out of there together. He didn't like the way she held on to his arm, which was humiliating, but he needed it and he let her. He felt as if he smelled, probably did. Booze and sweat and an exploding head. He was fucking rank and he did not want to go home. How long between leaving the pub and being hit? Fifteen minutes? Long enough for someone to tell someone where he was going.

Ten minutes' brisk walk to Di's house on a good day, longer now, with both of them blathering. Her name was Peg, she said, and she had a map. Showed where the pier was, she said; thought she would kip there and save the money, pretended to be looking after his rod, giggle, giggle. You look like my dad. Do you know someone called Di? No I don't, he said, no one knows her, not really. We should be going the opposite way, he said, I live down the other end, only you can't come in. Have you got a wife? she asked. No, not now, I never want to go home, that's my trouble. Mine too, Peg said. Dear God, she chatted on like she trusted him. A London child, she was, and didn't she know that this place was all about fish and feathered birds and the sea, all of that far more important than human beings.

Jones stopped and gestured expansively towards the waves, pointing back towards the pier. 'Innit marvellous,' he said, stumbling. 'I saw Thomas there at twelve, he said he was going home. I spoke to him, he said he was fine but he always said that. She didn't call the ambulance until hours after. What did she do?'

Peg looked at the map. 'Who are you talking about?'

'Di. Who lives up there.'

'Oh,' said Peg, 'That Di. She's a really kind woman, that one.'

Jones stopped, as if struck by lightning.

'Yes,' he said. 'Do you know what? You're fucking right. That's what she is. Kind. Too fucking kind by half. That's Di alright and that's all we need to know. It's as simple as that.'

There was nowhere else to go.

CHAPTER NINE

'I don't care if you're sick and tired, Saul. You have to go on talking to me. Say it again.'

Saul sprawled in Thomas's winter chair. It was upholstered in brilliant, faded blue, with scuffed arms and like most objects in this house, seemed to have an independent life of its own.

'I've been halfway party to this plan,' she said. 'But not all the way.'

'You couldn't be,' Saul said. 'Because you kept on thinking that one day Gayle and Beatrice were bound to inherit the finer qualities of their father and understand his passions. Can't imagine why you did.'

'Because I wanted to.'

'Because you think you inherited your own saving graces?'

'Some. A talent for concealing things. And I'm handy with a knife.'

'We stray from the point,' Saul said, carefully. 'Thomas and I hatched a plan to save this collection from the threat ·

posed by his children, who are led by Edward, who in turn clones his own bitterness. He's a failure in life who's wrecked his career by serial dishonesty and he has something to prove. Inherited qualities? If you had known Christina, you'd be better placed to judge them. But you didn't know Christina.'

Yes, I did, in a manner of speaking, Di thought. *I knew what she could do,* but it was an unspoken thought.

'At least I know *them* better now,' Di said. 'I hate them: Gayle, Edward, Beatrice. Although I don't know which I hate most.'

'Good. You're going to need that, although I'm sorry you found out in the way you did. That was no one's intention, although I must say, Edward's pre-emptive raid on the London flat was entirely in character and certainly endorses the rightness of the plan.'

'And the plan is . . . ?'

'To entrap them. To compromise them. To *give* them something, but make them work for it. To make *them* take a risk. To show themselves to themselves. Turn them into thieves, and soon. Otherwise, they will hound you into the ground. And it must be sooner rather than later, because they're going to look foolish when the Coroner exonerates you, and they'll think of something more extreme than putting you in prison. They'll get really vicious, and they won't stop. And it's urgent, because although Edward is my new best friend, I fear he has sources of information he doesn't share with me. Contacts, also. He'll go off on a dangerous tangent, like he already has.'

'We compromise them,' Di said slowly. 'We make *them* the thieves. Yes, I like that.'

She got up. They had been talking too long. The sky was growing light.

'Whatever the plan,' Di said. 'We need allies. Thomas always said the allies would arrive.'

Saul yawned, unable to decide between hunger and an acute desire for sleep. A loud banging on the back door brought him to his feet. It was a confident *rat, tat, tat*, nothing surreptitious about it. The first light was in the sky.

'Perhaps that's them, now,' he said.

Dawn had merged into morning by the time Di sat at the computer.

The small picture on the desk was one she had found upstairs and moved to the place so that she could look at it and record it in words. *A bowl full of old necklaces, odd earrings and beads.*

She wrote to him.

This is not my story, Thomas is it? It will never be mine, it will always be the story of someone else in which I play a part. I'd like it if there was someone else who knew me, but there's isn't.

Been talking half the night, Thomas, to a sick and weary man, too. You knew that Saul has been cosying up to your children since whenever. You always reckon that he had as fine an eye for personality as he does for a painting.

I think my father's back, Thomas, I think he's there, although I don't want to believe it. You thought of that possibility, but not what might happen if, by any chance, he should collaborate with your children. Saul says he'll put paid to that, but I don't know what else he might do. It's rich, isn't it, that he's afraid of me, because of what I know of him, and I am only afraid of him for the knowledge he may have. And because he never acts alone, he only ever carries out the intentions of others. Saul says, discount him, but then neither of us explained everything to Saul, did we? My father might indeed want to help in the way he knows best.

It was too soon to go to London, Thomas, wasn't it? But it gave me the anger I need. Saul's right: a little hatred goes a long way and I'd better hang on to it.

All I want right now is the sea and the sky and the bay, but the allies have arrived. You said they would and I think I know what they can do. Man the fortress. I mustn't be alone here. The house is under siege.

So, here they are. Saul has the master plan you devised together; Jones is obstinate and little Peg can read a map. And they've all been to prison. A bond of sorts.

Can I tell Saul everything? No, not yet.

I'll tell you more about the allies another time. For now, I'm going to the Bay. I wish you were with me. And Patrick.

I miss you so much.

The Allies. Di counted them up. The smell of bacon had driven them dizzy and, now replete, they were floundering round in the kitchen like so many soft toys. Peg, with the bruise on her forehead worn like a flower, full of pride for rescuing Jones, and him full of shame for being rescued. Peg, a girl on the run, not so much damaged that she could not believe in the kindness of strangers, a person of undiscovered resources. Then there was Jones, with whom Di had unfinished business and mutual, exasperated affection. Jones and Thomas, another story, friends of a sort. Thomas and Saul Blythe, another story, too. These were what she had to trust.

Skinny Saul, propped up in the corner in recovery mode, was the possessor of the kind of voice she could mimic, but never own. He was the one with the glib tongue and the charm; articulate even in delirium and sitting like an invalid acting a part. The one who now knew every painting in the house, reclining in Thomas's chair and looking at the nude with fond but objective appreciation, his eyes straying to the tiny painting up on the wall next to it as if measuring it. The house was always ready for guests, because Thomas wanted it ready for the army who never came. Thomas and Diana, wanting it ready for what it might become.

They gobbled breakfast of bacon and eggs with a variation of smoked salmon and chives for Saul, the burglar, if you please. The lump on the back of Jones's head was spitefully sore, would have been worse had he been entirely sober when receiving it, but the application of ice dulled the pain, if not the indignity of the event. *I didn't see it coming*, he kept saying. *What am I like? I should have seen it coming.* The vocal sympathy of Saul, with his exaggerated cries of *Oh no, of course you couldn't,* created an immediate empathy. Saul fussed and bothered and found remedies from the hypochondriac's arsenal in his bag: tiger balm, lavender and paracetamol, praising Jones meantime for his hardiness. It was rather well done, Di thought. Otherwise Saul, who managed a degree of elegance even when exhausted, would have been anathema to burly, homophobic Jones, even allowing for Jones's innate appreciation of style.

All Di required of her allies at this point was not loyalty or affection, but the ability to keep watch – and if they wanted to stay, which they did, because none of them had anywhere else to go for now, they had to come clean about who they were, if only so they understood one another. Di craved the sea and the sky and the keyboard, but she was in charge.

'I want each of you say why you're here and why you aren't in a hurry to move,' Di said.

She pointed at Peg. Peg was at the end of the line, shrugged, pulled her hair over her forehead, sat up straight and spoke fast.

'I'm Peg, eighteen, born in Borough, not that that'll mean anything to you. Tried everything, shoplifter, shop worker, tried everything I'm not good at, like stealing and being a tart. I was running away, anywhere, picked up the wrong ticket, got on a train and ended up on a fucking pier. I'm good at cleaning, love it and you've got a lotta house and I owe you fifty quid. And I like him.' She pointed at Jones.

'Fuck's sake,' said Jones. 'Why me?'

''Cos you were nice to me. Same for her,' pointing at Di. 'Goes a long way, that does.'

'You kept me warm,' Jones said.

'Always the best thing,' Peg quipped. 'Don't like being cold.'

'And you, Jones,' Di said. 'Speak up.'

Jones looked shifty and, deciding he had nothing to lose, saluted his audience and spoke as if reciting a police report in a court of law having taken an oath of limited truthfulness.

'Ex PC Jones, never rose further, retired copper, ever so lightly bent but not broken. Retired non-voluntarily, briefly in prison. Familiar with family Quigly: arrested Mrs P here, when was it, nearly ten years ago, when she was found in here and took the fall for the others, although there were other things going on in here on that particular night. Said officer acquainted with DQ when she was knee high, and conversant with fact she had a bloody bad deal and apologises for failing to keep her out of prison. Was flabbergasted when she came home and took up house with Mr P, even more when she married him. Reason I want to stay here? I don't like my own home, especially now, and I want to be needed. Miss Q has never needed me, but it may appear she does now, because Mr Quigly, her old dad, may have hit me on the pier. Besides, the cops are going to come back for Miss Q sooner or later. She isn't out of the woods there, and I'd better be here when they do.'

Jones was ever economical with the truth and always knew more than he was prepared to say. He spoke in his own code, and was about to say more but wilted under Di's stare and looked away. *Don't talk about my dad; he's my problem.*

'And,' he added, 'I know this house. Was one of the last kids to go to school here. I could catalogue the ghosts. Make an archive.'

Jones finished without a single fuck and turned to Saul.

'What about you then? Who the fuck are you?'

Saul inclined his head, graciously.

'Me, darling? I'm a long term acquaintance of one Thomas Porteous.' Saul was all flourishes; so camp he was sending himself up. 'It seems I share something with all of you, i.e. a criminal record from a not entirely misspent youth when I was a fairly nifty dealer in stolen goods, although 'goods' is too broad a description for the finer works of art which are my speciality. I specialise in the relatively obscure, the anonymous and I only deal with persons of taste.'

He adjusted the scarf round his throat.

'I am now an almost respectable dealer, one who abhors theft, except when strictly necessary. I simply want things to fall into the right hands, rather than the wrong ones. I want things of beauty to be honoured for what they are. And as such, I loved and admired Thomas, it was a joy to work with him and I knew what he wanted to do.'

'And what was that?' Jones asked.

'Don't you know?' Saul said incredulously, as if it should have been perfectly clear. Jones watched Di's face break into a grin and realised he was seeing her in a whole new light. Di, a fucking scholar.

'He wanted to put together a fine collection of English paintings, one of the finest. He wanted it to rescue the unloved, the unfashionable, things prone to destruction and neglect. He wanted to create an art gallery for this town. To educate and inspire.'

More flourishing of hands. Jones liked it.

Di turned her head away and blew her nose. 'Educate and inspire,' she said, fiercely. 'Just like he did with me.'

Jones laughed, embarrassed, because this was all too many fine words and pretentious crap for him. The man Saul was the kind of thief he liked, and Di Quigly might just be a sucker for daft talk and big ambitions, but he was moved all the same, giggled nervously and said, *fuck me.*

'Don't laugh,' Saul said, 'It's a noble ambition and what the hell's wrong with that? How else did we get the fine collections that civilise us, except through the efforts and passions of Collectors? Anyway, Thomas was exactly the kind of client I adore and they're rare as hens' teeth. His were the right kind of hands to hold precious things. A person in pursuit of quality rather than vanity, who collects what might not otherwise survive, let alone be seen, with a view to passing it on. Thomas knew nobody ever owns anything. So does she, I mean Di.' He looked at them all, especially Jones. Jones was getting the point. 'Collecting works of art and giving them a good home is a bit like fostering children, don't you think? You don't own them, either, but you have to make sure they're safe. You have to be ready to kill for them.'

Peg was falling asleep. Jones was staring at the wall and Saul buffed his nails on his scarf.

'Steady on,' Jones said. 'I'd kill for a child, but I fucking wouldn't kill for a painting. Fucking collectors, bloody mad. Do you reckon,' he asked Saul, 'that Thomas might have blown his marriage by this collecting malarkey? Left his missus right out in the cold by it? Women don't like that.'

The conversation was now between the two men. Saul thought about it seriously.

'I've known one or two collectors who would cheerfully burn the whole family for a square inch of Matisse. I gather that the late, drowned Mrs Porteous was insanely jealous of Thomas's interests, but far more jealous of his success. So jealous she was barking mad. A lot to do with being a failed artist herself.'

Di was silent, watching the dialogue between two disparate men like watching a tennis ball in play.

'Bored wives are jealous of a husband's jobs and outside interests,' Jones said. 'It's why so many police marriages go wrong, because the Job's so much more important and fucking interesting than anything and anybody else.'

'It wasn't his collecting, was it, Saul?' Di said, breaking into the circle.

He shook his head, smiling at her.

'No, it wasn't. He simply didn't have enough money and his daughters enchanted him and that wasn't a way of life Christina wanted. Only she couldn't admit it. She had to pretend there was a nobler reason for leaving.'

'I don't fucking get it,' Jones said.

'No reason why you should,' Saul said, smoothly. 'Now, Di darling, will you let us get some sleep? Tomorrow is another day and all that. This collection has to survive and thrive. Di,

I think you and I should go on a spending spree. It's time you came out of the woodwork as Thomas's successor. Collections have to grow. They can't stay static. You have to spend.'

He rose from the faded blue chair, knocking over a cup.

'A *spending spree*?' Jones shouted. 'That's the last thing she should do. She's being watched and she should keep her bloody head down, at least until after the inquest. She's under suspicion, she's got his daughters stirring the shit and waiting for a chance to pounce, she's got skeletons in cupboards ...'

'What did you say?' Di said quietly.

'Oh Di, love, Di, why did you wait those two fucking hours before you called the ambulance? I saw him on the pier in the morning, I saw him go home. I saw the ambulance go. You said he'd only just come in, but he hadn't. He'd been inside two hours. I had to tell them that. Why did you wait?'

There was anguish in his voice. Silence fell in the room. Saul was watching her closely. Di was pale.

'He was dead,' she said patiently. 'He was dead as soon as he came in the door and sat in the chair. He'd bought me a bunch of flowers.'

Jones remembered the flowers. Purple daisies, dying in a corner.

'He was dead in his own chair. I didn't want them jumping all over him and breaking his ribs to bring him back, so I waited. I wanted to talk to him.'

Jones closed his eyes. Three beats passed. He believed her, knowing that the doubts would return.

Saul settled back into the chair, hugging himself into it. Di left Saul asleep there, wrapped in a blanket. She took Jones and Peg up to the top dormitory and showed them where to wash and sleep. She was acting like a school matron, welcoming pupils at the beginning of term. Then she wrote to Thomas. Then she took her bike out of the back yard and pedalled down the back road to the bay.

She had been nursing him for so long, she was used to sleepless nights.

She paused to touch her head as she rode, felt a slight amount of soft stubble at the back. Flying along the coastal path on her old bike, feeling childlike and giddy with freedom, going faster and faster, on her way to the other bay, a hidden place, sheltered by the road and invisible from it, the domain of birds. Marshland stretched for a mile; Thomas loved the sound of the curlew as much as the cackling of the November geese and the crazy mewing of the seagulls and there was a purpose in coming to this place. This was where he wanted his ashes to be scattered – among the birds, because for all that he was an avid collector of art, Thomas valued nature more.

A cackling of bird noise filled her ears and she looked skywards to see a battalion of migrating geese flying far above her head, calling to each other, maintaining an effortless formation as they headed away, the sight and sound of them delighting her with the optimism of their pilgrimage and the energy of it. She stared at them until they passed, sick with anxiety for the stragglers on the edge, satisfied only when they regrouped, clapped her cold hands softly to celebrate and wish them speed.

Don't look down, Thomas; look up, she told him. *You got ten minutes to see this; look at them! They make you think you can fly and then you can.*

Only when they disappeared did she lower her eyes to sea level, dragging her gaze back across the distant sand of the beach to look for the earthbound wading birds she loved

almost as much. Long-legged creatures, stalking and peck-
ing, vulnerable and determined, picking their way like models
on a runway, foraging with patient grace. And then she saw
a figure walking across the marsh, invading their territory,
moving towards the sea, a pin figure of a man with a cap,
trespassing on sacred territory.

She knew it was her father, from his own peculiar gait, half
limp half affectation rather than a real disability affecting his
shuffling speed, like a Long John Silver. A bald head hidden
by a cap because the slightest hint of sun burned his scalp,
long sleeves and dark coats at any time of the year to shield
his pallor. A visitor, a stranger returning, drawn back like
the geese to home territory, a man who once lived in these
parts and went away, where the real work was. The unofficial
undertaker, who knew how to conceal the bodies, always
homesick, seeking revenge for disappointment. Sometimes
looking for the daughter he blamed for the wreck of his life,
sometimes not. Wanting to help, perhaps.

Di looked at the striding limping figure, remembered
another time when he had brought her here. Saw herself putting her hands over her ears and begging him not to shoot the
birds in the bay, screaming so hard that they got up and flew
and ruined his chance and then he had hit her. *What's wrong
with it?* he said. *It's only practice.*

He had no air rifle now, simply the speedy, limping step,
going north.

She felt a need to scream, stifled it because it would disturb
the birds.

*I am NOT that child. I am a Collector, a grown-up, a person
with a mission. I cannot afford to be afraid of you, but yes, I am.*

She looked towards the empty space left by the figure on
the landscape, turned away and went home.

Whom should she fear most? The one who shot the birds, buried the bodies, locked her in cellars and gave her away? The one who knew her, and was also afraid of her?

Waste time on fearing Him, whom no one would ever believe, or fear the ones with the greater power in the world, such as Beatrice, Gayle and Edward?

One at a time. Concentrate on them.

The two sad bitches.

Chapter Ten

> Picture: *A Victorian poster, showing a sweet little girl dressed in lace with rosy cheeks, advertising soap.*

What Patrick registered from the picture and the room was the kind of little girl he didn't like and the smell of patchouli which he didn't like either. Not that he really minded where he was as long as he could sit on the floor and scribble in his book and they all behaved as if he did not exist.

Edward and Gayle sat across the kitchen table in Beatrice's north London house which they did not like either. Beatrice's two children, Alan and Edmund, sat upstairs acting as young teenagers crossing the gulf between childhood and beyond, crouched over mobile phones, embarrassed by their elders as much as they were by *weird* Patrick who didn't talk much and always stayed with the adults and wasn't allowed his own phone. It irritated Beatrice that Patrick, in whom she had no interest either as a nephew or otherwise, should always be present at siblings' meetings, but the child was always there and since he was always preoccupied, she usually ceased to notice. He would sit cross-legged on the floor if there was not the luxury of a table, with a book propped up against his feet, silent and insignificant. The adults were gathered around the laptop, looking at an email from Raymond Forrest. Gayle was noticing that the surface of the kitchen table was grubby and, like everything else in this dark little house, sticky. Beatrice affected a martyred, biodegradable kind of poverty that was not quite true.

'Shall I read it out?' Edward said.

'Please,' Gayle said, trying to admire him. Edward did so love the sound of his own voice and she was trying to avoid the thought that that was all he had left. The good looks had run to seed: the jowls had grown, and his once handsome face was lined with petulance. Too bad he had not quite fulfilled his promise, dissipated what he had got on one get-rich scheme after another, gobbled the silver spoon with which he had been born and relied on finding another. It was never his fault that business ventures never worked; there was never the instant profit and no one understood his vision. Gayle had married him when he was full of promise, schemes and a voice; they had managed the last years by borrowing in anticipation of another fortune that she had promised and now he faced a chasm. Gayle had misled him; so had her mother. She had always said it was in the bag; she had blown it and she owed him.

Edward did not care whom he pushed over which cliff as long as he did not fall himself; he was trying to see what he could retrieve and, above all, he wanted the respect he knew he had lost. He wanted his wife to remember the man he was, not a man with a bitter spouse and a dysfunctional boy who should have been an athlete, but a man of decision, ready to take charge, go into battle, a man who made things happen. So far, he had failed. And all he had was a powerful body and a powerful voice, which could not sweeten the pill of what he read out loud.

'"I have to report that the Coroner, on receipt of the post mortem report, sees no reason to delay the funeral/ cremation of Thomas Porteous. The PM report concludes that albeit the deceased was unnaturally thin, he was not ill nourished and a degree of muscular fitness prevailed. He had survived far longer than anticipated, apparently due to excellent nursing care and imaginative nutrition. The ultimate cause of death was an embolism, coinciding, only possibly, with over exertion. Nothing untoward was discovered."'

'Over-exertion,' Gayle said. Edward continued to read. Gayle smelt her own acetone breath, disliking the word 'nourished'. She struggled to maintain her own slenderness; she was always hungry.

'"Your demand for a second post mortem is under consideration. The Coroner is sympathetic to it, especially in the light of your information received as to the background of the deceased's wife and her inappropriate behaviour at the scene of his death. Mrs Porteous remains the subject of enquiries."'

'So,' Beatrice said. 'She didn't have to poison him. She gets away with it. Oh, my poor father, poor man.'

Such an expression of sympathy for the dear deceased was so breathtaking in its hypocrisy that even Edward paused.

'He must be avenged,' Beatrice said, sonorously. 'It is our duty.'

Edward stifled his loathing for his sister-in-law because they needed her. Beatrice was stupidity incarnate what with her poetry, her long gone spouse, her macrobiotic diet and her refusal to contemplate anything as menial as paid work. There was nothing left but the moral high ground, which she occupied tenaciously. Whatever rocked her boat; anything to keep her on board, even though she was the one who had blown it, even more than Gayle, after that damn party.

'Look, another post mortem might exonerate her completely,' Edward said. 'Contesting the will remains an option, but even with all the dirt we've got on her, it takes time and it might fail. We can't rely on her being put in prison. We can't rely on driving her mad. We've got to outwit her, like Saul says. Get what we can, and get it soon. Get something, at least, and get it before Thomas is buried. Your mother died ten years ago next week. A good deadline, hey? What we can't do is just play a waiting game. And her father couldn't even get inside the house. We've got to go with Saul's plan.'

The urgency and the authority were infectious. Gayle looked at her husband. If they did not get a large injection of money soon, she was going to lose him. He would leave her and she would be everything she feared most. She would be like Beatrice in a house like this: she would be as mad and bitter as her own mother and nobody would rescue her. She sat with her arms folded, her nails biting into her own skin, thinking of the house by the sea.

'Wouldn't it be easiest just to get rid of Her?' Beatrice said. 'Burn the house down with her in it, ha ha. And get the insurance,' she added.

Beatrice, mistress of malice and the blunt instrument. Contemplating arson, but never subtlety, so destructive she was perfectly capable of turning herself into a bomb, which was a useful tendency, but not yet, because she would bring them all down with her clumsiness.

'Hardly practical,' Edward said, patiently. 'With uncertain outcome. And we'd only get a fraction of the value.'

'Her dad would do it for us,' Beatrice said.

'No, he wouldn't,' Gayle said. 'He's all talk. Go on, Edward, please do.'

He cleared his throat.

'Saul's plan is sure fire, short term. Thomas has a few priceless paintings. We take the best.'

'But there aren't any priceless paintings,' Gayle said. 'Raymond Forrest says not. There are a lot of paintings, but none of them particularly valuable, individually. There's an inventory, nothing of outstanding value.'

'An inventory that Di compiled. So it's false. There *are* paintings worth upwards of a hundred thousand, and either Di has lied about their existence or *she really doesn't know*. Saul does, though. He's earmarked two in particular. If we were to get them, we'd be bagging a quarter million, which is better than nothing from where I'm standing. And Di wouldn't be able to complain, because either she doesn't know what they are, which shows how ignorant she is, or she's lied about what they are and that makes her a cheat. She'll be hoist on her own petard. She'll have to be quiet about it, if she ever finds out.'

Gayle listened intently. Fifty thousand pounds, let alone a quarter of a million, would get their lives back on track. And there would be an element of revenge in the outwitting of that little bitch, whom she hated with a passion she never expressed, for reasons she never dared explore. A quite different level of loathing to the chanting malice of Beatrice.

'What's in this for Saul?' Gayle said.

'He's a dealer, he gets commission. He was Thomas's dealer, and now he wants to be ours. We're a safer bet, that's all.'

'So why doesn't he just bring us the paintings she's lied about?' Beatrice said. 'Just take them off the wall and bring them to us?'

Again, Edward marvelled at her stupidity.

'They aren't on the walls,' he said. 'They're hidden. And Saul couldn't do that. He's on site and he's got to go on being trusted, because it doesn't stop there, it's just the beginning. No, we have to go and take them, at night. He tells us how to do it, and we do it. Gayle and I will do it.'

'Why not me?' Beatrice pouted.

'Because Gayle will keep her head, Gayle can drive and she knows the house better than you,' he said.

'Do you, dear?' Beatrice asked sweetly. 'You went there more often than me when we were tiny, but do you really remember any more than I do? Bearing in mind we were both traumatised by events.'

'I don't know,' Gayle said, slowly. 'I don't know that I was.'

'Yes, you were. Mother said we hated it. We were frightened of Grandpa first, and then of Dad. Traumatised.'

'I do remember the house as it was. We've scarcely seen it as it is now. We rushed away and didn't come back.'

She turned to Edward.

'So, dearest, why should this plan work better than the last? We tried to get her arrested, and that didn't last for a minute. And that wretched father of hers couldn't even mess the place up. Our little informant. So anxious to help. So ignorant. Pretending to know what he doesn't. All he ever did was pass on gossip. He doesn't know anything.'

'I entirely agree,' Edward said.

Let them fight their own battles and reap their own rewards, without sharing.

'This plan will work,' he said, 'because it's foolproof and it relies on no one but us.'

'So I'm not fit to go on this expedition?' Beatrice said. 'What do I do? Keep the home fires burning when I'd rather put a bomb under hers? Our poor father. I don't care what they say. She starved him. The witch killed him. Ten years since our mother died, and then the witch killed him.'

Beatrice's singsong voice went down to a whisper.

'The witch didn't starve Grandpa,' Patrick said, his voice cutting across Beatrice's ranting. He was shouting and he never shouted: he was as quiet in his speech as his mother: he spoke so rarely and so monosyllabically, the voice unnerved them. 'Grandpa said she made him eat too much.'

Edward turned on him, incredulously. 'What?'

Patrick couldn't stop shouting. He hated it when his father shouted, but he couldn't stop doing it now.

'He said so. He said she made him eat, even when he didn't want to. They make jokes about it. Him and his nice brown witch. Di. That's what he calls her.'

The shout fell into a silence, and then Beatrice cooed at him.

'So when did Grandpa say that, darling? You haven't seen him in a while. You're inventing things.'

'No I'm not. I talk to him all the time, I . . .'

The shrill voice faded away. Gayle was by his side, standing over him, shaking him.

'When? How? What did he say? Who does he talk to?'

'To me,' Patrick said, his voice shrill. 'When I phone him.'

'When you *what*?'

'I phone him a lot, I talk to him.' His voice rose to a shriek. 'He tells me stories on the phone. I tell him about drawings,

I send them to him. And now I can't.' His face crumpled. 'Now I can't,' he wailed. 'I want Grandpa, I want Di.'

Gayle slapped him across the face so hard that his mouth wobbled open. He shook his head, as if dislodging a fly, and put his hands round his chin, holding his lips shut. That was all he was going to say. He tensed himself for the second blow; tried to remember she didn't mean it, she never did.

'Do you talk to Di, too, you deceitful little beast?' Edward shouted.

He shook his head again, more emphatically, mouth still closed but saying, *No*. It was a lie and they believed it. He made up a picture in his head, an outline of a face, thought of something he could draw, the shape of a fish, a table, and a chair. A picture of a witch and her cheery, brown face, who left him with Grandpa and then took him back to the train with something to eat. And talked to him, as if he was real.

'But you did talk to *him*,' Gayle said softly. 'All this time. You treacherous little monster. Go upstairs with the others.'

He went, taking his sketchbook.

'Christ,' Gayle said with an apologetic laugh, feeling her hand sting, redesigning her voice to descend to normal. 'Sorry about that. The viper in the bosom. How could he do this to me? He fell in love with a witch at a party. You're right, Bea, probably an invention.'

'Poor little soul,' Beatrice said in that same, singsong voice. 'Don't blame yourself, Gayle dear. Perhaps you leave him alone too much.'

'I don't,' Gayle said, 'We take him everywhere.'

She thought of the long evenings after school when she and Edward drank and rowed indoors, and banished him. She stopped. Thought of cash missing from her purse and the way her mobile phone ate money and went missing.

Thought of her own son phoning her own father and suppressed a silent scream. How free he was, how self-sufficient, her boy who bunked off school and whose cloying, clinging affection she had never wanted until she noticed its ceasing. Gayle felt on the brink of losing everything.

'Back to the matter in hand,' Edward said, recovering himself, while thinking at the same time of how much his runt of a son was left alone to listen.

'We have to plan against the eventuality of the police doing nothing. We have to get what we can before she spends it, or sells it. We rely on Saul, because we have common interests. Saul will help us obtain the two most valuable pictures in the collection. Soon. Before the anniversary of your mother's death. Doesn't that appeal to you, Beatrice? If we follow this plan, we've got working capital for the rest. We've got *something*.'

An eagle in the hand worth a flock in the bush.

'I'll settle for that,' Beatrice said. 'And it would be lovely revenge, wouldn't it. We steal from the thief who stole our father. Let us join hands.'

It was like they were plighting some troth. Gayle smiled conspiratorially at Edward and rolled her eyes, but still held her sister's hand over the table.

'I would rather there wasn't a fight,' Gayle said, finally, as hands were awkwardly un-joined. She meant that she knew she would never be able to trust herself in a fight. She was the calm one, privately afraid of her own, vicious temper. She had just struck her own son, for God's sake, this time in public: she knew her restraint was precarious, because *she wanted that house*. That house haunted her and she knew that it haunted Patrick, too. Where had he gone when he bunked off school? Beatrice went to make herbal tea in her sticky teapot with water boiled in a diseased kettle. The touch of the place disgusted Gayle – sticky soap, sticky everything, a vision of life as she might lead it without her inheritance; a vision of insanity. She adjusted the shoulders of her jacket, twitched the knees of her skirt and admired her shoes, rearranged her voice yet again. The vision of that house came back again: she was supposed to remember misery in it and yet that was a memory she could not find. She looked at the walls of this house, which were as bare and unadorned as her own. She had never been a homemaker; never had the knack. Gayle craved to own something in her own right.

Silence from next door. Fruit and nuts had been passed upstairs to those gangly, tall children of Bea's who looked as if they had been raised in the dark, younger than Patrick and yet twice his height. They would flee their mother soon, whereas miniature Patrick would always be hers; she would make it up to him, and he would always be hers. What was it he said? I WANT DI. That was the last straw. She turned to her husband – my, my, he was masterful.

'Are you sure about masterpieces worth hundreds of thousands, darling? You know nothing about art,' she said, 'any more than I do. Even though you've been hanging around dealers, trying to find out. Going to galleries with Saul. You've worked ever so hard.'

'Yes,' he said modestly. 'I've learned a lot.'

He was staring at the screen. Beatrice leaned over his shoulder. 'Look,' she said. 'We've missed another page.'

Mrs Porteous is amenable to the idea of a settlement, subject to advice, but is currently confused as to how to achieve it. Mr Thomas Porteous possessed many paintings and sundry works of art, but none of any great value, entirely in accordance with his practice. The collection has great, potential value only as a whole. The house is part of the collection: there are no disposable items.

'She denies it,' Gayle said, flatly. 'She denies the masterpieces because she wants it all. That proves they do exist.'

And she has been speaking to my son, she thought. *I hate her.*

'So we take what's ours,' Gayle said, beginning to feel the thrill of it, her long fingers twitching. 'We identify the pictures and we take them away. She won't be able claim them back if she's lied about them. Nor can she take back what doesn't exist. We steal what's ours. We enter the place and take them, and he'll fix it, right? Saul?'

She sat back, exhilarated.

'Saul's emailed images. He's going to tell me which pictures to take and where they are, down in the cellar. Believe me, they're already famous.'

'And no involvement from Di's father at all?'

'No. He keeps watch. He wants money up front, for everything, and we haven't got it.'

Edward could not say, *Quig scares me. I am out of my depth with a man like that. I am already disassociating myself from Quig.*

'I'd kill her if I got close enough,' Beatrice said. There was such venom in the voice, Edward believed her.

'Hush,' Gayle said, digging her nails into her forearms and bestowing a glance of adoring admiration on her husband which made him seem to swell in size and hold himself straight.

'Let's do it on the anniversary of mother's death,' Beatrice said. 'Or thereabouts. How fitting that would be.'

Edward wanted the morning meeting to end: enough was

enough, and yet he sat back at her sticky table and pondered while Gayle went to disentangle her son from his cousins upstairs.

'How was it our dear, perverted father made his riches?' Beatrice mused. 'When we were born, he was a humble teacher who tinkered with useless inventions. Whatever was it that catapulted him into riches?'

'Games,' Edward said tersely, putting on his coat. 'He invented games. Games for children, featuring dragons and witches and frogs. Stupid things, turned into computer games, worth millions.'

'Did he? Did he really, of course he did, didn't he?' Beatrice said, dreamily. 'He really adored playing games. Perhaps,' she said, more sharply as Edward withdrew his arm from her touch on his sleeve, 'we should remember that.'

I must not underestimate, he was thinking, just before Gayle ran back into the room.

'Where's Patrick?' Gayle was shrieking. 'Where's Patrick? Where's my child?'

CHAPTER ELEVEN

Earlier the same day, a small figure stepped inside the door of a smart auction house in a side street in the West End of London. She looked entirely at home. The entrance to the auctioneers was not auspicious and neither was the street, but a man in uniform opened the door for her and bowed to her interesting companion. The hidden entrance led into a foyer that would have graced a fashionable hotel, complete with wide TV screens, flowers, and a carpet so soft and wood so dark it muffled footsteps and voices. It was a setting of neutral luxury and could have been anywhere from the Business Class lounge at an airport to the boardroom of any successful corporation with the sort of ambience designed to comfort those who were used to it, or bring out the closet revolution-ary in another. The scenery was completed by a trio of women with uniform features sitting behind a huge and ancient desk that looked as if it had originated in a Venetian palace. Informed by their screens and half hidden by flowers, they were obeying rules and displaying appropriate manners, trained to react with equal friendliness towards the hopeful punter bringing in a valueless object as they did towards the rich client with serious business. People did not stumble upon this place: they had to know where it was and many did. A free valuation of your work of art was always available and courteously given.

Nevertheless, the patience of the messengers could wear thin towards the endless trickle of unbeautiful people bearing treasures gleaned from attics and back rooms for a free valuation: receptionists and the persons they summoned via the screen had learned that the giving of negative opinions to hopeful faces was difficult. Handling disappointment was better dealt with briskly to limit the hurt.

As Diana Porteous and Saul Blythe arrived, an elderly man was being ushered out, scarlet with embarrassment, having been audibly informed that the precious ornament carried under his arm was a cheap reproduction of an Egyptian head sold by the thousand to tourists in Cairo and not the priceless artefact he hoped it might be. The object was as valueless as the man now felt himself; it seemed as if judgement was made not only upon the item but also upon the person who carried it in. He had not been offered contempt, merely fact, but contempt was what his soul received. Di was hurt on his behalf.

'It's not fair,' she said, seeing the man scuttle out of the door with his bundle under his arm. 'It's just not fair.'

'We are defined by our taste and our ignorance,' Saul murmured. 'And we must bear the consequences. What else can they do but tell him?'

Mrs Diana Porteous and Mr Saul Blythe were warmly welcomed and looked fit to grace the place as buyers or as sellers of something worth the trouble. They were a handsome couple; an urbane man in his mid-forties with his mid-twenties wife, no doubt his second, or perhaps an indulged mistress, a tad vulgar. Welcomed inside for the preview of the afternoon sale; really to admire the rooms and be seen to attend.

The rooms were splendid in themselves. The colours of the walls changed by the week or the day and the lighting and the hanging of displays was itself a separate work of art. They were looking at the walls as much as the pictures and the people, looking at how everything was shown to their best advantage. They were out for the day, expensive art tourists, Mr Blythe perhaps continuing Mrs Porteous's education where her late husband had begun. Also to be seen as big spenders, and Di to absorb the ambience.

They emerged into the quiet street and walked for a while before the sale, Di adjusting the fur collar of her ostentatious coat against the cold.

'Did you see the way they dismissed that poor man with his sculpture?' she said. 'They made him feel an old fool. How could they do that?'

Saul tied his silk scarf and guided her across the road, speaking patiently.

'Telling someone that their loved object is not worth a penny is never going to be easy. They do their best, and there simply isn't a kind way to do it.'

'Yes, there is,' Di insisted. 'You sit him down. You tell him it's a beautiful thing and say thank you for letting me see it. Then you tell him that beauty doesn't always have a price. You let him go with his dignity and compliment him on his taste. You listen.'

'They'd be talking all day if they listened,' Saul said. 'Dealers and salesmen don't have time for such useless compassion.'

She turned on him.

'Yes, they do. They have all the time in the world. Yes, they should. If you've got time for the rich one wanting to flog a masterpiece, you should have time for the others as well and you should be *kind* to them at least. You should welcome them, express an interest.'

He shook his head, amused by her.

'Beg to differ, ma'am. They are businesslike, that's all. Places like this exist to make money out of beauty and aid in the general distribution of wealth. It's only a theory that they are accessible to all. Fine Art *is* a commodity with a variable price and this is a market place, not a charity. *We,* on the other hand, come to great places like this to see fantastic things we might not otherwise be able to see anywhere else, because they're hidden until the moment they come up for sale. You come here to see things that have lived in private hands in private houses for most of their lives. You come here to make comparisons, get an idea of values, but above all, to see what there *is.* Then you go scatting about. You hang around auction rooms so that people know you're look-ing. Then they come to you.'

He paused at a junction of rich roads, leading into richer roads, facing a traffic jam of rich cars. The environs of St James's, King Street, the nest of the big dealers in art, hand-some streets leading into squares and endless, secret places. The bright cold weather required good, warm clothes. They sat outside a cafe, wrapped up in the winter sun; Di smoked, rapidly.

'Look,' she said. 'Collectors like me and Thomas don't belong here, because we're too modest. We're hunters for quality, first, no matter who made it. It doesn't have to be a named artist. He wouldn't buy a bad painting by a famous person just because it had financial value. It's pointless, unless you're an investor. You have to start with thousands to shop here. This auction house isn't going to sell a picture for you unless it has a start price like that. They're dealing in named commodities, artificial values. Not real ones.'

'When this is all settled you may well have millions to spend or burn, Di,' he said, mildly. 'Shall we go back in? Watch the sale? You've got to learn to think big, look ready to spend the money and look as if you know how. It's part of the plan.'

'What I want,' Di said, 'is a proper learning job.'

'You have one. You're a curator and a collector. You learn all the time. That's why we're here. We're also here to look as if we're spending money before the relatives can get at it. That's what we're here for. Looking rich, acting rich, willing to spend if not actually doing it. No one can really tell which.'

She let out a peal of raucous laughter.

'Spending in the sky. Virtual spending. I like it. Better than the real thing.'

He leant towards her.

'Could you laugh like that again? Only louder? Only I know Edward haunts these streets, also his spies, and he may be in the vicinity, watching himself. Or someone he knows. He's been scouting for months, putting himself about, trying to find out what Thomas might have been worth, not know-ing he was in the wrong place and not learning anything. He's set his spies, including me. As you know, I report to Edward. Speak louder, will you dearest? And look at me as if you really trust me, body and soul?'

She touched his hand, playfully, gazed into his dark blue eyes. Thomas's eyes were translucent, pale blue, incapable of deceit. These darker blue eyes were full of guile. He was dressed for the day in a maroon waistcoat with a splendid watch, every inch the serious stylist and the very opposite of anonymous.

'The master plan?' she asked. 'Are they hooked?'

'We have set the hare,' he said. 'As Thomas planned, some time ago. Everyone knows that the late Mr Porteous had a semi-valuable collection of paintings and ephemera. What is less well known is that he had at least one painting of greater value than the rest put together. These paintings are not of course included in any inventory. I have been drip-feeding this information for months, long before he died. The hare is set. If we, you, are seen about these places, it would be assumed that we are scouting about for the best place to sell the really high-priced goods, whatever they are. By our very presence, we are announcing that not only do we have money to spend, but also *you* may have something to sell. You are putting yourself about. Our presence on these not-so-mean streets indicates that you are in *debate* with someone about something, ready to sell the family gold and pocket the money as soon as, so they better get a move on and get what they can. And they have to steal it. Thomas wanted that. It is entirely necessary.'

'Thomas didn't have any one thing worth a million,' Di said.

'Maybe not, but he does now,' Saul said, crossing his fingers. 'As of when I set the fable running, you are the de facto owner of an unknown masterpiece or two. Not an Impressionist or anything like that, nothing so obvious, but high value all the same. Something to gamble with. And you aren't willing to let it go, you've lied about its existence already, please remember that. Even you might not know how valuable it might be. The story is that I acquired it for Thomas many moons ago from an old lady who knew no better, someone who had possessed either one of them or both of them for years. Please also remember that you are a foolish child, a local girl made good and you would do anything for money. Now, let's go back in and watch an auction. It's a lovely game, even Thomas couldn't have invented it.'

The room inside was like a ballroom hung with paintings, a stage, screens, a quiet army, moving paintings from place to place around the people who sat as if watching a performance. The sound of phones trilled from the galleried corner at the back next to where they stationed themselves among the discreet, restless and alert audience. A tall, urbane auctioneer with tanned skin and white hair was standing on his lectern below a screen which showed the lot he was selling, the same lot lifted on to the easel on his left. Prices in six currencies appeared on the screen above and the screens on the walls, left and right, along with an image of the painting under the hammer, the price altering with each bid, from wherever the bid came. Phone bids, commission bids already logged, or a bid waved from the floor by someone nodding a head and raising a numbered paddle, bidding in person. The bidder knew the code, acting with nods and winks and understated gestures, a hidden understanding between them and the auctioneer at his rostrum in a shorthand of exchanges. One lot every minute, max, each minute seeming to last far longer. A sale of ninety lots with a minimum price of five thousand: a collection and a catalogue which had taken nine months to assemble, gone within little more than an hour and with it the crashing of some hopes and the raising of others. A minor sale in the scale of things for an auction house regularly selling in the millions.

Di marked her catalogue, desecrating the glossy pages with her pen. So many paintings not meeting their reserves by thousands: too many paintings by the same artist, so they all looked the same and lost distinction. She could see how the sale was staged and how on this occasion, the staging, the proximity of one thing to another had failed, and she could see how the audience responded. They watched and they waited; they did not scream or shout. Some had passion for the purpose, all the more intense for being curtailed by the manner of the place and the clothes they wore. Rivalries and tensions breathed life into the room and then died, alongside a text of quiet babble and suspense.

'There were only a couple of exceptional paintings,' Di said a little later. 'Only three. The rest weren't bad, but they just weren't worth the money. Not by themselves, not for what they looked like. Half of them weren't sold because they didn't meet the reserve price. Who says what a thing's worth?'

Saul enjoyed the role of tutor and observer, just like Thomas.

'The reserve price printed in the catalogue is an estimate. The estimate is often based on what the painting sold for the last time when it, or something similar to it, came up for sale at auction. The *real* reserve price, by which I mean the lowest price the seller will accept, is lower than the printed reserve price. Only the auctioneer knows what it is.'

'So the printed reserve price is based on records and hope. Nothing to do with intrinsic value. Like other commodities,' she said.

'Exactly. Now, the advantage of *your* hidden masterpiece, or masterpieces if we insist on the plural, is that it is something that has never been for sale at auction before. No one has seen it for a generation and there's no real precedent for it. They'll have to guess the value. No one will be able to predict what it might fetch. That's why Edward will go for it, because it will be priceless, in one sense. It could go for a fortune if there's a devotee collector or an institution mad for it. It will be a *discovery*. Some collectors can't resist that. Edward won't be able to either, because he's a gambler, but a lazy one. A man who doesn't do his research, out for the maximum buck. Willing to risk it, the promise so much better than the certainty. He is thoroughly informed and seduced by me.'

'Have you really seduced him?'

'No, dearest, he's too ugly. But I wouldn't put it past myself, otherwise.'

'And you've really sold him on this?'

'Yes. Hook, line and sinker. As for *moi*, I'm in it for a share of the profits, of course, a motive he can understand, although he'll already have thought about how to cheat me out of that. A contract to act as a double agent is hardly enforceable.'

'What about Gayle and Beatrice? Will they go along?'

'Yes. Because they want action, and want it soon, before dear Thomas is buried, in case stuff is buried with him. And they are realising that getting you arrested might not work, and yes, because they've been dominated one way or another for most of their lives and they crave to be led even if it means being lied to. But as far as the paintings are concerned, they'll have to steal them. That was always part of the plan. They won't get any sense of achievement, otherwise. Stealing it will be part of their revenge on you and him, they'll have outwitted you. It would give them such satisfaction. We have to encourage it, we have to turn them into thieves, make them show the courage of thieves. The only way to settle their hash is to turn them into burglars and then, compromise them. They must be thoroughly compromised. Thomas was clear about that.'

He looked at his watch, a flamboyant timepiece, hung round his neck on a black ribbon, half hidden by his tie. A beautiful object, like every single item of his apparel. An old, dull gold circle, an inch in diameter, with a black face and the numbers of the time of the day picked out in gold roman numerals, as easy to read as a book in large print.

'And now we go and look at the other versions of the paintings in question,' he said. 'I want your advice. Your eye. To make sure they're tempting enough.'

'Thomas selected them,' Di said. 'Thomas thought it would have to be something they *expected* to see. The sort of thing they'd expect him to have.'

'Edward *does* get it, and he's the prime mover. I've sent him to see them in the Wallace and the National. I've sent him images and I'll hand him transparencies. I fear he was expecting things more heroic. Both of them are real. Both of them are masterpieces in their own right and legitimately owned. Thomas knew exactly what they were. We are not encouraging them to be palmed off with a fraud. We are *not* cheating. Both of the paintings are entirely genuine. With the difference that they are not quite what they appear. They are glorious paintings, but they are not named commodities. Shall we go and check?'

The Wallace collection was in Manchester Square, halfway between Hyde Park and Regent's Park. Handel's church overlooked the collection housed in a big, fat, comfortable house as squat and British as any house could be. Enter the doors and find inside a colossal collection of eighteenth-century art, collected by eccentrics. Di knew where she was in the Wallace, in the company of the maddest collectors of them all. Francophiles, acquisitive nutcases, amassing good and bad with equal verve. They were standing in front of the best-known painting in the whole collection, the one on the front of the catalogue, *The Swing* by one Jean-Honoré Fragonard.

They stood before it, Di smiling and silently reciting the description she had already written of the equivalent painting in the basement.

> Picture: *shows a girl on a swing in the middle of a verdant garden/ forest, with plenty of hiding places. The girl is gorgeously clothed, with full petticoats and a bonnet; no underwear, they didn't then; the swing is at its highest as she kicks off her delicious little shoe; the breeze lifts her skirts and she smiles with glee. An old goat of a man, perhaps her tutor, hidden in the undergrowth, watches her with helpless fascination. A young man, stage left, looks up her skirt.*

'Knockout,' Di said. 'Girl without knickers.'

'You,' Saul said, keeping her on track, 'have an alternative version. Similar, but with the swing going in the opposite direction. The same hidden, satyr-like figure who is going to rape her innocence, the same boy who will be helpless to protect her. Your colours will be equally brilliant, it may even be a better version than this, a little naughtier, the girl more knowing, the predators more determined, more transfixed by lust. There was more than one version. You have one, the best one, better than this. Are you listening?'

She was.

'The only difference,' he continued, 'Is that *your* version was not painted by Monsier Fragonard, although he painted several versions. It was painted by his sister-in-law, Margeurite Gerard, who came to live with him and his wife in 1775. Ostensibly to take painting lessons. She learned to paint just like him, as well as.'

'I like our version better than this,' Di said. 'More colour, more bitterness, more edge. It was in the school. Thomas knew who painted it. So did his father. That's why he wanted to rescue it. Margeurite Gerard never had a chance to succeed in her own right, never had the limelight and that makes her Thomas's kind of artist. But he rarely bought anything French. Might they notice that?'

'I doubt it. Edward would never research carefully enough. Nor has he ever looked.'

They were back in the taxi. Di knew the way through the National Gallery; it was she who led Saul towards Gainsborough's portrait of his two daughters.

'Even Edward and Gayle will have heard of Gainsborough,' Saul said. 'They might even be able to recognise the style. Fragonard? You know if you know, and you don't if you don't. Gainsborough's the better bet. The forerunner of English landscape painting, almost the inventor. His great love, although he was a portrait painter. He put landscapes behind portraits. One of his most touching portraits, I think.'

Di had written that one down, too. She could recite her own description.

Two little girls, almost embracing. The one is almost a baby, the other, older, protective, holding her. Based on the same faces of a more famous portrait of the two of them, chasing a butterfly. Sweet, sweet, sweet anxious faces, transfixed by Daddy. One face full of intelligence, the other, pretty, slack-mouthed and vacuous. Vulnerable faces, bodies dressed as adults.

'They went mad,' Di said, saddened by it. 'Gainsborough loved them as much as any father of his time, but his love for them couldn't cure them. Perhaps life couldn't. Look at them now. They were happy then.'

Saul was on full song, ignoring sentiment; no time for it.

'Gainsborough was different from other successful portrait painters of the time. He didn't have assistants to do all the extra bits such as lace and shoes like most of the others he followed. He concentrated on the face, first of all, painted from life and got a real likeness. Then he painted the body, and the landscape.'

'The faces,' Di said. 'Always concentrated on the faces, a true likeness, done from life, almost a sketch. Only he didn't paint the one wrapped up in our cellar,' Di said. 'His nephew did. Gainsborough Dupont, nephew and only pupil. Who learned to paint exactly in the style of his uncle, only with greater freedom. He copied, but he copied honestly. May have painted the same things as his uncle, at the same time. Maybe not an inventor of techniques, but just as good, or better. Remained modest and unknown. Another reason why Thomas liked it. The unknown artist, in the shadow of someone else.'

They were out of there, walking, hurrying without reason. It was cold.

'Either of them,' Di said. 'Either. But the Gainsborough's bigger and the one where they'll know the name. I wish they weren't wrapped up in the basement. It went against his nature, keeping things hidden. They were on the walls, ten years ago. I wish Thomas wasn't so keen on playing games.'

'He knew about misguided children. He wanted revenge, too.'

'They'll go for the Gainsborough,' she said. 'They're welcome. They'll go for both, and we have both, but they'll go for the name. They'll also go for Fragonard, because it's semi-famous and they'll go for both because of the subject matter. Beatrice will, anyway.'

'How so?'

'The Fragonard's naughtiness, its theme. The old goat of a tutor, hiding in the bushes. The man looking up the girl's skirt, that's what they'll see. And as for the Gainsborough, what have we got? Two anxious girls, transfixed by Daddy, looking straight to camera, ready to strike a bargain, wanting to please before they stopped wanting to please. A confirmation of some sort of perversion on the part of the collector, or at least the expression of a tendency? That's what they thought of Thomas. That's why they'll expect paintings suggesting perversion. They'll see what they see. Those paintings were always there. Thomas's father had them.'

Saul nodded, following in part, realising yet again that, however much he had been trusted, there were things he did not know.

'Christina would have killed for those paintings,' Di said. 'She might have known them.'

'In terms of value,' Saul intoned, 'Marguerite Gerard's

version of *The Swing* would fetch a few thousand, but if by Fragonard himself, at least a million. The same applies to Gainsborough Dupont. They won't do badly. Just not nearly as well as they thought. Good commodity, wrong name.'

'So we aren't selling them a fraud or a copy. That's important. And we're letting them take away something of real value, which is what Thomas wanted, but we're making them fight for them, steal for them. It's cruel, isn't it?'

'It'll teach them a lot about themselves, Di. Come on, Di, you still don't hate them enough.'

'Oh yes I do. I didn't before, but I do, now. Problem is, I don't hate their children.'

She thought of Patrick, shuddered, as if a cloud had descended over the sun, and then, as if it was an afterthought, rather than a real one, she said, 'I've got go home. I wonder what they're doing at home? I feel as if I need to go home, There was a flood warning. Let's go home. Now.'

'Tell me things,' he said, urgently as they walked faster and faster. 'Tell me what happened to Christina when she came to call on Thomas. Tell me what he wouldn't tell me. Tell me more about your father.'

She was walking along, looking at a text on her phone, stopped so suddenly they bumped into one another. She was tight-lipped and pale.

'I can't,' she said. 'Christina jumped off a cross-channel ferry, everyone knows that. As for my father, he follows death. I can feel him. He knows the house. Something's happening. He's there, I can see him.'

'Nonsense. We can't go back, not tonight,' he protested. 'There are other places to visit tomorrow. The flat, Raymond Forrest, things to *do*.'

'It can all wait. I have to go home.'

187

'Why, for Godsake?'

'Because there's a shadow,' she said, shivering. 'He's watching. He won't come near me, but he would go for someone smaller. I told you the other night, Saul, my father won't come for me head on, but he might sneak round the back, he'll come in sideways, for something smaller than me.'

A boy who looked like a child sat on the train, sketching in his book for something to do, the way he always did. 'On your own, son?' the ticket inspector asked. Patrick stared at him. Of course he was on his own; that much was perfectly obvious. He was usually on his own, wherever he was, whoever he was with. He looked to either side of him, impertinently, and said, yes it seemed as if he was, so why did he ask? The inspector did not quite like his tone; strange little chap, with an old voice. Patrick was sick of explaining that he was older than he looked. Twelve, and the size of an eight year old, the year he stopped growing. But he was growing now: he could feel it surging beneath his pale skin, making him six feet tall, already. Getting dark out there, didn't matter, he had a map, a watch with a compass. He wanted to see the sea.

He had kept the map for years, the way he kept so many things, ever since Di gave it to him. It had come with the invitation to the party. When he grew up and could choose what to do, he would make maps. When he was a baby, a hundred years ago, when Mum and Dad still visited Grandpa until they stopped, they came by car, squabbling all the way. When he came for the party, he came on the train with the horrible cousins; part of the adventure, and that was how he learned the route. And then, Auntie Beatrice, coming in there screaming. *Pervert,* she screamed, *fucking pervert.* She just didn't get it, did she? Nor did the cousins, they never got the magic at all.

Didn't matter: he knew the way to the house from the station like the back of his hand. Anytime, Di said; but you must tell your mother. That's what she said at first, anyway. Then she gave him food and put him back on the train.

Money for the ticket was easy. He siphoned a little from his mother's burgeoning purse every day. She was useless with it, never knew how much there was. She never noticed much and nor did Dad. They wouldn't even notice he was gone. Should have kept his mouth shut, though. Shouldn't have said anything to the stupid cousins, although he doubted if they heard.

Patrick loved trains. He went on one every day, only the Underground on the days he went to school, on the days when he didn't bunk off. Di worried about that. No one else did.

'He's gone *where?*'

'Said he was going to Grandad. What's wrong?'

'She's done it, she's abducted him. It's her. She's a spider and she got him into her web.'

Beatrice was so thrilled, she was clapping her hands. 'We've got her now, we've got her, abduction, kidnap, the lot—'

'Shut up,' Edward yelled.

Shouting, screaming, fury, distress. Edward held up a magisterial hand.

'Wait,' he said. 'Wait.'

'He's gone,' Gayle said, so quietly she was almost inaudible. 'He's gone to *her*.'

'Our boy has eyes in the back of his head,' Edward said.

'This could turn out fine. Should I ask Di's father to look out for him? Just look out, not do anything? He's there, isn't he?'

'No,' Gayle said, knowing it was too late and he'd already done it. You undo that. We phone Raymond Forrest. We phone the messenger boy.

CHAPTER TWELVE

Peg loved this house, she really did. Even the cold bits, because it was the sort of house that hugged you. Peg was tired, in a good way. It came from all that cleaning. She had started at the top in the wide-open attics; it was such an open house, windows everywhere, light even when it was dark. She had done all the windows on the inside, worried about how the salt blurred the outside, because of the wind that carried the spray and plastered the salt against the glass. *It won't last*, Jones said; *the rain'll see to that.*

The place wasn't dirty as such, although much of it needed spring-cleaning and Peg reckoned she'd been born with a duster in her hand. There wasn't anything bad about being paid to do work like this. There was a linen cupboard the size of a small room, warmed by a hot water tank: she was in love with that room, full of enough old cotton sheets for an army. She folded them with care. *Look at me*, she said to herself, *a few days here and I'm well at home.*

The feeling of being alright without being uneasy really

began because Di had given her clothes. It was not the fact that Peg had woken after the first, full night she had slept there to find a pile of them by the bed, it was the choice of them, not any old stuff, not clothes that would never fit, but carefully chosen, good stuff. Di had left the best and told her to take anything else that she liked. Cosmetics, perfume, make-up, help yourself, you know, just go in there and get it whenever you like, so that it didn't feel like charity; it felt like a gift. Today, Peg was wearing a red sweater and black leggings with boots. She and Di were the same shoe size. It gave an uncanny sense of belonging, stepping into Di's boots and finding them fit. It meant this was fate, and she was *supposed* to feel at home.

Peg was told what to do, did it willingly and then found other things to do on her own initiative. Jones tinkered and mended locks on windows and screwed down floorboards, did things with drains, muttered about installing a security system, kept on tinkering around as Saul ordered and was an excellent handyman and cook. That left Di free to closet herself with Saul and do stuff on the computer in the big room. The house was so large that hours could pass without any one of them being aware of where the others were, but Saul and Di were likely to be together, moving things about, organising quietly. When they all ate together, they talked easily of nothing and everything, mostly about the house and the virtues of the town which Di banged on about because she certainly liked the place. They did not talk about pictures and paintings, or the future, but they did talk.

Peg loved the pictures, but felt shy about passing comment, not wanting to ask the kind of questions that would make her look stupid. There were other things she liked much more than the things hung up the walls, and paintings were by no means the only things collected here. Peg loved the stash of old suitcases with labels she had found on the top floor: then there were the map books, the drawers full of watches, and after that, there were the trunks full of children's toys, and the other one full of fancy dress costumes ... it went on and on. She even found a wooden box full of shells. *Just make things better,* Di said. *Make sure nothing's got moth, or rotting.* Nothing was.

Peg just wanted to be where she was with no one else in the world knowing she was there for the time being. She did not want to know what would happen next, so it was nice when Saul and Di went away to London and left her and Jones. She really, really liked Jones; she was dead easy with Jones as Jones was with her. They were in the same boat, homeless but at home. With Di and Saul out of the way – and she liked Saul OK, he was funny, but there were buts, such as the way he looked – she could ask all she wanted and say what she thought. As if she would.

The bruise had faded, but her hair was such shit, and she had a thing about her hair. She really needed to get it fixed – the state of it troubled her, so bloody thick it was out of control. It was the only feature of herself she could not sort out and it made her feel like a slag, now she had clothes and a job. One of the good things about Jones was that you could talk to him about stuff like that.

'So go and get it done, why don't you?' Jones said the morning after Saul and Di left. 'Monica's never busy on Tuesdays. Go on, girl, you've worked hard and you've got your pay. Monica will fix you up. Get out of here and get straight back before the rain sets in. It's going to be nasty later. You haven't seen real bad weather yet.'

He showed her where to go on the map. Peg didn't want to go out alone, yet, but the hair was too important and the place would be easy to find. She wrapped up warm in one of Di's jackets, the nice green one. The colour combination of red and green reminded her of Christmas, she felt jaunty and free to please herself. When she came back, she would tell Jones what was really bothering her, because she really was in the shit, except it didn't feel like it right now. She felt OK.

The sea was too vast for Peg: she did not really like walking alongside it with all that noise it made. It was better seen from the inside of a window; closer than that, it was threatening, and she had no wish whatever to pass by the pier, so she followed the back way via a wide and well-used path which sent her uphill first, skirting the backs of the big houses, and then down into the town. It kept her away from the stirring wind, which sounded better in trees than it did with the crash of water. Sweeter in summer, perhaps: would she still be here in the summer? What did it feel like on a warm day, would it be that different? She didn't care. If this would keep her safe for a bit, that was fine.

Monica's was dead easy to find and when she did, it was half empty and it made her feel like a kid because the three other customers were ancient. Monica was an old crow, obliging although hardly friendly to a stranger without an appointment, nodded her to a chair, and said, *yes, you'll have to wait a minute*. She did.

Peg waited and listened as Monica fastened rollers into an old, grey head with a mouth that talked all the time.

'So where's that Jones when you need him?' Delia said. 'He was supposed to be fixing my door. Left his rod on the pier all night the other night. Someone came and stole it.'

Peg opened her mouth and closed it again, sitting very still, thinking of the rod leaning against the back door. Di had gone and fetched it that first morning when they all slept. Peg looked around. When she was small, she had a burning ambition to be a hairdresser. That way you got to make people happy all the time, like cleaning, you could only make things better. You couldn't go wrong with that, even though this Monica was not exactly a bundle of laughs and she seemed a bit stressed out.

'Jones knows when he's in trouble,' Monica was saying. 'He goes walkabout. He's good at hiding.'

The old head nodded.

''Cos old Quig's hanging around, is that it? That who he's running from? You were sweet on him once, weren't you, Mon?'

'Shush, you. That was a long time ago,' Monica said, finishing off. There was a cackle of laughter.

'Get on with you, you'd still give him house room, you would.'

The lid of the hairdryer came down. Monica turned to Peg. 'Hair needs cutting right back,' she said, abruptly 'Nice jacket, that. Where did you get it?'

'Charity shop,' Peg said, defensively, without thinking why she said it.

'Clever girl,' Monica said. 'I suppose you got the jumper there, too. Thought I'd seen them before. Got to be careful about what you give away in this town. Cut and blow dry's ten pounds today, alright?'

It wasn't easy being in there, because Monica never said anything else and kept interrupting her styling to answer her phone and Peg was glad to get out of there even if she was pleased with the result. *Nice jacket*, Monica said again. *Have you signed the register? Only I got to keep records.* Peg signed her full name without thinking and then, instead of looking at the other shops as she had planned, bought a packet of three-inch screws from the hardware shop and other stuff on a list as directed by Jones, plus a bottle of wine, and then she lost her nerve and began to scuttle home, again avoiding the sea as far as she could. The sky was huge and threatened rain. There were flood signs in windows, sandbags outside doors; she had heard warnings on the local radio when she was working in the morning, remembered Jones saying about how it would get *nasty*. None of that worried her, no flood could possibly threaten that house which had so quickly become hers, but she wanted to be indoors near a fire. She dreamed of cheese on toast as she walked faster, trying to look over walls into gardens, meeting no one but a man and a dog hurrying home, all the time afflicted with the feeling that someone was following her and knowing that was absurd; no one knew who she was, or where she was, and Jones said there were no police in this town. All the same, it did take all the pleasure out of light, floating, freshly cut hair.

When she got indoors, marvelling still at the possession of her own key to the place, locking the door behind her as instructed, she shouted for Jones.

Jones was in the cellar. She could hear banging.

They were getting on well, Jones and she. No silly business, no touching up. Just like having an uncle or a grandad, only one who never criticised. He praised her instead; ever so keen on the way she worked. He'd say things like, *my word, Peg, look what you've done, you're a right grafter, you are. Where'd you learn to polish like that, Peg? My mum,* Peg said. *She was a cleaner. Ah,* Jones said, *that's what you and Di got in common, her mum was too*. That boggled the imagination, but it did explain something. If you got to live in a place like this purely for the price of cleaning it, life had all sorts of possibilities. Did the man who owned it give her mum the house or what? The truth was, that although Peg liked Di, big time, and was curious about her, Di was a bit scary and she didn't really want to know too many details of her life history, not yet, except perhaps the romantic bits, not until she'd proved herself. It was Jones she wanted to impress. It was Jones who was going to save her from her own sense of shame and realise she wasn't really that bad, despite what she'd done and that fucking warrant for her arrest: Jones who would say it's OK to skip bail, I'll hide you, 'cos Jones knew the inside of prison, too.

The encounter with Monica had upset her more than the walk home in the rising wind, and she went over it in her mind. Lovely short hair from a nasty hairdresser who thought she was a thief, asking her about the clothes, for shit's sake, making her sign a register, and yes, she had signed her full name, never mind. And then someone following her home, and the house beginning to rattle and make noises in the north easterly wind she had heard about. It was Jones she needed and Jones was in the cellar, yelling up from the other end of those creepy stairs, telling her to come down. She obeyed.

Never liked cellars, or basements, for that matter. When Peg got her own place, it was going to be on the sixteenth floor, with windows on all sides. She did love heights, even though living in a fourth floor flat with a stepfamily had proved to be a nightmare. She wanted to tell Jones about that: she wanted Jones to know about *her* life. Jones was a person you told things, but Jones was preoccupied, banging around down here. That worried her. He wouldn't be doing that if Di was here, she knew it. Di never said that anything, any room, any corner, was off limits, not even her bathroom, but Peg had the feeling that the cellar was. She herself had once looked round the door and gone no further. It was just too big and she had to confess she had never been down a cellar before, except in a pub and then it was small.

'What are you doing?' she said.

'Testing, just testing. Ah, I see what he did. Bricked off the far room to keep out the sea and left the door.'

Peg smelled the smell of the place, surprisingly warm for being underground, like being in a Tube station on a cold day. Good enough for storage, things wrapped in canvas, more bloody pictures perhaps, as if there weren't enough. Jones was looking at the table in front of the door, a nice thing, wasted down here. He'd been banging at the walls, installing something small on a hook, and his face gleamed with sweat and she had to admit she had seen him looking nicer.

'Look at that,' he said. 'Look at this ceiling.'

She looked. The ceiling was arched and the arch disappeared into the wall. The brick above her eyes was old and rust-coloured while the wall was proper red. The graceful brick arch of an old wine cellar ceiling was abruptly cut in two. Yeah, she could see that. So what?

'Wasn't like that when I came to school here,' Jones said. 'Beautiful ceiling when you could see it all. We used to come down here to smoke. I guess he tanked it up against the water coming in, gave up with the front bit. Shame, spoils the ceiling.'

He turned on Peg, his face illuminated by the overhead light. There was enough light in here for an interrogation room. His face was haunted and she didn't know why. There was a creeping, whispering sound, as if of someone breathing. You could hear the sea down here, and she didn't like that, either.

'That's where the sea got in, on that side,' Jones was saying, talking more to himself than to her. 'Nineteen eighty-seven, famous flood that was. They seem to happen about every dozen years or so. The water creeps in underground with a high tide and the north easterlies. A boy almost drowned in the back cellar, hiding down here. You can't keep the sea out, you can only contain it. Houses are high, this end, but it comes in, under the sand.'

She shivered.

'Come on upstairs,' she said. 'I got us a bottle of wine.'

He shook himself.

'Di left us plenty of wine, but it was nice of you to think of buying some, pet.'

He was tidying up, piling old crockery on to a table.

'Mustn't fiddle with what they kept down here. Blimey, what a waste. But I fixed the camera, like Saul said. Hope I got it right.'

Jones shook his head like an old warhorse demented with flies, followed her back up the stairs, turned off the cellar lights and sat down in the snug. The sprung door to the cellar closed automatically unless it was left propped open. Peg offered the wine and watched him screw off the top.

'I reckon the old boy, William, kept the naughty stuff down there,' he said. 'Smugglers' stuff. The best brandy. Probably collected that, too. Sodding collectors, they're mad.'

She gazed at him. He needed a clean shirt. Then he changed the subject. 'You know, Peg, if you learn to cook and clean, and maybe learn to drive, you can get a job anywhere.'

'S'pose. How long have I got?'

'As long as you like, if you keep your nose clean. You're a great girl, you are.'

The subject was now herself and still she couldn't tell him. He might stop approving of her and she could not bear the thought of that. Yeah, she was good, but she had a warrant on her head.

'Do you like my hair?' she said instead. 'It was ever so cheap.'

'You look terrific, girl. You really do.'

He got up and stoked the fire. The wind was howling round the place. She suddenly felt less safe and wanted to know more. She was hungry; Peg was always hungry and it was dark outside in the hinterland of the day. Days here were timeless. There was no timetable for eating. Jones started doing food, the sort of solid food she liked. He was peeling potatoes; she helped, clumsily, and listened. She had come to realise that he was better at talking when he was doing something with his hands.

'I think someone followed me home,' she said, trying to get his attention. 'And your friend Monica recognised Di's clothes on me. She'd have known where I came from. Who's Quig?'

She told him what she had overheard. He listened and went red and she didn't like that, either.

'Bugger. Maybe that wasn't such a good idea, getting a haircut. Still it does look nice. Look, girl. Things you oughta know. Di's mother used to clean this place, first when it was a school, then when it wasn't. Di came here with her mum. Di's dad was as sly a bastard as ever lived, chip on the shoulder a mile high. Beat up mummy and kid, mum died of pneumonia after an operation, he went inside, kid runs free.

Di's dad? He could shoot a bird out of the sky when he was a boy and he could dig for England. He wouldn't come near Di unless he caught her alone, he'd go by the back door, pick on someone close ... Oh shit. Big bastards like that, they're never short of work.'

She waited, disappointed. Not another rotten story about a rotten dad. It took the novelty and shock value out of what she wanted to tell Jones about her own life and her own excuses for being such trash. Jones stopped.

'Another time, girl,' he said, somehow understanding. 'Another time. And there will be another time, promise. There's a time for listening and a time for hearing, and if you want anyone to listen to you, you have to listen first. I'm like you; no one listens to me either, although they might, in time. You like garlic? Well, you do now.'

Whatever he cooked smelled good to her.

'What do you think of all these paintings and stuff?' Jones asked her, as if really wanting her opinion, while keeping busy with food.

'I think it's a bit weird, to be honest, having so many,' she said. 'But I like it. Everywhere you go, something to look at. You could spend hours just looking, making up stories about them, forgetting where you were. Just looking.'

'Entering another space,' Jones said. 'Looking at other worlds through someone else's eyes. That's the whole point. Thomas used to say you needed other peoples' eyes as well as your own. Life was too short to learn enough, otherwise. Same for reading. Having the experience without having to do it, a shortcut. Learning about other lives. God, he did talk rot. But the idea is you come to a place like this, and you look, and you lose yourself. You learn something without thinking about it and you go away without realising you've forgotten your own snivelling little life for an hour or two.'

'I can see that,' Peg said, surprising herself. 'I like the paintings of children the best. There's a lot of those, aren't there? Kids playing, kids doing stuff. I like the one of a bunch of kids playing in the sea.'

'Yes,' Jones said. 'There's plenty of kids in this collection, come to think of it. That was Thomas's dad, the teacher. He collected pictures of children in particular. Some people found that suspicious.'

'Why? Kids are beautiful. I love kids. I like looking at them. I'd rather look at a kid's face in a painting than some fat old rich lady in a frock.'

Jones laughed. 'You're a tonic, Peg, really you are.'

She felt flattered, emboldened to continue. The wine was nice too, although she would have preferred vodka. It worked quicker.

'Are there more paintings down that cellar?'

He nodded. 'I reckon. They've been moving things round. I don't want to know what until Di sees fit to tell me. Just wish it was more secure. God, will you listen to that wind?'

They listened. It was no more than a booming sound, comforting their safe seclusion. It would be noisier at the top of the house. Peg wondered about sleeping down here. She didn't want to go to bed for a long while yet and where was the telly? The wind rose, with a shriek behind it.

'It was a dark and stormy night,' Jones began, using a dark, dramatic, rumbling voice, 'and the captain said to the mate, Tell us a story, and the mate began ... it was a dark and stormy night ... And we're all going to DROWN.'

'Stoppit,' she said, frightened. 'Stoppit. Just STOP that.'

'Sorry,' he said, but he was no longer quite in the present.

He was no longer in this small room. He was somewhere else. She noticed he had drunk most of the bottle.

'Shall I tell you a proper story? Only you mustn't tell anyone else.'

She nodded, not sure. 'Just don't tease me like that. It's not fair.'

He nodded back. No, it wasn't fair. The child wasn't used to sounds like this, but he had to talk. He talked while he washed up the dishes, made it easier to think things through, funny how he needed an audience to think.

'The first time Di came to this house was probably when she was a kid, came here with her mum. The first time she met Thomas was much later. She was in a gang. She was the smallest and mad as a snake long after her mum died. She got stuffed through the grille at the back with instructions to nick money if she could, but mainly to find car keys, so they could nick the car he had. Only, there was a tip-off, and she got caught. I was there, watching. It was a night just like this. Thomas didn't want her arrested, but he had no choice. He kept saying, she saved me, she saved me, but he was delirious. He'd been hurt, but he swore it wasn't her. He said the knife on the desk was his, but it wasn't. Di always had a knife. She was taken away.'

He paused, shuddering like a dog shaking off water.

'Then all hell broke loose, because the seafront flooded. People marooned in houses, waves crashing over the pier, cellars filling up with water. A nightmare night, like this might be, no it won't, it hasn't happened since. We had to go off and leave Thomas to it. We made the arrest, let the others go and fucked off. What a night that was. The High Street was under water, the Bank, too, and that was more important. So we left Thomas on his own.'

Peg lit him a cigarette, spellbound. No rules about smoking in here. The snug still smelled of Di's cigars.

'Which is why I never found out what really went on. Because there was someone else here that night. I know there was. Someone else who ran away and hid.'

'One of the gang?' Peg suggested, trying to be helpful. 'Someone who came in with her?'

Not someone who ran away after, like she had done, from a place she'd trashed. Shame made her skin mottle.

'Who knows? Maybe, but I don't think so. I knew who most of them were. Thomas had rope burns round his wrists and marks round his neck. He tried to hide them and he did, from everyone else. Di hadn't done that, she didn't have a chance. I'm good on timings, I was there.'

He looked at her blearily, a long day, plus wine. Not used to it, preferred the steadier influence of beer. He regretted this talking, it wasn't right to burden her, but still, he couldn't stop.

'I've been dying to get down that cellar ever since, never had the chance. Must have flooded that night, for sure. Everywhere did. Think I'll have a coffee.'

The wind seemed to have eased, leaving a lull. Peg was interested, thinking all the same that old blokes were such fucking dreamers. Talking about things that happened before she was born and when she was what? Six years old? Why was everyone's else's life so much more interesting than hers? She thought of her baby brother, not seen in years.

Jones's phone rang at the same moment that they heard the crash downstairs. They gazed at each other and failed to answer the phone.

'Someone's got in,' Peg whispered.

Jones sprang to his feet: they looked towards the open

cellar door, equally scared. Then, of common accord, and without a word, they went back down the steps to the warm part of the cellar where Saul and Di had shifted stuff only yesterday, part of some strange reorganisation they had conducted over two days, moving things from high to low. Di said they were putting things away until they found a place.

Creeping down, somehow expecting to find water although there had been none before, Peg was thinking of a film where people were trapped in the bottom of a boat, knocking against the hull. There was the same breathing sound, but no water and the same relative warmth, although markedly colder than the kitchen and the snug. In a room of once vast proportions, bigger than either of the rooms above, there was a small boy, sitting on a box, looking scared in the harsh light. He had kicked something over. The light glinted off his owlish spectacles. He looked like something out of a cartoon, so harmless in relation to the sound he had made that Peg almost laughed in relief.

'Oh, shit,' Jones said, stopped in his tracks.

The child stopped eating.

'She wanted me to come,' he shouted. 'Grandpa wanted me to come. Someone wanted me to come, or they wouldn't have left the chocolate.'

'You silly little shit,' Jones growled. 'Don't you know that Di leaves food for any bloody down and out who knows their way in here? It wasn't fucking meant for you.'

The boy began to cry. Jones looked as if he was about to wring his neck, moving towards him threateningly. Peg elbowed him aside, saying *shh, shhhh*, squatted down on to her haunches to make herself the same size and held out her hand. He looked like one of the winsome children in one of the paintings she had liked best. Only a fucking lost kid with specs.

'Hello, poppet,' she said. 'Who are you? You're ever so welcome, but we weren't expecting you. What's your name?'

'Patrick,' he said.

Upstairs the phone rang on.

'Oh shit,' Jones said, again. 'Now she's really blown it.'

CHAPTER THIRTEEN

> Picture: *Head and shoulders of a boy in silhouette, look-*
> *ing south through a window, framed by light. Looking at*
> *someone.*

A washed out morning; a long night.

Here I am. It's not my life, is it, Thomas, it's always someone
else's. I don't think you thought this would happen. Not part of
the game.

Perhaps we shouldn't play with other people's lives.

It was never the plan to put a small one in danger. You would
never have wanted that. Patrick drew a picture of my father,
Thomas. He said Quig was waiting at the station. I followed
instinct and came back.

I don't know what my father wants: I don't seriously think he
wants me dead, but he wants a hold on me, and he could certainly
get it through Patrick, the smaller target. Saul is very angry,
because Patrick running away here again gives his parents extra

ammunition against me and puts the master plan at risk. He's angry too, that he didn't know about Patrick's earlier visits when you were ill, and he's only slightly mollified when I say we were both implored to secrecy. Are there more of these secrets? *he says, and how right he is to wonder.*

I worry that Patrick could be a target for my father. He would always go for something he could hold to ransom: he would always shoot the smaller birds for practice. It hurts to send Patrick back so soon, but he has to go.

I wish you could tell me what to do. You said I'd know, but I'm not sure I do.

Di and Patrick sat at Thomas's desk in the long gallery. The storm was long subsided and the day was clear and cold. Rain had washed the windows clean of salt, and the distant retreating sea was murmuring, no harm done. They were looking at Patrick's sketchbook, Di alongside, entirely absorbed while Patrick sat in Thomas's chair, as if he belonged.

'How many of these books do you have?'

'Dozens.'

'Well, just you make sure you don't throw any of them away,' Di said. 'People will want to see them, one day. Anyway, you have to keep them to show yourself how you change and get even better. Do you still keep the diary?'

He nodded. 'Yes, but not much.' He pushed his spectacles back up his nose. They were loose. Di took them off him, bent the frame in the centre and put them back. They fitted better and he didn't notice she had done it.

'The drawing's like a kind of diary, I s'pose, but I do what Grandpa said.'

'"Write something every day, draw something every day. Collect something beautiful whenever you can."'

They chorused the lines, laughing in unison.

'What a bully he was,' Di said. 'He once told me that the Latin word for education was the same word as torture,' she laughed. 'He would never quite stop being the teacher, you see. That's what he should have been, what he was, until he invented things instead. There were weeks when I never moved from this room. Here, I like this one, best.' She pointed to a sketch in the middle of Patrick's book. 'Who looks at these? Your parents?'

She could not bring herself to refer to them as mum and dad. She was too angry with them for that.

'Not any more,' he said. 'Not unless I show them.'

Patrick had such a talent for caricature that she could understand that they might not like what they saw. He drew shapes with ridiculous ease. The shapes became figures, the figures became cartoons, or not. Sometimes the shapes gambolled across the page; other pages were devoted to earnest, detailed drawings of objects, while the back of pages and the corners of pages were devoted to hands. He often began with hands and got no further, while on other sheets he simply drew noses. The one she was pointing out was a full face, with a big nose and thick neck descending into collar and tie. Her smile grew.

'I know him, don't I?' Di said. 'He's a ticket collector from the train.'

Patrick smiled too, pleased with the recognition of it.

'I didn't like him,' he said. 'Bossy boots. Sometimes it's easier when I don't like them and I do it quickest. Besides, he had a funny face. Not like the other man at the station. The one who stared at me when I was sitting down, looking at the map, so I could remember the way. Big chin and a cap pulled down. Not a funny face.'

That was the drawing that made her blood run cold. They had passed over that one, quickly. *That man*, she had asked him, *what was he doing at the station? Was he on the train?*

Don't think so, he was just waiting in the waiting room. I stopped there, and drew him pretending to read his book. Then another train came and he got on the train going the other way.

Are you sure?

Yes. He went the other way.

Di went back to the ticket collector. Patrick had drawn a sketch of her father. Her father, *going away*. She wanted to believe it; made herself believe it. Quig would not like to be photographed, or drawn.

'I've got other books where I just do *things,* you know tables and chairs, because I like the shapes,' Patrick went on. 'Anything I can see when I'm sitting on the floor. Stuff I do when people want to look, and I need to have something harmless to show them. That ticket collector? You know what? He doesn't like his job.'

'A lot of people don't like their jobs,' Di said, 'Any more than you like going to school.'

'School's OK. I cracked it,' he said. 'I do drawings of people and they like them, so they leave me alone.'

'Do you know what you are, Patrick? You're a fucking star. A right clever bugger.'

'I still don't want to go home,' he said. 'This is home. This is where everything happens. I like it here.'

'No one wants you to go home,' Di said. 'Not me, not Peg, not anyone. I'd do anything to keep you. But you do understand, don't you? It's the only way you get to come back.'

He pushed the glasses back up his nose again, vaguely surprised to find there was no need. She knew better than to point out that she had adjusted them because it did not do to offend an old man or a young one. He calmed down and she found herself resenting the fact that he was so used to obedience.

''S'ok. Yes. I always knew it would be like that. I knew you'd have to phone them, get someone to phone them, whatever. I understand a lot of stuff. People say things around me thinking I don't understand, but I do.'

'And they do love you, your mum and dad.'

Don't mouth clichés to a child too wise, she told herself. *Don't give him divided loyalties.* Her heart ached for him. A boy his size was the size of a man: a boy aged eight was fully formed, Thomas said.

'S'pose they do, in their way,' he said sounding old. 'But Mum just wants me in manacles, away from harm, and Dad wants me to have growth treatment therapy. They'd like me better if I was different. I'm not what they wanted. He calls me a pansy, Dad does.'

The spectre of her own father rose before Di's eyes and she banished it. Gone. *He had gone the other way.* She was like Patrick towards his father, perhaps less afraid than ashamed, and perhaps they were both wrong.

'Beautiful flowers, pansies,' she said. 'Grow well in winter when nothing else does.'

'I never draw flowers.'

'Well,' Di said. 'Good taste doesn't seem to be your father's strong point. Everyone else thinks you're damn fine as you are. Doesn't matter if you never grow an inch, but you will, I promise.'

He smiled at her with Thomas's soft blue eyes and they shook hands, formally, making a pact. Then his eyes strayed to the paintings on the walls, resting upon Madame de

Belleroche, who gazed down on them imperiously whilst eyeing up her courtier on the other side of the room.

'She's just like you,' Patrick said.

She bowed towards him.

'Why, thank you, kind sir. I wouldn't mind looking like that, although maybe not for a few years yet. And he hasn't quite got the hands right, has he? What do you think?'

'Not really. There's always a bit the artist doesn't get quite right. Something he's not so good at.'

Everyone else was still asleep. They had both been up early. By the time Di and Saul had got home, Patrick was petted out of existence and fed to bursting point. Such high excitement: such fitful sleep, so many arrangements. Raymond Forrest instructed, parents informed, all that. Di had found Patrick wandering in the morning, exploring the whole terrain, touching, admiring, looking in and looking out. To everyone else he was a child, but here, he was artist and critic, waiting to speak his mind.

'I had to come,' Patrick said. 'I hated what they said. And I wanted to prove that they couldn't just drag me around. They'll have to listen to me now. I know I have to go back, but I still don't want to. I did think I might be allowed to stay a couple of days, though.'

He looked at her, hoping again she would change the plan, let him stay longer. She shook her head. He was quickly resigned, deciding to make the most of time.

'There's plenty of time yet,' he said. 'Walk to the pier, the way I did with Grandpa?'

She wanted to say no, but she couldn't. She wanted to walk with him, prove there was nothing to be afraid of, so they did. It was an easy transition from there to here, walking along, side by side, not linking arms, not close enough for that, but close enough for it to be possible to do so. Cold and bright, today in this waiting period, post all the hysteria, post the making of arrangements. It was early yet. Raymond Forrest was not expected to collect the wayward child before noon. There had been no flooding, only a false alarm. The sea was flat and exhausted, robbed of triumph.

'Will you look at that? You didn't get your way, did you?' Patrick yelled at it, waving at it as if acknowledging a friend who had failed to score a goal. 'Never mind. Next time, my turn soon.'

The sea responded with a growl. Patrick grasped Di's hand briefly and let it go, a gesture to say she was forgiven for making the adult decisions while not treating him as a child. They might hug, before parting, but not in public.

'Grandad loved the sea, didn't he? He said so.' Grandad, Grandpa, he used both. Thomas would have answered to either. 'And he liked me, didn't he? He *really* liked me.'

'Liked you?' Di said, hearing an echo. 'He loved you to bits. Far more than he loved the sea and believe me, he loved the sea a lot. He admired you, too. He loved talking to you. He said you see things.'

'Like you see me. Do you see me?'

'Yes, I do. Like a true colour. Like the sky.'

'I know you do. Like Grandad did. At home, I'm no colour at all. They don't have colour at home.'

They detoured off the concrete path and walked on the shingle; hard going and noisy, so they turned back after stooping and collecting a stone or two, repeating the challenge to find the one with the hole all the way through and they kept on, detouring on and off the shingle, hunting, until the pier stood before them, sticking out of the low tide water, looking like a giant grasshopper with many legs, showing more knees than an old girl should. Di felt self-indulgent: it was delirious, even in these circumstances, to be talking about Thomas to someone who loved him. There were things that puzzled her, things she needed to know in order to evaluate her enemies, but she would not press. She kept looking behind as well as forward, walking backwards, looking; he copied her.

'So what all went wrong, do you think?' she asked as the pier came closer. 'There you were, only a few years ago, you and the cousins being sent to visit sometimes, all right you were under escort but you were left alone with Grandad. Your mum and dad thought that was OK, and suddenly it wasn't.'

'I found one with the hole all the way through,' Patrick said, holding a stone aloft. He perched it on the top of his little finger and transferred it to his pocket. An achievement. Another collector.

'I think we were brought here first to "keep Grandad sweet",' he said, mimicking an adult voice. 'Granny told them to take us, go and wave babies at him, rattle his conscience, he can't resist kids and he won't be dangerous now. I heard them say that later. I was very little then, but I remember those times though I don't remember Granny except that she shouted and cried and I hated her. We didn't come after she drowned, much, and I only remember coming in the summer when you were here. That party. You were the cook and you made games, too. And I was his favourite, like I was when I was a baby.'

'Was that a problem?'

'Well, I *was* the favourite,' Patrick said, with a swagger. ''Cos my cousins are sooo stupid. Never noticed the paintings, never noticed anything much. Just sulked. Never noticed anything. Grandad walked with me, we did this . . . '

He raced down to the sea shore, picked up a stone and flicked it over the calm water, watched it skitter, twice, before disappearing under the grey water: she followed suit, better at this than he, but letting him win. She could feel the mounting of his distress, the crowding in of what he had to tell, grabbed him before the force of his repeated throwing overbalanced and took him right into the water.

They staggered back up the bank.

'It was that party,' Patrick said. 'You know, that party you had? With the King Frog and the witch, and us all getting dressed up? I tried to draw it all afterwards, that's when I started, I wanted to remember it and drawing was the best way to remember, and Grandpa made us draw stuff. Cousin Ed teased me about being the favourite. He was magicked too, but he had to pretend he wasn't. Not cool.'

She only remembered that they all seemed equally entranced. The cousins, Monica's young nieces, the other local kids, all treated to fantasy tea and stories, because Thomas wanted his protected grandchildren to mix with ordinary children and all of them to enter another world for an afternoon.

'Beatrice came to collect you,' Di said. 'She took one look at little girls dressed up in floating costumes, like something out of a harem, and she didn't like it. She couldn't take you away fast enough.'

Patrick nodded.

'All the way home, she kept egging us on to say something. She kept saying, just to me, now you can tell me, you must tell me, what did he do to you, what did he do? Why did they make you change your clothes? Did you take them all off? I said he didn't do anything and none of the girls took any clothes off. But cousin Edmund said they were running around with nothing on, and then he said you don't have to worry about what he does with little girls, mummy. They're quite safe. It's what he does to little boys. Edmund said that Grandpa Thomas got his thingy up when Ed was sitting on his knee. Said he bounced him up and down and felt for his willie and touched his bum. But he *didn't*, Di. No one sat on his knee. He wouldn't let it. We had tea in that tent. It was Edmund said he was touched. Then Alan joined in. But Edmund, he liked everything really. He just doesn't like sharing. He likes getting attention.'

Di flung another stone, and thought, *darling Thomas, you were as naïve as I was, wanting to bring sheer fantasy into life.* Remembered her instructions before that glorious party. *Dress in many clothes, guide children, never touch them, never push or shove. Welcome them in; bring them to another world of colour, and stories. Give them magic. If you touch, touch lightly.*

'And Aunty Beatrice told Mummy and Mummy went quiet. That's when they said we would never come back. That Grandad was a pervert, like he always was. Like Granny said he was, until she said he was too old and they'd better be nice to him anyway.'

'It isn't true,' Di said gently.

'No, I know it isn't,' Patrick said, impatient and relieved, wanting the subject to be over. They had reached the pier. A lone fisherman was packing up and going home, nodding good morning as he passed. They paused and counted clouds. The boats on the horizon made her want to move; the sea below made her want to stay. She looked back. No one, the town still asleep.

'And I just wanted you to know,' Patrick said, 'That it wasn't *my* mum, it wasn't her, it wasn't. It was Beatrice and them. It wasn't *my* mummy. *She* doesn't say bad things, she tells Aunty Bea to stop.'

'I hear you,' Di said. 'It's all right. Do you know what?' she said, leaning over the side, 'I really, really want to learn to fish.'

'Oh yeah, so do I,' Patrick said, fervently.

'Next summer, hey? When all this fuss is over.'

They walked to the end. In the absence of anyone else on the brink of the day, it felt as if it was their own domain. They looked back at the sweep of the land, the tall houses and the small. Then they looked at the sky. This was home. This was better than any painting.

'Some people collect clouds,' Di said. 'You can do that anywhere and its free.'

'I collect all sorts of stuff,' Patrick said.

'Everybody sane does,' Di said. 'C'mon. Let's run back, it's good for us.'

He did not register the fear in her voice; it was only another part of the game. Di had seen him in the distance, from halfway down the pier, watched as he was ducking into a shelter on the promenade, still a long way away. She was glimpsing a limping figure with a stick coming towards them from the town end, moving slowly and purposefully towards the pier, the hat pulled down over the eyes. She had been looking around all the time since they set out and had not seen him. He was skulking in doorways, seemed to emerge from nowhere, looking towards the boy, who was playing airplanes with his arms; speeding up himself as if he was planning to greet them at the narrow gate of the pier. Di did not want Patrick to see him or recognise him and she did not want Quig any closer. She did not know what he wanted, or even if he had seen them, but she knew the distance between them was far too small for comfort. He may have been sent; he may have been looking for an easy target: he may simply have resented a boy who had drawn his face.

'Race you,' she said. 'All the way home. Last one's a sissy.'

Patrick responded, running ahead out of the pier, turning for home, running faster with clumsy speed and waving arms, she in his wake, spurring him on, overtaking him, until the house was there, and they slowed down to a walk. Safe now. Quig could not run like that.

They walked the last stretch in a breathless stroll. The adrenaline waned and Di slowed her steps and so did he. Patrick took her hand as they approached the house, and then, when they were at the gate, he let go. She looked back, one last time, into an empty space.

'It wasn't my mum, it wasn't my mum, Di. It was Aunty Bea and Edmund did it. What shall I tell them, Di?' he asked once they were inside and the door shut and they were back upstairs.

'You tell them whatever you think it's best to tell them. Tell them anything that makes them listen to you. Tell them you want them to stop fighting.'

'I didn't mean that,' he said. 'I meant, what do I tell them about the paintings worth a million. That's what they'll want to know about. The ones on Daddy's computer.'

'Paintings like that don't exist here,' she said. She could not tell him a lie.

'But shall I tell them that they do?'

'Tell them whatever they need to hear, I would,' she said. 'You must tell them whatever you want, no less, no more.'

'So I won't say nothing, then. They wouldn't believe me anyway. As long as you know it's not Mummy.'

Her heart was fit for breaking, the fragments of it cold. She envied Gayle her loyal son.

Treasure him. Let him come back.

They were safe indoors. Quig could not penetrate these

walls, not even to kidnap a boy. Even a boy could outrun Quig.

The others foregathered to make picnics and fuss, crowd round and say goodbye. Patrick was seen off like a king and she was lost in the crowd, waving until the car holding him was out of sight. Di went upstairs and looked out of the window, wanting him away and wanting him back.

Then she shut herself away with Saul. There were sounds of argument, upstairs and down.

Always the messenger boy. Raymond Forrest was furious with his client and her instructions. He drove into the town in a bad temper, not improved by traffic jams on the way. He hated his solid car and his solid frame, and he hated the way she was right. His wife, that is. *Just act as mediator*, she said. *Give Di my regards. Met her once and liked her very much.*

His ears buzzed with the conversation that had begun yesterday morning and lasted until well into the evening, when Gayle and Beatrice and Edward forgot he was there, listening on the speakerphone to everything else they were saying.

He's there, he must be there.

No, he must be at the flat. We took him there, didn't we? Go there.

We've been there.

No, wait.

Wait? It's your son we're talking about.

Wait. He's perfectly capable of getting home by himself. Gayle's voice.

All that way?

He's been there before. He's been in cars and trains. Are you there, Raymond?

Beatrice's voice. *Di's abducted him. She's taken him away.*

She's been speaking to him and telling him to come. I want to call the police.

His own voice. *Is he in danger?*

Can't wait. Yes, He's in danger. Di's a pervert, too.

Beatrice, again, before the voices melded in the background, Edward's uppermost.

Wait, he could be useful . . . Use him, the little shit . . .

He won't come to harm. Don't you see, we've got her? She lured him there, she's a kidnapper. We can use it . . . if that's where he's gone, he can be our spy. Let her hang herself.

Beatrice. *WE'RE GOING TO PHONE THE POLICE.*

'Good luck to you,' Raymond Forrest said and put the phone down. Picked up the other one and called Diana Porteous. By that time it was late and there had been more conversations. Why didn't one or both of these parents just go and fetch the beastly child if they knew where he had gone? Why weren't they out searching? Even if there were flood warnings on that part of the coast, dammit. If it was his child, he would have got in the car and driven through hell.

It followed, he told himself as slowed down to turn into the High Street, looking at the litter of a storm, wishing he knew a better route, that the parents of the boy were not worried about him at all. As soon as they knew where he was, they knew he was safe. There was another agenda. Edward had refused to speak to Di, *the bitch,* such an overused word for anybody and anything, only a name for a female dog. They would only have him as an intermediary, and Di agreed. *I've just got back,* she said. *Sorry to have missed your earlier calls. Yes, he is here and well looked after, not by me. Please tell them that and please tell them that yes, of course, he must come home as soon as possible. I agree it isn't appropriate for him to be here. They won't want me to bring him back and they won't want to come here and collect, so could you do it, Raymond?* Third party, adult, neutral, utterly responsible lawyer. Trusted by all. Tasked with the impossible.

What had he said to her? Keep your nose clean, keep good company. And what did she do? Failed to respond to the draft of a will he had sent her, surrounded herself with riff raff and treated him like a servant. Here he was now, chauffeuring a silent child who sat in the front seat of his solid car on the way back, drawing things in the book he got out of a canvas bag, the only luggage he had apart from a picnic for one. Raymond felt neutered. All right, he was paid by the hour, but not enough for this. He felt as if *he* had been kidnapped rather than this child who was not exactly a child, more of an alien.

The boy started to hum as they approached the outskirts of London. Then he started to talk, a slight improvement on silence.

'I like Jones. He's going to teach me to fish. He's bent, you know.'

'Is he? Bent like what?'

'Bent like bent copper. Not gay bent, like Saul is. And Peg's going to teach me stuff. She's going to tell me about sex.'

Raymond Forrest shook himself and groaned.

'Jolly good,' he said.

Peg was that surly teenager with spiked hair, who covered the lad with kisses. *Bye, bye sweetheart, come back soon.* She had bosoms hanging out, like flower baskets on a balcony, not good for a boy; not good for Raymond Forrest's own temperature either. Such undesirable companions Di had chosen.

Raymond felt heavy and clumsy, his emotions, such as they were, in conflict, and what made him most uneasy of all was the sometime presence of Saul Blythe, briefly glimpsed at the door of the kitchen, that trusted friend of all, the hell he was. Raymond slowed down. Sat nav told him his destination and there was precious little time to talk.

'And Saul?' he asked. 'What's he going to teach you? What was he like? Was he nice?'

'Dunno. Not sure. Peg says he used to be a thief, but he isn't any more. He could teach me about that.'

Raymond groaned again.

'And what are you going to say to your parents about this motley crew?' he asked in his unconvincingly avuncular fashion.

'What's a motley crew? It sounds pretty. Shan't tell them anything about them,' he said. 'They won't want to know. You won't tell them either, will you?'

'No.'

Patrick leaned forward, breathing into Ray's ear. 'Just as long as Di knows it wasn't my mum. My mum's smart.'

Duty was duty. He drove slowly. Raymond Forrest had been instructed to deliver this child to the safe territory of Thomas's London flat, and that was what he did. Duty did not extend to saying anything. The child was in good condition, speaking for himself. His client was in control.

There was no need for a key. The door was open. The interior was a scene of dereliction, nothing like the state Raymond had seen it in before. Everything had been taken down off the walls or out of boxes and systematically torn and smashed into pieces. It must have taken some time. Gayle sat in the wreckage of broken things.

Patrick looked at her, sadly. She did not run towards him, or he to her. Raymond watched as the boy walked across the floor and hugged her knees. She began to cry.

'It wasn't me did this,' she said, waving at the room. 'It

wasn't me. And it isn't fair. My own son runs away to another woman. Everyone hates me.'

She glared at Raymond.

'I hate her,' she said softly. 'She stole my child. Why does everyone love *her*?'

The child is father to the man. Raymond looked at Patrick with new respect. There can be no sadder moment for a child when they realise that not only is their mother deficient, but that they have wounded her deeply. He stood there, battling with pity. Everything was broken.

Gayle wiped her eyes and stood up, smiling at the boy.

'Well,' she said. 'Did you find them? That's what you went for, isn't it? Tell me that's why you went. You went all that way to help us, didn't you? That's why you went.'

'Yes, Mummy. Yes, I did. They're there, Mummy, the best things.'

She turned to Raymond with an unnerving, glacial smile.

'Thank you, Mr Forrest. You can go now.'

He did not want to go. He did not want to see if she struck him; he did not want to see a child so desperate to please. He left. Patrick's high voice followed.

'I found them, Mummy. I found them. There's two of them. I found them. Granny's paintings. I drew a map.'

'Good boy,' Mummy said.

Tell them what they want to hear. Love your mother. Even when you know she is very bad, and smashes things up. Make her happy.

'Gayle will hate you for this,' Saul said to Di.

'Will she?' Di said.

CHAPTER FOURTEEN

Picture: *An oldish man with fluffy hair, seen in half profile, waving a pen, gesticulating. Brown eyes, and an open mouth, as if speaking. A teacher. A dreamer? Subject William Porteous, headmaster. Small dimensions; X cm by X cm.*

Oil on canvas, dated on the back, looks like 1960. Style more like 1890s. Possibly portrait of a headmaster by a pupil.

'You do have a roundabout way of going about things, Di,' Jones said, standing next to her in the furthest attic room, later in the morning, looking at the picture of Thomas's father. 'Seems like you can't think unless you're looking at some fucking painting or other. Or writing summat. You sent for me, madam?' He peered at the small picture. 'Lovely man, old William Porteous. Not like your dad, eh? 'Cos that's who we're talking about it, isn't it? Not this old fella. And we gotta make it quick, because that Saul's got me that busy, installing cameras and such. I've got my work cut out as it is. And Peg's not happy.'

'I look at pictures to clear my mind of other impressions,' Di said. 'This man calms me, because he looks like Thomas.'

'It's only the sea clears my head,' Jones said. 'Nothing else does it. Get on with it, Di, love.'

She lit a cigar. It was nice up here, out of the way. These, and the laundry room, were the ones Peg liked best. Hot in summer.

'Like I told you, Quig was on the pier, walking towards us. I just had the feeling that he was going to snatch Patrick and I was afraid that I'd be paralysed and not able to stop him, though I could have stopped him, easy. Now you tell me that he might have followed Peg home, that he might have tried to get in that night when I was in the nick. And it might have been, might have been him belted you on the pier. What do I do about it, Jones?'

'You mean what do *we* do, girl. My problem, too.'

'OK, what do we do? What does he want?'

'Don't fucking know, can only fucking guess. But before I do that, you've gotta come clean with me about what you feel about him. Like you might try telling me that it was him who led the team who stuffed you through the shutters here, when was it, ten years ago this week. You always said it was someone else, but it was him, wasn't it? Oh, all right, he wouldn't be the leader, he never is, but he was there. Am I right, or am I right?'

She nodded.

'He was there. He wasn't the leader, but he was there, standing back.'

'And ain't that typical of him, and ain't that typical of you,

Di, never to say. You couldn't shop your own dad, could you? You know there's one clear way of getting rid of Quig. You can shop him now, for that and God knows what else. He's buried a few bodies, your dad, and you know where they are. You can make a call and send them hunting, but it would have to be you, and you can't fucking do it. What's he got on you, Di?'

He looked at her. She looked at the picture of William Porteous, as if searching for a clue.

'He knows things. He knows . . .' she faltered, and Jones thundered on.

'Nah, you couldn't shop even the lowest of the fucking low, 'cos you think anyone'd rather be dead than go inside. You'd kill him first before you told on him. Right,' Jones scratched his head and took refuge on the view from the window. 'Now I think I've got it straight. There's no point trying to fucking psychoanalyse a screwed-up bastard like Quig, and you're not going to deal with him by telling the cops, so we just have to deal with the fact that he's here. And with the fact that he's kept tabs on you all these years. Got someone in this town to keep him informed.'

Jones decided not to tell her who, and omitted to mention that Quig had been outside the Town Hall on the day Di got married. Later, maybe. There were a lot of things they were going to have to cover later, such as what really went on the night of the storm, all that, but Jones was transfixed by the present and highly excited by Saul's plan, which he thought was pretty damn fine and made him feel indispensable. It was really going to work. He looked out of the casement window and saw a lowering sky, God he would like to be on the pier, but then he liked where he was, too. Being fucking useful. Get this over and then think about Quig: don't let Di lose her bottle. And don't remind her she was still subject to those police enquiries, which his contact told him had gone quiet at the moment. Gone quiet, but not gone away. They didn't like Di; they'd be back. One thing at a time.

'I don't know what Quig wants, Di love. He might want his daughter back, he might want money, he might want to hurt you. He might just want to help, but lets look at what he *is*.'

Another deep breath.

'Take it in order, he don't work for anyone unless he's paid, and Thomas's kids aren't going to do that. Nor would that Edward have an inkling how to deal with someone like Quig for long, he ain't even got the same fucking vocabulary. So Quig's on the sidelines, probably doesn't know what he wants, apart from being homesick. Might also be sick as a fucking parrot about his kid living up at the big house.'

Jones took a dead cigar out of the ashtray, lit it with his own lighter, found it disgusting and put it out, glad of the distraction all the same.

'Look at what he is,' he insisted. 'You're not afraid of what he might do to you, you're afraid of him for what he knows.'

She looked at him, blankly, opened her mouth to speak, closed it again.

'But you're only afraid of him for what he knows about you, about this house where he went to school. But look at what he *is*. He's a busted flush, love. He can't run and he hasn't got a gun and he's frightened to be seen. All right he clocks me on the pier, but only because I was pissed and halfway down already. He might chase you and Patrick, but he can't outrun you. He might try and get in when he thinks the place is empty, and he'll bury anything already dead, but he never comes at anyone full on, never comes on to someone who might hit back. So what's the worry? Think of what he is.'

Di gave up. The moment passed. It was knowledge that she feared, not brute force.

He shook his head, walked to the window at the other end, raised his binoculars.

'Quig won't be here long, unless he gets an instant result. And what you've gotta fucking remember, Di, he won't hurt you unless you're lying down first, all by yourself, waiting to be kicked, and that's not going to happen, is it? You're not going to be alone, not once.'

She was listening.

'Quig gives up easy, Di. Runs as soon as he's spotted and he's been spotted. Ignore him, get on with the main stuff.'

'Any way of telling him that I'm never alone?'

'If he's still here, he'll find out.'

He thought of Monica. Better not mention Monica: he wanted to wring her neck. Monica, the contact, the informer, who always knew where Quig was. Di looked better: she was suddenly businesslike and smiling at him, accepting reassurance like a good girl.

'Anyway,' Jones said, grinning back, 'gotta get on with stuff. Get yourself back to the control room. Saul's in overdrive. All this with Patrick and bloody Quig, just makes everything more urgent. And Di, after this, we're really going to talk, aren't we?'

'Yes,' she said.

'And pigs have fucking wings, right? In the meantime,' he said, 'I take orders from Saul, do I?' He was still grinning. 'It's a pleasure. We're sorting out the details. Good plan. Concentrate on that, hey? Forget your fucking Dad.'

*

Back downstairs in the gallery room, she began to write to Thomas, only to find that beyond a few lines, she couldn't.

Accusing a man who reveres children of abusing the trust of a child is a worse accusation than murder. I can see why you can't forgive them, or her. You want to hoist them on the mast of their malice and greediness. And yet you want them protected from the knowledge of what their mother was like, and the worst she could do.

You said: tempt them, make them steal something; make them fight in a way they never have. Give them something and make them take risks.

I think I understand, but I don't always know where you are.

She turned to the inventory of paintings instead.

Di was still writing in the afternoon of the day that remained dull after Patrick had gone and she had talked to Jones. Before that, there had been an argument with Saul and then with Peg. *You* can't *send him away,* Peg had yelled. *Let Patrick stay, he can hang out with me.*

No, he has to go home.

And what about me, what about me, will you do the same to me? Hysteria lurked near the surface.

No, Peg, I won't. You'll go when you're ready.

Peg was rude to Raymond Forrest, Jones, as well. All of them had retreated to the various ends and heights of the house, and even after she had talked to Jones, there was still the retreat position of the back yard. Best to let it all simmer down.

Saul came in. He stood by the desk and looked at the description she had typed. *Old man with kind eyes.*

'Back at the addictive keyboard, are we? When do I see the personal diary? You're getting on with the alternative inventory, I see. I do love your descriptions, Di. They're so flippant and frivolous. Not a great help to a valuer. They're written for a collector. Nothing about the quality of the fucking paint, abstract qualities, only about the narrative. Like they were all fucking stories. Sorry, I've been talking with Jones. It gets infectious.'

He moved to the window and looked out towards the sea, in which it seemed he had no interest, except for the changing colour of it. The rain had removed the salt from the windows and the view of the sky was painfully clear.

'Have you sorted it out with fucking Jones? I thought so. He's a good man for the purpose. Mustn't let Daddy distract, nor any other neanderthal. I must say, my dear, that if your fortunes and your chances of winning through were to rest entirely with that lump of a lawyer, I don't know where you'd be.'

'Raymond's a good man,' Di said. 'And much abused.'

Di had a tendency that annoyed him. If you criticised anyone, she defended them: if you sneered, she praised, if you denigrated, she supported. It was the same when they looked at paintings. If you said something was valueless, she pointed out the virtues in it; she said what it could be, not what it was: she existed to defend people, things, even pieces of flint which excelled hand-hewn sculpture in her eyes, it was all the same. If you put it down, she would try and bolster it up.

'Raymond's everything a lawyer's supposed to be,' she said. 'Solid, dependable and unimaginative. He's a properly responsible man. Doesn't dabble. Hears what he wants to hear, does what he's asked to do.'

'Unlike me?'

'Definitely unlike you. You are profoundly irresponsible.'

He paced between the windows, restless, speaking as he moved. He was dressed in olive cords, belted at the waist, bulking out the extreme narrowness of his frame. Saul was never just dressed; he was costumed.

'Well,' he said, 'I think everything's going OK, all things considered. Just had a long chat with that dangerous, half-educated buffoon, Edward. Patrick is safely home.'

She turned quickly, anxiety written large.

'How is he?'

'He's fine,' Saul said, carelessly. 'Safely delivered to the flat and into the arms of doting mother, for whose sanity her husband secretly fears. He will no doubt pump the boy for information and I've hinted that nothing would ever result unless the interrogation was gentle. And I have also, not so gently, hinted that should your dreadful daddy be in touch, they'd better choke him off. Said they'd be blackmailed for-ever if they didn't. Have I done well?'

'There's nothing Patrick can tell them,' Di said. 'He's not a pawn to be used.'

'No, I know he isn't, but Edward thinks he is. I've never met such an immoral man. He was all for leaving Patrick here longer, using him as a spy. He didn't think twenty-four hours, or however long it was, was enough for the boy to confirm the whereabouts of certain *things*. Like the paintings in the basement they are going to steal. The odd thing is that there's them sounding off about Patrick being in danger from *you*, and Edward never thought so at all. Nor I suspect, does ghastly Gayle. She never really believed the myth. This pae-dophilic *myth*.'

'It can't be great, being Gayle,' Di said, after a pause. 'Can't be easy.'

'You're doing it again, Di.'

'What?'

'Always taking the other side. Can't you sustain a good bit of hatred? Listen, love, they really despise you. Patrick coming here will have made that worse. They're going to come back and raid you, just as planned. That's what Edward wanted to finalise. Shall we give them the faux Fragonard or the faux Gainsborough?'

She was struggling with the thought that Patrick, whom she loved, had come with a mission, rather than arrived spontaneously. She decided it did not matter either way.

'Both, of course, we decided both. The collection can live without them, especially the Fragonard. They were part of Thomas's inheritance, rather than his choice, even though they're exactly the kind of artists he liked. Shadowy people, the cousin, the pupil, artists who never had the limelight. My kind, too, but they're slightly tainted, somehow.'

She was talking like a Collector again and he was nodding agreement.

'Slightly dubious portraits of innocence on the cusp. Edward has the images, he's seen the famous versions, and I'm taking him the transparencies this evening. He's such a philistine, attention span of a gnat, always looking for the bottom line in euros. Encouraged to think he's an expert.'

'By you, I suppose.'

Saul shrugged, elegantly.

She joined him by the window. Clouds were better than anything. Clouds and flint. She felt nothing. She wanted above all to bury her husband having done what he wanted, with the freedom to do more of what he wanted. She could not enjoy conspiracies as Saul did.

'You're enjoying all this,' she said. 'Why does Edward trust you so much? I trust you because Thomas did and I believe in Thomas's judgement. If I were Edward, I'd never be sure.'

He laughed out loud.

'I do notice your sideways glances, don't worry, and I'm not at all offended. Your plump little lawyer man, Raymond, what a common name, he's puzzled, too. Edward trusts me because he's greedy and he doesn't like me, in fact I'm anathema to him, but he trusts me, within limits of course, because I correspond exactly to his idea of what a shady Art Dealer should be. Effete, lounge lizard, morally bankrupt, ready to do anything for a commission. He thinks he found me, whereas I lured him in, like Thomas asked me to do, to find out what Goneril and Regan would do if they inherited, would they honour the collection? Would they share with you? The hell they would. They'd sell the lot, soonest, and the house for development. And spend it on anything other than the education of their children.'

'I think Beatrice is the worst,' she said. *Pervert, paedophile;* the words ringing back like screaming seagulls.

'Do you?' he said, surprised. 'Oh, good. Because on current arrangements, it's Edward and Gayle who are coming to take the designated pictures in the basement, a couple of nights hence. Lovely Patrick hasn't got in the way of that at all. My word, that boy can draw.'

He held aloft two sheets from the sketchbook Patrick had left behind, one showing the ticket collector and one showing Quig.

'Look at this,' he said, pointing to the latter. 'Now there's a man who could skin a kitten but not a lion. Couldn't do a thing unless someone shot the beast first. Is this a subject for discussion?'

'No.'

She peered at the screen and wrote another line as if her fingers were connected to the keyboard. He waited.

'Can I ask you something?' she said. 'What did you really think when I came on the scene? The thief who came back?'

'I was absolutely appalled,' he said. 'Until I knew the truth of it. That you're a born connoisseur. And Thomas needed another pair of eyes.'

She bowed her head. 'Is that all?'

He sat down, hitching up the immaculate cords to save them bagging at the knee.

'No, of course not. We both met Thomas on our own road to Damascus. We are both his missionaries and apostles, and over the course of time, you've learned what the words mean. You'll do.'

He rose.

'And on that note, my dear, I'll be about my Machiavellian tasks, shall I? Including prepping the sulking staff. Expect me back tomorrow. I think we can expect a visitation, possibly the day after. A crucial date, isn't it? Peg and Jones will be there to protect you. Obviously, I can't be here; I have to be elsewhere, ready to receive the stolen goods. I have to be out of the way so that *you* do not know that *I* had anything to do with it. A crucial date, n'est-ce pas? Beatrice thinks it's perfectly poetic. Ten years since her mother drowned.'

The truth was on the tip of her tongue, and then the coughing began again. He had never been quite free of it. In public, he could make it discreet, but not here. She got up and stood behind his chair with her hands free, until she stroked his hair, as if he were Patrick, or Thomas, or any ill, restless child. There was no point offering patent remedies; Saul had his own dispensary of those.

He let her do it, relaxed for a minute, safe in her hands.

She might not know the cause: she might not know the extent of the illness, but she knew when a person was ill. He pulled himself away, hugged her fiercely and impersonally, and went downstairs.

'Got to prep the staff,' he said.

I must not be afraid of my father, she wrote, her hands steady on the keys. But I am. *Tell me Thomas, out of Beatrice and Gayle, who was the favoured child? Who was the one you loved best?*

The old steel shutter had never been properly secured. It looked fearsome, but to the initiated, it was easy to penetrate by a simple twisting technique. Patrick, that weird boy, had known how it was done. It followed, to Jones's mind, that either someone had taught him or he had learned it himself. It was perfectly possible, Jones thought, that this was not Patrick's first clandestine visit to the house since he was banned; not the first from that enterprising little man who could easily have slipped away for a day. Jones was only annoyed because although he had seen so much, he had missed out on the boy, while he knew about the others who came here, too. Jones had watched from the pier, knew who was drawn to this house, just as he was, like people always had been, three generations of them. Lost souls, kids, waifs and strays, rather than thieves. There was the old down and out fisherman, who came here about once a month when he could not find his way home: so did Monica's cousin at the end of one of his benders, so did a very few, disparate people, who had known the house in some other context of their lives, and they were all tacitly permitted to take shelter in the basement, as did an intermittent parade of children. They came and went silently, and when they were gone, Di cleaned

up and left it ready for the next. Jones both approved and dis-
approved. It might be an act of mercy, but it was a silly thing
to do, leave your house open like that, although he had to
concede she wasn't taking much of a risk. Any intruders via
this route had nowhere else to go and they could not access
the house itself unless the door into the kitchen was unlocked.
That was a heavy sprung door, which swung on itself so that
getting in from below was not an option unless it was
propped open. Di could confine her secret overnight guests
to the makeshift comforts down there, which were enough
for the temporary respite of sleeping it off. A washbasin with
a single tap, water, blankets, enough.

Not that she needed to have worried about the contents of
the spacious cellar, either. No tired drunk or runaway child
wanted old things hidden in boxes or wrapped in canvas,
even if they could be bothered to investigate. In fact, as Jones
thought aloud to Peg, the lack of temptation applied to the
whole fucking house. A big old house was not always a
beacon for thieves because there was nothing new in it; even
the white goods were old, there was nothing anyone could sell
immediately down the pub or the car boot fair. No money,
no jewellery, no state of the art technology. Your ordinary
thief would not know what to do with a thousand paintings,
collections of suitcases and dressing-up clothes.

'It goes like this, Peg,' he told her, sermonising. 'You're
pretty safe in a house full of valuable stuff, provided it's specialised. Art's a pretty safe thing to own. What you've got to
guard against is the casual thief who gets in and craps on it
out of sheer frustration because none of it's any good to him,
does damage 'cos he's pissed off. As for your professional,
specialised thief – well, if he's any good, he'll know what's
there before he sets out. He'll have a list of what he wants,

he'll have reconnoitred, he'll know what to do with the stuff and he'll be in and out in a jiffy. There's nothing you can do about him. He's not some silly little trasher, he's got a brain.'

He lit a cigarette, surveying the back yard and the leverage of the shutter with the eye of the expert. 'I reckon our Saul was a thief like that,' Jones said. 'A proper thief, stealing to order.'

Saul emerged behind them, quiet as a cat, touching Jones on the shoulder, making him jump. Peggy sat on a pot of withered pansies by the front fence. The rain had flattened everything.

'Jolly good analysis, old chap,' Saul said with irritating joviality. 'And how many thieves like that have you ever caught?'

'Not a one, I don't think. Not without inside information,' Jones said, cheerfully enough, totally unembarrassed about being overheard on his pontificating. 'Like I was saying, I'd never have caught the likes of you. Only the stupid ones get caught. The idiots. With you, it'd be like catching an eel with bare hands and no net. Besides, I wouldn't have wanted to, really – you've got to respect a proper thief.'

'Only the stupid ones get caught,' Peg echoed, so quietly no one heard. 'People like me.'

Saul looked up at the sky. Jones looked at the ground.

'There's another kind of thief who doesn't get caught,' he said. 'And that's the one who's allowed in. The ones who are *encouraged* to get away with it. Even if they don't know it. And that's what's going to happen here, isn't it? Like an insurance scam. Those bastards deserve everything they get.'

'Not quite like that,' Saul said.

'You going to bless me with the final details, or what?' Jones asked, sarcastically, but with a level of humility. There was some instinct in him that looked upon Saul as the leader and Jones was always looking for one of those.

'Yes, when I've seen Edward. When I come back. By phone, OK? I'll phone first and explain.'

Jones nodded.

'Just tell me what to do. And just so's you know, Di's not off the hook with the police. I'm getting static on the news, but she's still in the frame, always gonna be. So the sooner we do this, the better.'

Saul's coughing began again. It swayed him on his feet, and he made a parody of it with exaggerated gestures of patting his chest and adding extra noises.

'Filthy cold here,' he said finally when it subsided and he made them laugh with his pantomime. 'So what on earth are you darlings doing out here, anyway? Not sulking, I hope.'

Oh Lord, he thought to himself, how much they need a master and how much he would rather not be one.

'A bit,' Jones said. 'See, Peggy here thinks Di shouldn't have sent Patrick home.'

'In case she should do the same to you?' Saul said, practically kneeling at her feet. 'Why on earth would she ever do *that*?'

Because I'm one of those stupid thieves, with a proper warrant out for my arrest. The one who left fingerprints and did damage. Not just a pickpocket. A drunk who trashed things for fun.

She could not say it aloud. None of them would listen anyway.

Saul patted her hand and she looked towards her cold feet on the ground. He smelled cologne-sweet. He said, 'She wouldn't ever send you away until you are ready to go. And she'd never give anyone up to the police, even if they pulled her teeth out.'

Peg nodded. She was going to tell Di. Di would listen to someone wearing her clothes. No one else would.

Chapter Fifteen

All right, Saul said to himself on the train. I am going to see Edward. I am going to see this through. I have organised a burglary. All that matters is the Collection, and although I am a coward, I do so love games. This is about me. And about what I know. Have to get it right.

There was a sour-faced ticket inspector on the train, who eyed Saul with distaste as if he was inedible. Maybe not the same man as the one in Patrick's sketchbook, left on the kitchen table overnight: perhaps they were all like that. Patrick; now there was a boy with a talent for depiction which might well develop into something else. Another reason for compromising his father who might otherwise ruin him.

Saul arranged himself comfortably and got out his laptop. He might have dressed in some ways like an elegant old fogey but he preferred his equipment to be streamlined. The laptop was carried in an envelope of old, soft leather, found in Florence. He wanted to read, but he had read too much and his eyes were tired. He would have liked to read what Di wrote on her old computer in private: he would like to know what she hid from him. Something niggled; an area of ignorance, like an itchy patch of skin he could not reach to scratch. What troubled him on his way to organise Edward into the other end of the burglary that was going to liberate the Collection, was the personality and whereabouts of the late Mrs Christina Porteous, who was somehow fixed upon his inner eye, disturbing his vision, as if she had anything to do with anything.

Most of the material he had gathered on the first Mrs Porteous was inside the laptop. He had been collating it for years, noted it now into bullet points, the way he did with a description of a painting he was trying to sell. He did it to put her into perspective. The first Mrs Porteous had been a vibrant art student in the conservative nineteen sixties, with the sort of face and figure which courted adoration and got it. She wanted the world, and got instead studious Thomas Porteous, teacher, son of a teacher, dallied with him, dropped him, took him up again, married him when life did not quite fulfil its promises. Had children, hated the process, disliked her life, loathed her dull man of duty, left him, came back, left again until she finally left for good; regretting it thereafter, since the new man was made of straw and the old one got rich. Won her custody battle for the two little girls hands down after she had cited Thomas's 'unnatural tendencies' towards them and the merest hint of that untested evidence was enough. After that, no contest, not in those days. Thomas paid generous support for his girls and wrote to them, often, in sweet, undemanding letters which were returned, without postage. They had gone to expensive schools at their mother's behest, but not the sort of schools that taught a girl the value of work. Saul had a desire to press these handwritten pages back into the hands of their intended recipients. One day, perhaps he would.

So; Thomas got rich and the now-ex Mrs Christina P got poor. She wanted to come back; she thought she could undo the past, but she had gone too far and the door was closed. She beat against it until her knuckles were raw and then she got angry, possessive of people and things long after she wanted them and could not bear to be caught out in a lie. The grandchildren were the next opportunity to blackmail Thomas but she had really boxed herself into a corner on that one. Too late to say he's old and no longer dangerous, and then expect to be believed. She wanted what Thomas had and she could not bear for him to have it. She hated him enough to want him dead: she found his serene existence intolerable. All recorded in the scribblings of a deranged woman that Saul had recovered from the little flat where he was now bound to finalise a plan with her son-in-law.

What else of Christina? She had liked the sea, if only to sail across it to France on day trips, and that was where she would have liked to live. She had announced her intention of going there on the day she was last seen and she never came back. Saul told himself that she was no longer relevant, and yet, there she was, glued to his inner eye and this was stupid. He moved his mind on.

For the purposes of his investigations into the minds of the Porteous daughters and Edward, Saul had conducted research that was less than scholarly. Burglary was so much quicker. He had been inside their houses, finding photos, mementos, notes and diaries, first in Beatrice's messy place, then in Gayle's white-walled, sterile environment. He was, after all, a born thief: old habits really did die hard and he never intended to relinquish the talent he had honed in his youth, or the adrenaline rush that went with it. He had always been in love with attics, rooftops and cellars, the extremes of a dwelling: exploring other people's houses in their absence revealed uncanny familiarity with the inhabitants, so that he felt he knew them better than they knew themselves. He no longer took anything away, except what he learned.

Such as: Gayle and Beatrice had no talent for anything and no appreciation. They had been nurtured to be decorative and never forced to study. Their homes were ridiculously easy to penetrate and he shuddered at the very thought of them. Edward and Gayle in an ugly, high-status apartment unsuitable for a child; Beatrice in her dank, artisan dwelling, both of them revealing an appalling dearth of pictures or books, and oh, dear, they had not been trained to work, just like their mother, only they were in the wrong generation to be kept. No telling what Gayle would have been if she had not married Edward. *His* place told of a man who always made the wrong investments and while Saul did not particularly relish the level of concentration he would need for their imminent meeting, he found he was approaching it with a degree of malicious enjoyment. Such a game.

He paused to examine his own motivation, albeit briefly, liking to check on himself, occasionally. His motives were far more straightforward and solid than anything as ephemeral as love, personal loyalty or anything like that. He was a Collector, that was all, and this was a fabulous collection. He'd been terrified that Thomas would behave like others who succumbed to sentiment in old age, leaving a life's work for a family to chew up and consume like junk food, such a waste. Saul recognised the limits of his own emotions and knew he had no idea about the unconditional love one individual could hold for another, because nothing, absolutely nothing, came anywhere near the way he felt about a picture. And although he could find himself transfixed by the body of a boy, he knew how to turn his face away from that, too, unless it was on canvas.

Alighting from the train, tucking the leather envelope beneath his arm and steeling himself for his prearranged meeting with Edward, he rather wished they had fixed the meeting for somewhere else.

Check: Transparencies of the pictures in question.

Check: Potential values (don't over-egg your pudding.)

Check: Remember how to make a stupid brute of a man look clever.

Check: Remember the purpose of it all, i.e. you relinquish control of two paintings in order to preserve the rest from gross interference. You are going to outwit the claimants by giving them something of enough value to settle their bogus moral claim, and you are going to compromise them in the process so that you can threaten them with blackmail thereafter, and thus enable the Collection to thrive and grow with the best curators it would ever have, Di Porteous and Saul Blythe.

After that, deal with the other matters. Keep Di alive and out of prison. The Collection needs her eyes.

He was early, stopped for a coffee and longed for a whisky. He admired the vaunted ceiling of the station: it held such promise, like the cellar in the house. A pigeon pecked around his feet and he did not chase it away. Thomas had been fussy about coffee: the taste of it reminded Saul of the first time they had met. Sipping coffee. The reason he was regretting the meeting place was because of associations. Saul had first tried to cheat Thomas in that little flat, before he loved him and his collector's eyes. *Will you help me, honestly?* Thomas had said, *and be honest with it, no point otherwise – will you?*

Yes, he would.

Saul coughed and dabbed his eyes, suddenly angry. *Oh, Thomas, why did you have to die?* Walking towards the flat through the dark and quaint streets of King's Cross, he remembered how Thomas had said what it used to be like when he was a student here: teeming tenements, alive with noise, children playing in the street and mothers calling from windows. It was silent now, apart from the distant city hum. He had loved the presence of children, any children, and these were the innocent longings of an only child, brought up in a school. Saul could not give a damn if Thomas had buggered half the underage population and raped the rest. He tucked the pretty leather case containing the laptop under his arm and moved on.

Inside the studio flat, Edward tried to mend the damage, picking up one smashed object and putting it down again. The mess and the damage would not make a good impression but why the hell should he care about *impressions* with a nancy boy like Saul Blythe? Gayle said someone else had got in and wrecked the place all over again, but he knew she had done it while waiting for Raymond Forrest to come back with their son. He was late, she said, and she hated waiting. Edward looked around, uneasily. Strange how they foregathered here, staking territory as soon as they knew Thomas was dead. Awful place; he hated it. He heard Saul come in only when he was inside the door. The man was so quiet it was uncanny.

'Bit of a mess, isn't it?' Saul said.

The damage was comprehensive and deliberate.

'Patrick did it,' Edward said tersely. It was a lie Saul chose to ignore. That child could no more wreak such havoc than he could fly. A child who could draw and who looked at paintings could never do that. The lie made him dislike Edward more than ever, but he smiled at him all the same.

'We're in business,' he said.

'I already know where the two paintings are,' Edward interrupted.

'Yes,' Saul said. 'You do. But I'll tell you again.'

A pause.

'You'd better look at these transparencies, so much clearer. Take both.'

Edward looked, closely. The girl on the swing. The two faces of Gainsborough's daughters. He seemed a little disappointed. Then he looked again, checked the dimensions, scowled, and leered at the images.

'Naughty, naughty. The old rogue. Pictures of kids ... he would, wouldn't he? Are you sure you can't simply collect them and bring them here yourself? They're small enough. Save us the trouble?'

Saul shook his head. 'We've discussed this. You know it's impossible. They have to be taken, without my knowledge, or I can't help you later. No, I stay out of the way, I set the scene, make it easy. You collect, you and Gayle, you said.'

He wants to cut me out already, Saul thought. *Patrick was down that cellar for quite a while: I wonder what he told them?*

'How much will they be worth?'

'I don't know. It depends on when and where they go on sale. It depends on the provenance. A million for the two's possible in the right auction, with the right provenance. The sooner they're in your hands, the better. Two nights hence is really ideal. An anniversary – Di will be thoroughly preoccupied. You and Gayle slip in and collect.'

Edward hesitated. He was excited, but he did not like taking orders. *He's nothing without Gayle*, Saul thought.

'I have a map of the house,' Edward said, importantly.

'From Di's father, I presume? Ignore it, and ignore him.'

'I've sacked him,' Edward said, as if the man had been on the staff. 'He knows nothing about any of this. The boy brought it back.'

Saul nodded.

'You don't need a map, because you don't have to go into the house. In fact, it's vital that you don't. There'll be people in the house. You get in through the steel shutter at the back, down the ramp, I'll make sure it's open. You don't need to go further than the cellar. Don't go into the house. On no account do you go into the house.'

'Gayle's cool with that.'

'Your wife is a cool customer,' Saul said, deferentially. Edward laughed.

'What on earth makes you think that?'

Saul cast a slow look round the fragmentation of everything in the room. Edward shuffled, uncomfortably.

'Did she do this?'

'No, of course not. I told you, it was Patrick. Shall we go through it again? You're sure Di won't be alone?'

'No. Di's never alone these days. She'll have her rabble upstairs for a birthday party. A dubious uncle and a girl, celebrating. They'll be upstairs in the gallery room, getting drunk as they often do, or sleeping it off. I fear Di has rather taken to the bottle. But the uncle fellow, well, he's nasty. That's why you mustn't go into the house.'

'I'm glad she's not alone,' Edward said.

'The cellar's a biggish space. I'm afraid I shan't be able to label your packages with neon stickers, but you'll know where they are. In front of the drawers, in front of the door ... I've photographed it for you.'

He held out his phone, which Edward accepted with indifference and then looked at closely. He seemed mesmerised by the presence of the wall and the door.

'What's behind the door?' he asked.

'I've no idea. Water, I suppose.'

They went through it again, and then again. If only Edward would offer him a drink, if only he would finish this and go.

'And afterwards,' Saul said, 'Once you've got them, you keep them safe in your own attic, or somesuch. Then we'll work out the provenance. And the best sale programme. Might take a while.'

The delay troubled Edward. 'And what will Di do when she knows they're gone?'

'She won't know immediately. Trust me. And when she does find out, it'll be too late. She won't be able to claim back something not on the inventory, and you'll have retrieved something before she spends it all.'

'I heard. Day after tomorrow, then,' Edward said. 'Gayle and I. Inside for five minutes max, you said.'

'Two days hence,' Saul said. 'Confirm by phone. More like three minutes than five.'

Edward had been getting steadily more restless, Saul noticed. He actually wanted this adventure; a proving of self, as if stealing back his wife's property would make him a man. If Saul got up to go, then Edward would do the same. Saul had the knack of predicting people and Edward rose unsteadily, still trying to maintain the upper hand.

'Shame about the mess here,' Saul said lightly. 'Don't worry, I'll tidy. I'll stay here tonight if that's OK with you. No one will know it's been done over. Housework's my other speciality. I'll phone you.'

Edward went. Saul let out his breath, thought, *yes, we've got it right. They have to do it this way.*

Then he set about the tidying, wondering exactly who had done such comprehensive damage, which daughter it was, but he did not think about it for long, because he had never really taken to ceramics, although there were exceptions. Ceramics had never been Thomas's passion, either.

He had the ironic thought that what had been destroyed might have been the last relics of Christina, and that they had only broken what was hers.

How ironic was that? He laughed out loud.

Chapter Sixteen

Peg had given herself the task of household washing because she liked the smell and the usefulness. The laundry room was another secret place she had discovered, not that it was that secret; just not what you'd think it might be. The building was full of insignificant doors that led into meaningful rooms like this, especially on the middle floor. There were rooms that were not in the place you expected them to be, such as next to the kitchen. Daft place to put machinery, Peg thought, but you may as well carry washing upstairs as well as down. There was a vintage, industrial-sized washing machine, with incredibly simple instructions, a pulley suspended from the ceiling on which to hang clothes, a sink, a fireplace, a table and two chairs and all the impedimenta for ironing, plus a radio and a kettle. There was even a press for sheets. No pictures, except that one of the maid with the copper and the view from the window, and she looked happy enough. Peg could hide in here, listening to the hum of the machine and music on the radio, feeling right in the hidden heart of the house, but apart from it. She liked it even better than the linen cupboard two doors along, where there was a picture on the wall of clean washing pegged out on a line, but she couldn't stay here all day, could she?

It felt as if something was going to happen. Something was going to burst and she didn't know what it was. It had been nice the evening before, without Saul. Peace was fully restored. They had sat in the gallery upstairs with the fire on, Jones and Di teaching her how to play cards and she hadn't missed her lost mobile phone or the telly, and she finally stopped aching to talk. Wanting to tell them stuff, about her being in more trouble than she said, and not being quite what they thought she was. It wasn't so much wanting to talk as wanting to be asked. She was sick of their politeness, and her own: she wanted to shout and she wanted Patrick to come back, for the sake of having someone younger around. The old ones weren't pushing her to talk, they were respecting her relative silence and she wished they wouldn't. She wanted them to be curious enough to draw her out, and they just didn't do it. They were waiting for her, and she was waiting for them, especially for Jones. He had at least hugged her goodnight, so that was something. But would he have done it if he had known that she was one of *those* kinds of thieves he'd been talking about with Saul, one of the stupid ones, who got inside people's places and trashed stuff? Fucking trash.

She left the washing humming and went to find Jones, but Jones had gone out mid-morning. That left Di, who was in the gallery, sitting at the desk and talking on the new phone, not the big old phone that must have been around for a hundred years. Di used the new phone for household stuff; she even ordered the food by phone. Peg would have liked to do the shopping but it was mainly done that way. She knew she wanted to tell stuff to Di, and she was suddenly tongue-tied again so she retreated quietly. She went right to the top of the house where she had stood with Jones and let him teach her to focus through his binoculars which he left up there. She scanned the sea and the sky, concentrated on the pier, where she could just about make him out, walking towards the caff at the end. He seemed to be walking alongside a woman and the sight of them made her feel lonely. She wanted to cry and focused on something else. Binoculars were magic: they brought the world inside your brain.

Di came in, touched her on the shoulder and made her jump. Peg yelped.

'Sorry,' Di said. 'Were you looking for me?'

'No, not really.'

'There's a telescope downstairs,' Di said. 'Even better. What were you looking at?'

'I was looking at the boats,' Peg said, suddenly emotional all over again. 'I'd like to go on one of those. Sail away. Maybe a job on a boat.'

Big boats on the horizon, looking so sleek and beautiful and small against the clouds, they looked like toys. She felt Di's thin arms around her and consented to the embrace. Yes, she could talk now, but all the same she wished it was Jones.

'Dirty old town,' Monica said, looking back from the pier.

'Only for the dirty-minded,' said Jones, taking her arm by the elbow. She shrugged it off.

'It's a shithole.'

'Just look at it, Mon, will you? Raise your eyes to the skies. Look at those boats. Look at the sea. Look at the old houses.

It's beautiful, this place. My, my, you were born and raised here and always wanted to get out, didn't you? Well, it isn't too late. You can still go.'

'Wouldn't matter to you either way, would it?' she said.

He took her arm again and this time she let him. They strolled on. The caff looked shut. It always was when you wanted it to be open. It was too cold to sit around in the open for long, but neither of them had long.

'Course it would, Mon love, and a lot of other people besides.'

'A lot of little old ladies who need cheap perms. A couple of old men like you who like a drinking companion and an occasional lie down. This town's bled me dry.'

He sat on a concrete bench and felt the cold on his thighs. She sat with him.

'Never could get a man who'd take you away from it all, could you, Mon? The ones you loved were the ones who wanted to stay. But I'm not having this crap. Who'd miss you? Hundreds would, you know. You've never done a damn thing except make people happy, you don't know how much I envy you that. Everyone who goes in your place comes out better, you know that? For a lot of your punters, you're the difference between staying alive of a morning or not bothering. Even if it's only for a day. Go into yours feeling like shit, come out feeling OK, that's quite a fucking contribution.'

She laughed without any real mirth, slightly mollified.

'Yeah, I daresay I cheer a few people up. Like that little tart you sent down for a fix up? Honestly, Jones you've got a nerve. You go fucking missing and then you send in the scrubber you've gone missing with, leaving a clear message about where you've holed yourself up. Couldn't have been clearer. She's wearing Di's clothes. You wanted me to know where you are. You're rubbing my nose in shit.'

'There's no contest with Peg and you, love. She's just a runaway kid. You know I don't do kids. Stop messing about. Quig belted me. The kid was there. Di took us both in. Anyway, it was you phoned me earlier, remember? Are you going to tell me about Quig? Look, I know he's here and you've been feeding him information.'

She leant into him to light a cigarette, a well-worn routine.

'The man you really wanted to take you away, even though you knew what he was. Is he still here? He'd always come to you, because you were the only one fool enough to take him in. I'd have married you long since, Mon, but you were always stuck on Quig. Must be something about the glamour of muck. Come on, tell me. Where the fuck is he?'

She moved to the other side of the pier with her cigarette. It was a clear day: they could both see the ferry boats on the horizon, standing out like emblems; the tanker, the cruise ship, the ferry from Ramsgate going to France, the link that was more real than any tunnel. She laughed.

'Remember them days out to France, Jones? Good old days of duty free and booze running? That was fun. Going over for the day, loading up a van, filling the cellar and coming back? Christ, that was the furthest I ever got from home. I loved those ferries.'

Jones nodded. 'Quig did a lot of that, long time ago. It's not the same now. You get penned down in the hold like a whole lot of cattle fit for nothing but eating and shopping for rubbish. You can't even go on the top deck. We went last year, remember?'

'Yes. The whole pub went for a day of getting drunk afloat.

I thought you were trying to romance me, and all the time you kept saying how easy it would be to jump off.'

He remembered, felt a little guilty, couldn't stop thinking.

'Jumping off them boats mid-channel must be the easiest way to disappear in the world. Pick a moment halfway across, the ferry can't stop and most likely no one would notice. That's why they close the top decks. Health and fucking safety.'

Christ, he was good with useless information

'I wanted to jump, Jones. I really did. I still do. When you're on that top deck on a nice day with a drink aboard, you think you can fly. Fly away and sink, before you hit the realities of coming home. It looks painless. Must have looked like that to Christina Porteous.'

'Yes, that's what they reckon. Her and a few others. Are you going to tell me about Quig? Is he helping the daughters to stiff Di?'

They watched the boats, miles out but as large as life. Closer in, the more recognisable craft, small vessels, plying for fish, maybe bringing in other kinds of contraband. Looking pretty. Different kinds of fishermen entirely from those who fished off the pier.

He put his arm around her, wanting to comfort her, short of time. She was one of those invaluable, blind, angry women who didn't guess at her own worth, because she wasn't what she wanted to be and life was passing so fast she had lost control of it. And all the time, anything he had ever told her about Di Quigly had been passed on to Di's dad, wherever he was, near or far. That's how it went; Jones told Monica, and Monica told Quig. The wonders of the mobile phone never ceased to amaze him. Poor old Monica, always hoping to lure him back.

'Tell us about Quig,' he urged. 'You've got to tell me. Or
warn him off. Those Porteous kids are bitches. They'll screw
him and they won't pay. Tell him.'

'He already knows.'

She threw away the cigarette. Christ, she hated this pier,
where she had courted, been bored, loved and lost. Never
even try to love a fisherman, you always came second. Never
love a man with a passion for something else; you always
lose.

'He came back,' she said. 'He came round mine the night
we had a drink and you went back to the pier. Just as well you
weren't there. He was raving. Talked in his sleep. I knew he'd
hit you, he said so.'

Jones waited. *And you told him where I was.* She took out a
handkerchief and dabbed her nose. He was losing pity for
her. He loathed fucking informers.

'Said he was homesick. Said he wanted to see Di, wants to
make it up to her, but he knew she wouldn't have it. He's sad,
Jones, sad and spiteful. Nor was she going to give him anything, so he'd only got together with Di's stepkids, hadn't he?
He was going to help them. They reckon Di's place is full of
their mother's stuff and they want it back.'

'And he would have helped them, and helped himself as
well? Leave off, Monica. There's nothing there he could use,
not even a gun.'

'That was the plan, and he was going to help. Only they've
fucked him over, told him they don't need him no more.
And once he knew you were staying up there, he thought he
wouldn't bother. He's afraid of you. You hit him when he
came back for Di's wedding.'

'Which you told him about, and that's why he was there.
You've never forgiven me that, have you? First I knew he was

afraid of me. It isn't me he's afraid of, it's Di. And he only knows I'm up at the house because you told him.'

She hung her head.

'He'd have found out anyway. He's been watching the place.'

'While bunking up with you. You've been his spy. Don't you know Quig would bury you as soon as look at you? Or is that part of the appeal? Well, perhaps he wouldn't unless someone paid him. That's how Quig earns a living. He gets paid to hide the fucking bodies, and then he gets paid for blackmail and information. So, who's going to die this time? Or what fucking body is he after?'

'Don't,' she said, 'Don't. It's not true. He wanted to help her, Jones, he really did. He thought there was something he could do for her; he said it in his sleep. And he knew what them kids really wanted to do, one of them anyway. He said one of them really wants to kill her. Only that man, Edward, he was never going to pay. Called him a cunt, and Quig doesn't like insults.'

Monica got up and walked away. He followed her, stopped her and stood in front of her.

'Where is he now?'

She put her hands in her pockets, feeling for the cigarettes, the tears coursing down her cheeks running furrows in the blusher.

'He's gone, Jones. Got an offer of a job somewhere, with a lot of dosh. Got an offer on his iPhone. Very technical he is these days. So he's gone.'

He would not have believed her, except for her ugly grief and the feeling of a weight, lifting. Jones trusted his feelings. He looked out at the ferries crossing. Another world, so close. Why were they all so slow to move away and find opportunities somewhere else? Why fester here if you didn't love the place? All you had to do was go a few miles down the coast and get on a fucking boat.

'He's really gone, has he?'

'Yes,' she said, pointing towards the closest of the ferries. 'He went off on one of them, this morning. And he didn't take me.'

He wasn't sure he could believe that, and decided he just would. Jones went indoors and whistled. *Fuck me, people had better level.*

Di was unpacking the food the deli and the out of town supermarket delivered. Peg was out of sight. He came in through the back gates that led on the yard and the blankness of the defective steel shutters.

Midday. No sign of Saul and he was sorry about that, but he had been briefed by phone. He looked at the apples in the bowl.

'Listen, Di. Do you hear me? Quig's gone. Reliable information.'

She packed things away, quietly and efficiently, the sag of her shoulders showing relief.

'Are you sure?' she said.

He smothered hesitation and said, as sure as I can be.

'I would so like to go shopping,' she said. 'I get some of the right things and a lot of the wrong ones this way. Next week, I'm going shopping.'

The sheer silliness of this took his breath away. Jones hated fucking shopping.

'Did you hear me? Quig's gone for a job with money. I've been talking to Monica,' he said.

She dipped her head, bending from the waist to retrieve a paper bag from the floor. She was as supple as oiled rope.

'I know,' she said. 'I saw you. Sit down a minute. I can't talk to you when you're standing up, that's not levelling. And you need something to eat.'

Jones sat.

'OK, I'll believe Quig's gone for a while. Makes it easier to breathe. And thanks for being here. Thanks a *fucking* million.'

He felt ridiculously pleased.

'Look, you've got the outline of what's going to happen, and Saul's got the details. It's tomorrow. I don't want anyone else to be in danger. Especially Peg, and you've got to talk to Peg.'

'What date are we on?' he asked, reaching forward for the bread she was offering.

'The anniversary. Ten years ago tomorrow, when *I* came in through the shutters.'

'You were good at stealing, you know,' Jones said. 'And I'm looking forward to tomorrow. Always wanted to be a thief.'

Saul came back in the late afternoon, full of insouciance. He found Peg and Di sitting at the computer. Peg was learning how to use it. She was learning how to write. He saluted them and went away. They could hear him whisking round the house, checking every room, singing to himself, very light of foot. Peg and Di raised eyebrows and smiled at each other. He really was a nutcase, that Saul. A bit silly. *A Dreamer*, Peg said. *But a clever one*, Di said.

You won't tell Jones, what I told you, promise you won't tell Jones?

No, I never tell. You tell him yourself. And just you remember, no one gets arrested in my house.

Then it all lulled down, such peace and tranquillity, everything quiet, as if the castle keep had gone to sleep, quietly.

*

Saul Blythe and Diana Porteous sat in the gallery room, admiring it. In the last week, they had re-hung the lot, revising the format, as if preparing for an exhibition. It was part of refining, it was what collectors did, a way of taking stock. Madame de Belleroche occupied the same place as always, a small creature, demanding a lot of wall space, as if she was alive. That's what they all were to Saul; alive.

'They'll do it tomorrow. And when they've been and gone,' he said, 'we can really organise the cellar.'

'Can't keep you out of there,' she said.

'Fantastic space down there, wonderful ceiling. Look, darling, when we really expand, when this collection is bigger and better, well, that would be a great place. Early Victorian brickwork. Changing exhibitions in a wine cellar, under a great big arched ceiling.'

'Perhaps,' she said.

'You seem so much more confident,' Saul ventured. 'But you're always so diffident about the potential of that glorious cellar.'

She said nothing.

Another cigar; another log falling *thump* into the fire, a feeling of peace. She stirred.

'Whatever happens, I don't want them to be here for long. They need to take the pictures and go. I want it over. I want to be free to bury Thomas. With plumed horses and a gun carriage, he would have liked that.'

Her voice trailed away. Saul coughed as he looked at the text on his phone.

'They'll come in about eleven tomorrow evening. They have strict instructions. We leave the steel shutters part open, to make it easy. You and your horrible friends will be up here, either asleep or aggressively drunk. They know you're guarded and I've told them Jones is fierce. So you do the lights and the music, and they never enter the house. Lock the door to the cellar, and they can't get in anyway. They come, they see, they conquer. Later they learn, so Thomas said.'

'And where will you be?'

'I don't quite know. Guarding from a distance.'

'Gayle and Edward,' Di murmured. 'I'd be more worried if it was Beatrice.'

Saul thought of the smashed-up flat he had not mentioned: said nothing.

'It'll be fine,' he said. 'As long as you aren't alone. And there's no question of that.'

The fire was dying. She got up and rebuilt it with a single log. They needed sleep; she would let it die out and begin again in the morning. Logs from the pile in the yard, more in the basement, firelighters, twigs to get it going, the same method for fifty years. No shortcuts.

'Poor Gayle, poor Edward.'

Saul coughed.

'You're doing it again, Di,' he said.

'What is it I do?'

'Defend people, even the indefensible.'

'No one's indefensible,' she said. 'Except me. Shall we go through it again?'

The echo, like the sea, was uncomfortable to his ears.

Chapter Seventeen

It was a nice, calm day. What a terrible and useless word, *nice.*

You're getting blurred round the edges, Thomas, Di wrote. *Don't go away.*

Today's the anniversary. Ten years ago. I don't regret a minute of it.

There was one thing I wanted to ask you. Was there a favoured child? Was it Beatrice, or was it Gayle? Which of them did you love the most? It was Gayle you talked about most. Gayle made you laugh, like I did.

'We're having a party tonight,' Jones said to Peg at breakfast. 'Fresh fish.'

'Yuk,' Peg said.

'All right,' Jones said. 'Burgers and chips, if you like. It's my birthday.'

'Fuck off, Jones.'

'No, not really, but it's about time to celebrate. Been working hard.'

'Can we have real music?'

'OK. You teach me to boogie and I'll teach you to waltz,' Jones said.

'"Boogie"?'

There was music from the radio in the snug, noises in the cellar, with Saul down there, doing things. He wasn't coming to the party. He was going away soon.

Peg said, 'You all keep going into huddles and I don't like it. How do I know what to do if you don't give me any idea? OK, I've done a bit of listening, so I know half what's going down, and Di's told me stuff, but I want it from *you*, and I know it's not just a bloody party.'

Jones put down the coffee down in front of her, patted her shoulder in a condescending way meant to be reassuring.

'"Cos it's like this,' he said. 'This evening we are going to eat, drink and make merry. Bottle of vodka, anything you like. Matter of fact it might be better if we all got a bit tiddly, not too much, and then went deaf.'

'Suits me,' she said. 'And then someone's going to come along and do something we aren't suppose to notice. Like stealing something. Like them proper thieves you talked about. Is that it? Why can't you tell me exactly?'

Jones was serious, trying not to patronise.

'Because it's better for you that you don't know the details so you can't ever tell anyone else even if someone asks. And we've got to be very careful because these aren't *proper* thieves. Fucking amateurs and although they know what they want, being amateurs makes them unreliable and they don't like Di, not much they don't and we don't want them getting frustrated, do we? Di doesn't like them either and she's got a temper, too. So we've got to keep her upstairs and guard her. Close the doors and take no notice. Keep the music

loud. Don't want no violence, and there won't be as long as
she doesn't see them and they don't see her.'

'You mean you think it's Di might get violent?'

'Don't know, love, don't know. What they'll expect to hear,'
Jones said, 'is a party upstairs, and nothing downstairs. It
won't be till late on. So we eat well and drink up. You up for
it?'

'There won't be no police, will there?'

'Only me,' he said, and got serious. 'No question of that,
Peg. No question of that.'

'Not like the other time, then,' she said, 'like when you
arrested Di. And what about them coming back for her, and
all? Isn't she still in the frame because of her old man?'

Him and his big mouth. Jones slapped his head.

'Yeah, she is, too, but they're only thinking about it. It
won't be like any other time at all, oh no. Pity Saul won't be
here. Come on, girl, move yourself, this is going to be fun.'

A lot more fun than a walk with Di. *Got to clear my head*,
Di said. *Come with me, Peg*. So she walked with Di, wearing
Di's boots. It was nice, at first, walking with someone who
knew what a pickle she was really in and still wanted to walk
with her, but when Di said a walk, she meant a hike, right
round the corner of the coast and into the bay. To see what?
Birds, only bloody birds, I ask you. Peg preferred boats and
dreams. If she stayed here, she was going to have to learn to
ride a bike. They talked about Patrick; they talked about
spring and Peg's future and they looked at the sky. *Plenty of
time*, Di said. They didn't turn back until Peg begged and the
light began to go. The geese flew over their heads, cackling
like mad things. *That's the last of them for this year*, Di said
sadly, and whatever she was looking at, she kept on looking
around, Di did, as if she was watching out for somebody, and

Peg thought she was looking out for her, and then she made them both jog home.

Peg was exhausted. Not used to moving fast, and on that last run home, with Di almost skipping, Peg guessed that what Di intended to do was to wear them both out and she was right about that; you couldn't think of anything else when you were knackered. Maybe that was why she liked work.

A milky sky as the day faded. The house smelled sweet on every floor with fresh washing and Peg embraced the deep interior, knowing she was all right as long as she had hiding places, the linen room, the laundry, her favourite places, any-where but the cellar: she could never hide there. She soaked in a bath and changed her clothes, enjoying the ozone after-math of the cold air and deciding she just might do it again, because it really did fog up your head and make you want a drink, and yeah, there really was time for everything, and it was going to be a party, and whatever else happened was nothing to do with her. There was a slight celebratory air around the place downstairs; someone even mentioned Christmas. Only six weeks away; better plan for it and she reckoned she was safe until then and she started feeling good. She and Jones started cooking.

He left out the fresh fish. No fine-looking mackerel straight from the sea, grilled for a minute, and left on the plate with wide, staring eyes, that was what Peg had dreaded. Chili con carne, with oven chips, salads for the grown ups but not for her, followed by an old fashioned apple crumble Di got out of the freezer and put into the microwave. Vodka and coke, wine, and at the end she was feeling full and happy and it all took so long, it was already late. Jones was loading a tray with drinks to take up, went with the first consignment and came back for the rest, humming to himself, turning on the music, which she could hear from upstairs. They were all going to get lathered, and Jones was going to listen to her. Then all other sound was drowned out by the noise of the front door bell.

There was a bell pull on the outside, connected to the row of bells in the kitchen Peg had never noticed before. *Clang, clang, clang*, from that grand front door that was rarely used. Jones knew the door: it was how he had once come in to school at the beginning of term via the sea-side door, with grand steps and railings leading up to it. The ringing of the ancient bell on the wall was as loud as a fire siren. All of them stood and stared, not quite believing it. Jones put down the tray. Then the knocking began.

'Shit,' Jones said.

He went down the corridor from the snug to the door, peered out through the side window, and then went through the stained glass. The view was distorted but the colour of uniforms instantly recognisable.

'Police,' he shouted back. 'How do you open this fucking door?'

He knew he couldn't tell them to come round the back. He had to let them in. Jones followed instinct even when badly shaken. Like if any policeman knocked at the door like that, best let them in soonest; otherwise they'd bash the door down and he had done it often enough himself to know. It was difficult to turn the key and open the winter-damp door. Doors swelled here in winter, you wrenched them open, and slammed them shut, until they shrank again in summer. He pulled and they kicked, and the thing opened with a loud noise. There were two large men on the doorstep.

'Evening,' Jones said. 'You'd better come through. And you'd better have a fucking good reason for being here at this time of night. A very good fucking reason indeed. Otherwise you're right in the shit.'

It was an empty threat. Jones was in a state of shock. No one had told him about this. Di was getting in the clear, second post mortem refused, he knew; they were looking at nothing, even if they were still looking. He'd checked with his contact, it was all sweet, that end. His man had told him. Mrs P had fucking questions to answer still, always would have, but nothing yet and his man had lied. Fuck. They had come for Di, *again*.

Jones yelled his way back to the snug by shouting ahead of himself all the way, announcing the two uniformed men. Once he had led them back into the snug, he recognised one of them, the older one who had been there on the afternoon when Thomas had died in that chair over there. He watched as the man looked around, puzzled by uncertain remembrance and a touch of wariness. Been here before. Old man dead in chair, with a shabby girl, not nice, looked dodgy, didn't like her then or now. He fixed his eyes on Di. Must be her, all dressed up, it was her who had to be the one they wanted. He continued to fix his eyes on Di, who stood, supporting herself on a chair, looking back, challenging them. Jones looked too. He could see the door to the cellar was open. He felt the presence of Peg, lurking on the top of the stairs, hiding. *No police.* He'd promised.

The bigger, older man in uniform advanced a step towards Di and held out a piece of paper.

'Got a warrant for your arrest,' he said. 'For—'

'No, you fucking haven't!' Jones screamed. 'No, you fucking haven't. That's all been cleared up. Fucking warrant for fucking what? She didn't fucking poison him, she didn't. She might have waited, but she didn't kill him, she *fed him*, for God's sake. You can't fucking do this. You can't come arresting her NOW. No one told me. You've got it wrong, mate, wrong, fucking wrong.' He swung round to Di. 'Unless you really have found something new. Could they?'

The older one hesitated and then took one step further forward. The younger one hesitated, also, sensing trouble because there was this mad old geezer in front of him, talking shit. He had never been here before, found himself in a smallish, snug room full of good food smells that seemed so innocent. Got to get it right. He consulted his phone screen, verifying details better than a piece of paper.

'Hang on. We got a warrant for Elisabeth Smith. Otherwise known as Peg. For burglary, in London. She's here, isn't she?'

'Fuck me,' Jones said. 'For fucking *Peg*?'

Di stepped forward.

'You're in the wrong place,' she said. 'No one of that name here.'

The younger man looked at her and saw a young woman with awful hair, with a fierce, defensive voice, who looked as if she might spring to attack. She had to be the one. There was no other female in the room. He took another step towards her.

'No,' Jones said. 'It ain't her, fuckwit.'

He looked towards the open door to the cellar. That was where Peg had vanished. The door had been firmly closed before he left the room. Peg had panicked and taken the nearest exit and Christ, if she wanted to hide, that was the worst place tonight. Couldn't let her stay down there.

'She's not the one,' the older man said, his memory clearing.

'She's that widow Porteous. Come on, Di, where's the other one? We know she's here. Peg, she's called Peg. Wanted for theft and criminal damage.'

There was a horrible pause, in which Di said, 'No one of that name here. Some mistake, surely. Would you like a drink?'

'Shuttit, Di.' Jones went to the cellar door, shouted. 'You'd better come out, Peg.'

She was already halfway there. She had gone no further than a few steps down because the cellar frightened her as much as what she was going to meet upstairs, what shit, there was nothing frightened her as much as that. She had a fleeting, longing thought of the laundry room: should have run up, not down, then Di would have hid her, like she knew Di would have done. Di would have hid her until they could sort it, she knew she would, only she couldn't now, could she? Fucking Jones.

Peg came out from behind the door and Di saw in her face the unbearable terror of being locked away, the reality of punishment, and oh God, there were better ways of learning than this. Diana Porteous felt like the biggest traitor under the moon. *Traitor; one who betrays others.* Peg was shaking so much she could scarcely stand, and all the same, she was fighting tears. The question was in her eyes. *Who told on me?*

She looked at Di, pleadingly, then at Jones.

'What did you do, Peg?' He asked so softly.

'Warrant's for a dozen shop burglaries, criminal damage. I wouldn't say anything if I was you, Miss. Not yet.'

Peg opened her mouth, facing Jones, forcing the words out. She had so wanted to tell him. Di didn't make her feel ashamed; Jones did.

'All right, I tried to tell you, only you wouldn't listen. I

trashed some places, right? Not houses, shops. And I'm fucking ashamed of it. I didn't steal stuff, I just trashed it.'

Jones laughed, a great big bellow of grating laughter. It
went on and on.

'Is that all? Jesus, Love, I thought you'd fucking murdered
somebody.'

He turned to the first officer, calmer now.

'Can't quote what she said,' he said. 'Not without a cau-
tion, so don't even fucking try it.'

The man nodded. Jones looked at Peg.

'I'm sorry love, if you've done it, you've got to face the
music. Otherwise you'll be on the run for the rest of your life.
Look, mate,' he appealed to the older one, 'can't it wait until
tomorrow? I'll bring her in.' And even as he spoke, he knew
he'd blown any chance of that, 'cos he'd pissed them off and
so had Di.

'No, it's got to be now. Got to get her inside. Skipped bail
last time.'

Peg began to cry. 'I can't go now. I've got to be here . . . I've
got a *job*. I gotta be here, right now.'

Her terror was all-consuming. Everything else was forgotten, such as it being half past ten in the evening, thieves
coming in soon.

'If you've got to go, you're not going alone,' Di said.
'Jones'll go with you. Stay with you until you get bail. You're
not going alone. Jones, tell them I'll stand bail.'

'And what relation are you, madam?' the younger one said,
trying to keep the sneer out of his voice. 'Looks like you've
been harbouring a fugitive.'

'So?' Di said. 'Any time I get the chance. She's a great girl,
and she's coming back soonest, aren't you Peg? Go with her,
Jones. Bring her back.'

'But I can't . . .' Jones began, looking at Di, thinking of his promise. *Don't leave her alone, not tonight.* Saul said, she must not be alone when Gayle and Edward come.

'Please, *please*,' Peg wailed. 'Please come with me. Please.'

He looked at Peg, knowing what could happen, knowing that if she was alone, she was the kind to fall apart and beat her head against the wall of the cell until she drew blood and go mad, like Di did, and he couldn't bear it. It would be so different if she knew someone was waiting; it would make all the difference in the world.

He looked at Di and Di nodded back.

'Course I'll go with you, love. You're looking smashing, Peg, you really are, sweetheart, that's half the battle. Only you'll need a coat.'

Di's coat was on the back of the door. She handed it to Peg.

'What about you?' Jones asked Di, the decision already made.

'I'll manage. Just go.'

'I'm sorry, Di, I'm sorry,' Peg was saying. 'I'm sorry.'

Di touched her necklace, lightly. Peg's necklace, announcing her name.

'I know you are, Peg. Pity we couldn't do this our way. See you soon.'

They went out the front door. Di went with them as far as the front door, stood in the corridor, feeling the draught from the door, and then leant against it, trying to shut it. The door stuck and wouldn't budge. She left it, went back to the snug and felt sick. Should have hidden Peg, should've, should've, should've. Peg had already paid plenty; Peg was already mortified; Peg had already had her epiphany of self-loathing and

272

shame, just as she had; Peg was a person on her way to coming right, without prison. She was already making amends, she was learning, but Jones was right. If she did not go now, she would be on the run for the rest of her life. There would always be a warrant. But hell and damnation, going to prison was hell. She could not ration her own terror of the prison van, felt Peg's horror, and it made her want to shout with grief. Yes, there had to be punishment, but there must be better ways for those already punished.

Got to get her out of it.

Di lit a cigar and felt the silence. Remembered where she was.

Looked at her watch. Ten forty-five. The enemy were advancing, and she was entirely alone and suddenly, as the anger and pity faded, profoundly afraid.

Tell me a joke, Di, tell me a good one. Make me laugh. She had always been able to make him laugh. She could not laugh now. She counted on her fingers. Two people who hated her were about to enter Thomas's house. They must not know she was alone. Instinct told her not only that, but also told her it was all going to go horribly wrong. It was her time for punishment. For being a thief in their eyes, for taking away what belonged to them.

Panic struck her. She was so used to waiting for the axe to fall, for waiting for Thomas to die and dreading it, she could not bear waiting any longer, raced upstairs to the gallery room, to find that Jones had set the scene. The fire burned, the music played, the lights beamed on to pictures and how she loved this room. She changed the CD in the player so that it was not the music Peg liked, but Thomas's choice. She heard the sound of William Byrd's triumphal marches swelling to fill the room.

Then she ran.

Down the stairs, out of the house via the front door which was stuck looking shut, but not quite shut. It needed Jones's weight to ram it closed. She ran halfway to the pier along the footpath that skirted the sea, feeling the wind, stopped and ran on. Got near to the pier and stopped. She wanted to stay there all night, bunk down in one of the shelters, wait it out, go back at dawn, but she knew she could not. It was not a real choice. Running away never was.

Fishing competition, the pier full of men, fishing. Lights and radios, alternative life, a big swell on the sea. Men dressed for weather. She was icily cold in her almost party clothes; no phone, no boots, no coat, only responsibilities.

She jogged back. Went through the front door, pushing it as far towards shut as it would go, warped in winter, shrinking in summer. Needed a kick to close it. Di knew as soon as she was inside that *they* were there already. She tiptoed up the second set of stairs which led into the back of the gallery room, turned the music up even louder. Poured whisky out of the decanter, logged onto the computer, and waited.

In the last months of Thomas's life and since his illness, he had felt the cold, although nothing much else had changed, except the speech. She had found him a fur stole from the dressing up box which was still draped over the back of his chair. They joked about it. *If the Elizabethans could wear ermine, why not you? You look like a king.*

She looked at her fingers. Her fingers were covered with scars. So clumsy. Such a silly, corruptible girl. She drank the whisky.

They were here, in the cellar.

She looked at Madame de Belleroche, who nodded back.

The wind had got up. She lit another cigar, and talked to him.

Do you know Thomas, I loved you to extinction. And now you do this.

You invented a bad game.

She faced the screen and wrote, remembering that the door to the cellar, opened by Peg in her run to escape, was still open. She did not dare use the phone.

The camera winked discreetly in the furthest, hidden corner of the room.

She really could not care less.

Talk to me Thomas. Don't tell me this is what you meant.

She sat and wrote, fingers moving automatically over the keys, the screen her confessional.

She was back. Ten years ago. All it needed was a storm.

Chapter Eighteen

Set out too early, get there too early. Gayle was like that, always trusted to be early. Gayle was the one for the task; slim, sleek, athletic. She did not say how much she remembered about the house she was not going to enter.

You want to get there late rather than early, Beatrice said. *Get the goods and go. If there's any problems with the shutter, phone Saul.*

'He says not. No calls to be traced to him. He's the one who calls, never the other way round. If in any doubt at all, abort the mission.'

'Take Patrick, then: he knows the way in. He can do it.'

'NO. He stays with you, Beatrice. You're looking after the children. He's never going to go near that place ever again.'

Beatrice smiled and raised her eyebrows. Gayle was afraid that if darling Patrick returned to that house, he would never come back.

Do I lock him up, Beatrice asked, and Gayle said, *Yes, if you must.*

It sounded so simple. Park up the back road, go through the gate, into the yard. Prise up steel shutters, go down the ramp. Find two pictures, loosely wrapped in blue canvas, propped against a chest of drawers in front of a door. They're the ones, take and run, put them in the back of the car, drive away. Di and her mates would be drunk upstairs. Leave them alone. Take a torch if you want, but the switch is just inside the shutters, don't worry about the light, no one can see. You should be inside five minutes, max. Then, go. Gayle travelled equipped, a sheathed packing knife in the back pocket of her jeans, and a length of rope with a knotted end, the remnant of an old swing which she had found and looped round her waist. She would surely need neither, but they made her feel credible.

Easy, peasy.

Instead they were sitting in their big car, the one with the payments still owing, in a car park at the back of the town, waiting because they were early. *We must be precisely on time,* Gayle said.

Edward was not good at waiting. They should have eaten more than a sandwich; hunger was bad for the nerves. When they finally moved the car to the right spot, both of them were brittle with tension, Edward realising that it took more than a bit of bravery and expertise to be a burglar even when reclaiming your own. They parked fifty yards away from the fence that led on to Thomas's back yard, shuffled along the wall in silence. Rubber-soled shoes and the rope and the existence of the knife empowered Gayle. They found the rickety gate that led into the yard with a view of the downhill ramp and the shutters. *Remember when he had that vintage car he never used?* Edward said. Gayle did. *Sold it, never gave the money to us.* That gave a bit of extra anger, as if she needed it. This is *my* house, she repeated under her breath. Mine.

The tension eased a little as they approached. There were lights from the upstairs windows. Gayle thought she could hear music, although she could hear nothing but the sound of wind and the sea from the far side of the building and it was otherwise too silent. Once he could see that it was all exactly as it had been described, Edward felt easier, too. There were the steel shutters, which moved upwards with hardly a sound and fell back as quietly; there was the master switch that filled the room with light, or more aptly, the uplighters illuminating the vaulted ceiling, leaving the contours and corners of the place in various degrees of shade. A soft surface underfoot, almost sandy. It was all as it was supposed to look, and more than enough light to check a wristwatch. Five minutes, and then they would go. And then something changed. They started looking around instead of straight ahead. A spell came over Edward: his eyes grew wide.

The briefest of inspections showed that there were any number of objects and paintings down here. It was what they expected to see, but then it wasn't. There were a hundred paintings here, if all the objects wrapped in canvas and stacked against walls were paintings, but there were also things of different shapes, something which could have been a figure, something else which could have been a chair. Two parcels stood prominent against the rest, leaning against the old chest of drawers with others behind. Take them: Go.

Edward was peering into the corners where he could not see in this strange light, looking for more. He could not go with just the two. Gayle could not, either. She was not really on the same errand any more; it had turned into a mission as soon as she was inside and she knew it was where she had been before, playing as a child in a secret, wonderful place that had somehow been changed. Half a ceiling instead of a whole ceiling, lit to show the brickwork rather than the detail, and that strange sound of breathing that made it sound as if there was something live behind the wall, a voice from somewhere saying, *shush, shush, shush.* The memory of how she had loved this damp, smelly place. Compounded by the more recent memory of how Patrick had described it, albeit under duress.

Liar, liar, pants on fire, tell us about it. And his response. *I want Di. I want Peg.* Anyone but you. The cellar is full of wonderful things.

This place was seductively warm. Lit and warmed, full of treasure, bigger in diameter than their own flat. They were in the bowels of a treasure trove, and upstairs sat the Queen, holding court. Gayle had a dim memory of something else, of feeling safe and hearing music. She wanted to hear all the echoes, but Edward, in the meantime, was going mad. Eyes bigger than his stomach, that was Edward, amateur thief, suddenly seeing what else might be had. *Everything* here was valuable, otherwise why was it here? Why stop at two?

'Stop it,' she said. 'Stop it now. *Stop me.'*

'Got to check,' he muttered. 'Got to check. Are these the right ones? Are they really the best?'

Gayle was frightened of herself, remembered the instructions. Take those two and go, only to do so was beyond him. He started slashing at the canvas covers of the other things, carefully at first, and then fiercely, pushing stuff aside to see what was behind. It made Gayle want to scream. Five minutes had long gone. He moved faster and faster

'Ok, check these,' he said, selecting the most likely he had flung to one side. They looked well preserved in paper. They were not the two in front of the chest. The sea breathed from behind. He slashed at the paper. She shone the torch.

Two hideous, acrylic portraits by her own mother. Gayle gasped. Anger surged back. Edward was in overdrive, ignoring the original mission, consumed with greedy curiosity about the rest. How did he know Saul was giving him the best? Why was all this hidden if it was not equally precious, and what more precious things were behind the door? He could not stop moving and he had found a mallet. She knew then, that he was going to stay until he had either revealed or desecrated everything in this cellar. That he would even go through the wall in case there was more.

'There's better stuff down here,' he grunted. 'I'll find it, I'll find it.'

Di did this. Did this, did this. Di's making fools of us. My son wants Di. Everyone loves Di. The thief of souls, Gayle was chanting to herself, digging her long nails into her own arms. It was hot in there. Edward slashed and grunted.

Gayle could not stop him, moved away from him. She had lost him, just as she had lost herself. She walked in a circle and saw the stairs going up to a light at the top. She remembered that, too, the feeling of being three years old and falling down, rescued by Grandad and Father, lifted to safety.

She went up the stairs, dragged by memory, propelled by a white force of anger, looking for revenge for everything she had lost. Moved through an open door into a smallish, snug room with a dying fire and walls full of paintings, a room she remembered. Soft lights and warmth and nourishing food smells, the sort of ambience she wished she had ever created instead of the sterile places she had made. It was warm, even with the draught from somewhere. She paused, uncertainly, wanting to sit down, going on instead, propelled and possessed.

Two sets of stairs from the corridor beyond, up to the gallery room, where there had once been parties, when she was so small she could not remember her own size, before mother took them away, up and up, no longer caring who discovered her and what she might find. She had a knife, she had the rope round her waist, and she would hang her. Di did it. Di had planted the wrong paintings. Di corrupted everything. Di was the thief.

Gayle was weaving and unravelling, looking at things as she went along. This stairwell was full of paintings. She saw paintings of children on the beach, she saw herself, running free and innocent. She saw beauty. Little paintings on this stairwell, beach scenes with children, small paintings of sky. She saw that she had been lied to all along, that she could have had this, just as she could have had a father who loved her.

Ten minutes gone, and they should have been gone, too. The sound of the music penetrated from beyond the open door. It was always like this, Gayle remembered, full of soft sound, a childish memory of being taken to see Grandad, a terrifying treat becoming a pleasure, because he listened. Had he ever listened, had Father ever listened? Memories blurred into the day when Mummy said, don't go near them. Not Grandad or Grandma. And then, *Don't go near Daddy. Daddy's going to take you away. If you go to Daddy, you're on your own.*

The house was so opulent, in a Spartan way. Hard wood underfoot up the stairs, muffled by a runner of a carpet, the crooked walls full of things she had never dreamed of. And there was Di, so confidently, impudently alone, sitting with her back to the door. The biggest liar of all, look at her, she had even lied about the fact that she would not be alone. Di, who, in the absence of anyone else, was the root of all evil, the one who had taken away her father and was going to take away her son as well as her birthright. And who looked, now, disgustingly tranquil and self assured, in command of all she surveyed, with her back to the door, gazing at a screen, with a fur stole round her shoulders, dressed like a Duchess. Di, who had everything Gayle had ever wanted. Gayle touched the rope round her waist, could not wait to untie it as she tiptoed across, picked up the nearest thing, that heavy old phone on the desk, and smashed it over Di's head.

Di was not asleep. Better to sleep, if only she could, far preferable to wait out the hour in dreaming. They would be gone, soon, surely. No, they wouldn't. Nothing ever worked like that. She was dreaming, lost in déjà vu, ten years younger. She was writing now, in the same place as Thomas had been, ten years before. That night, long ago, when she had been fed through the steel shutters to find the keys to the old car, with the same music murmuring, the same sense of fate prevailing. Someone had come in and put a silken noose round his neck, bound his hands to the arms of the chair, and that was how she had seen him. A slow flashback running through her brain as to how she had found him then, when she had first entered the room, how she had felt when she had come in that time, how soon she had noticed him sitting with the light on his tears and seen the stillness of his bound hands. How ashamed she had been not to notice it first, transfixed as she was by the vision of Madame de Belleroche in her hat.

That was when I knew it was utterly wrong, Thomas. That stealing is always wrong, unless for the starving. And you were afraid for me. You wanted me to run, whatever happened to you. There was a maniac in the house, and I was just another child.

She was going to burn the house down. You wanted me to run away and leave you.

Di roused herself too late. Rubbed her eyes with the heel of her hand.

Felt a blow to the back of her head, a shattering crash and a black vision.

When she came round, there was a noose round her neck and no sign of the old phone. Her hands still covered the keyboard. The screen looked blurred. The instinct was to cover it, but she could not move. The light on the desk was angled towards her, blinding her. There was salt on her face. Gayle was hitting her and hit her again, swinging the knotted rope, catching Di's cheek and leaving a raw graze. The next blow was better, drew blood from the lips, the third, better still, opening a cut in the eyebrow. Gayle was not about to be moved by the evidence of the tears.

Gayle was looking at a face with smeared eyes and bruised lips, and Di's slender neck fastened to the chair with rope. The sight of her helpless made Gayle pause, unsatiated. She had made Di ugly and she was breathless: she could wait for a minute.

'Where are they?' she kept saying, 'Where are they, where's the really best pictures?'

'I don't know.'

'The hell you don't know. Patrick does.'

Angry again, Gayle yanked on the noose, exposing Di's neck, wanted to hack at it, felt around for the knife in the back pocket, could not find it. Oh God, she had given

284

Edward the silly knife. Then, from far below, there was the distant, dull sound of banging, hammering, reverberating through the house. Gayle paused, listening intently.

'That's my Edward,' she said. 'Thought you'd fooled us, didn't you? He's trying to get through that door.'

'No,' Di said. Her voice sounded like the mew of a cat in pain.

'And what's behind the door?'

'The sea,' Di said. Gayle slapped her, withdrew a hand sticky with blood, recoiled. She wiped her hand on her trousers and hid it behind her back.

'Why did he build that wall? What was he hiding behind?'

'The sea,' Di said. 'Only the sea.'

Gayle leaned into her, breath smelling of hunger.

'Edward doesn't think so. I'll have to go and help him and he pinched the knife. Then I'll come back and kill you.'

She tweaked the rope she had tied inexpertly to secure Di to the chair by the neck. Tight enough, she wasn't going anywhere. Gayle was as vicious as a dying wasp in autumn.

'Your husband is a fool, and you a fool to believe him,' Di whispered. 'Take what you came for.'

Gayle hit her again and then stopped. Enough done to vent her fury for a little while and now she wanted an audience. She wanted someone to watch her; she wanted praise for this and someone to say, *Look at what you've done, you clever woman.* The feeling of hysteria rose and fell and she was hungrier than ever. Her own house never had enough to eat. There had been good smells downstairs. She was distracted by the noise: she wanted Edward to see what she could do, and she wanted the knife.

'Go,' Di said, 'Please go. Please go before they find you. Go while you can.'

'You don't want us to find the best things. What's behind the door, then?' Gayle taunted. She ran back downstairs. The camera winked, unnoticed.

Di stared up at the ceiling, blinking. She could move her head downwards and she could write without looking at the keys. Only her fingers moved.

Your mother is behind that door, she wrote.

Blood burst from her cut eyebrow and trailed down her face.

She had kept faith. She never said it. *You must never tell them, Di. Better they think badly of me than know that their mother was mad. That she came in that night, bound me and beat me. She was going to set the house on fire – remember the kindling in the basement. The paraffin . . .*

Her hands moved slowly across the keys.

And then you arrived, my dearest dear. And She ran into the cellar to hide. Then the water came in.

Di heard the rain, pattering gently against the windows. No storm tonight, simply rain.

Don't let them set a fire. There is no paraffin. They won't be able to do it, but they might try. Don't, Gayle. Your mother's body is behind that door. Has been for ten years.

She tugged at the rope round her neck, tried to reach round to the back of her waistband to find her own little knife, could not reach. She stopped, exhausted, blinded, hearing nothing but the sound of her own breath. How long had Gayle been gone? One minute? Two? And she could she could feel a draught of cold air, touching the back of her neck. Her own, cold hands, clawing at the rope, and a murmured voice telling her, *Don't let that happen to you, girl. Remember how strong you are.*

The touch of a ghost and then her own, strong fingers

busily moving, more sensitive because she was half blind. She felt herself begin to black out again, fought it and then found she could move, wriggled like a fish in a net, fell over with the chair. She crawled towards the furthest door. She turned back, and saw her father walking out of the room.

'I only wanted to help,' he said, looking at her. 'I know about bodies. I know where she is. You never did tell on me, Di. I only wanted to help.' And then he was gone.

Hot as hell in the cellar. Edward was running out of steam, coming to his senses, sweat pouring into his eyes and making him pause to listen to himself, panting like a dog. STOP this, take what you came for. Remembered what Saul had said, two parcels wrapped in blue plastic canvas. *Blue* canvas. He looked around wildly. Another chest in the corner, another door behind. *Every room in this house has two doors.* There they were. Stop this, now. He looked around for his wife and Oh, God, she was gone.

Not gone. She was standing by the stairs they had been told to avoid and she was giggling and pointing.

'Come and see what I've done,' she said. 'It's quite a pretty picture, and I'm just going to go and finish it off.'

She darted back up the stairs. Edward picked up the two items wrapped in blue, unable to leave them even as real fear was lending wings, what had she done? Killed them all? *Don't go into the house – take two pictures and go, five minutes max.* They had blown it, mustn't blow it all. She should have stopped him. He should have stopped her.

Saul had promised he would not be far away. He was on the pier, increasingly uncomfortable. Jones was going to phone if anything went wrong, but he was also going to phone if everything went right and Saul's mobile was completely inert. He could not stay much longer on the pier, where he stuck out like a sore thumb, even in the almost dark. He looked like a thief doing a survey or some kind of official, with his binoculars and dark blue coat, when he should have been wearing the waterproofs in neon colours all the others were wearing. There were too many people fishing on the pier and a stern rain had begun. Saul pushed away an unoccupied chair and leaned over the rail and trained Jones's binoculars on the house, wishing there had been a vantage point where he could watch the back of the place rather than the front. Seeing lights in the upstairs room told him little, but he focused on the front façade all the same, better than nothing. Felt cold, very cold, looked again.

The redundant front door was open and light streamed from it. That damn door which was never open, was open now, it even had a security light and as he watched, the light seemed to increase. Saul stared in disbelief, frozen to the spot for a minute until someone tapped him on the shoulder and said, *Oi, mate, what are you doing, you're in the way of my line, do you mind?* and he found himself apologising, moving further down the pier towards the exit gate before finding another spot and bringing the binoculars to his eyes again. In time to see what looked like a figure, standing in front of the front door of the house, simply standing, before walking back down the steps again and moving away into darkness. Framed against a door that should never have been open.

Saul wanted to run away. He had never wanted to be in on the action, which was all going wrong, not according to plan, but hell, Di was tough, better at fighting than he ever would be. He tried to kid himself that he could just walk away and wait for the call with the excuse that he was not made for this, but then, he thought of the damn collection, the wonderful paintings and his heart missed several beats. Never mind Di, what about them? Saul left the pier and began to run. Five minutes on his long, grasshopper legs. He thought of the precious paintings in one of the most innovative private collections he had ever seen, ran faster, stopped, winded by coughing. His phone bleeped in his pocket and he was too breathless to answer. He straightened his cravat, like someone about to enter a grand front door.

Edward shouted after her. *Don't do it, Gayle, you silly bitch.* He should have gone faster but he could not let go of the paintings until he reached the corridor outside the big, long room he scarcely remembered from the last time. The paintings he carried were light but cumbersome and he was glued to them until he reached the door of the room. Should have listened. Don't go into the house: don't let Gayle go, either. You don't know what Gayle might do. Oh yes he did, he should have known. He found Gayle crouching by the door of the long room, whimpering and it was only then he dropped his burden and stared inside. A screen shone dully from the desk at the other end. The chair facing the desk was upturned. There were spatters of blood on the screen, blood on the floor and fragments of an old phone broken into pieces. The lights lit the paintings which furnished the room, made them look like living things gazing accusingly on to an otherwise empty space. He recoiled from it, wanting to shield his eyes. Gayle was holding the little knife she had grabbed back from him and her hand was trembling.

'What have you done, Gayle?' he whispered. 'What have you done?'

He heard the patter of the rain against the windows. The music stopped and the second, smaller phone on the desk rang, into silence. The answerphone message clicked in. Di's voice unnervingly loud. *No one's here at the moment, please leave a message*. Gayle screamed. Edward advanced into the empty room uncertainly.

'Behind you,' a voice said. 'Always look behind you.'

She was there, behind them, standing in the second doorway. She staggered and held onto the doorframe. Her eyes were smeared black, her face lividly bruised and bloodstained. She waved at them with her free hand, her face made infinitely worse by a ghastly smile and the whole presence of her made ever more awesome because of the unnerving calmness of her voice.

'Point made, hey, Gayle? You're the dangerous one, not Bea. Hope Patrick doesn't get the same treatment when he's naughty. Put the knife down.'

Gayle dropped it, watched Di, mesmerised. Why didn't they simply push her over, knock her to the ground, trample her into it and run? They didn't. A man and a woman with a knife against a hurt and skinny girl who looked like death and both of them paralysed. Both of them exhausted; an element of guilt and shame coming from sideways, maybe, and in Edward's case the dull knowledge that they would never get away with it. They had fucked up and they had smothered the place with traces of themselves. It was then he noticed the camera above the door. Di saw him looking, smiled her awful, sad grimace.

'At least you didn't set a fire. That would have been the worst.'

*

Saul came up the stairs, noisily. He was fighting for breath, stood wheezing in the doorway and even then they did not move.

'My, my,' he said, taking in the tableau with amazing aplomb even as he recovered his breath. 'Temper, temper.'

He looked at Di with indifferent concern, his faith in her limitless. She was still standing, after all.

'And with one bound, she was free,' he murmured. 'Really, this was not supposed to happen. This has really gone too far. This time we really will have to call the police. You have rather torn it, Edward. Can't you control your own wife?'

Di had moved across the room to lean against the desk, hiding the screen from view. Gayle stood behind Edward, put her arms round his waist, and hid her head in his back, weeping. He tried to dislodge her, but she clung like a limpet. Edward stopped trying to push her away, raised his eyes to heaven and glared at Saul.

'Definitely the next step,' Saul said. 'Shame about it, I loathe the police, but. Theft is definitely OK, but not bodily harm. That has to be punished.'

He moved towards the desk and lifted the phone. Di put her hand on his.

'No,' she said. 'No.'

'Why on earth not?'

'No one goes to prison.'

Even in extremis, Di could see he was acting and oddly triumphant; that he considered her indestructible and already halfway in command of the situation before he arrived and besides, an extremely distasteful sight at the moment. He would examine her later as he might a wounded canvas. For the moment, she was functioning and

Madame de Belleroche was still on the wall and that was all that mattered to him.

'No one's going to prison.' Di said.

'Oh, Di, how idiotic. Not even someone who's tried to kill you?'

'No one goes to prison,' she repeated. 'Especially not Patrick's mother.'

'Don't you see, Di?' Saul said eagerly, embracing the revised scenario. 'It's the perfect solution. That way, they're absolutely, thoroughly compromised. Just think, convicted of violence, whoever's going to believe any claim they make after they see what's on the cameras? And you don't even need to give them the paintings.'

He was suddenly excited by the idea, and in that moment, Di found him repellent.

'You cunt,' Edward said. 'You shit.'

Saul nodded. 'All of those. For God's sake, Di, let me phone.'

Even now, he was teasing them. Di could see the old, familiar terror in Edward's eyes. Gayle was weeping.

Di wiped her eyes again, and pinched her nose with two fingers, making the mess worse. It was difficult to see clearly, her head hurt and her knees were buckling. She looked towards Madame de Belleroche.

'Do you think you're safe to drive, Edward?' she asked him over her shoulder.

'Yes.'

'Did you find what you came for? Whatever it was?'

He hesitated. 'Yes.'

'Take Gayle home, then. And take whatever you want with you. It really doesn't matter what it is. Just GO. Go out the way you came in, but just go. No one is going to call the police.'

Saul stepped aside and allowed the two of them to stumble past. Edward shouted at Gayle to go first. Without a backward glance, he picked up the paintings he had left in the corridor. Saul followed them downstairs. As a precaution he followed them out of the house, chatting amiably, as to departing guests.

'I'll send you the DVDs,' he said. 'And do let me help you sell the paintings. You'll need a provenance and a legend to sell them highest and I am the best, you know, the very best.'

The rain had eased. The sky was calm and clear and a distant church clock struck the hour.

Saul walked back, closed the steel shutter firmly and went in the back door. Really, one could not get the staff these days, but all things considered, it had all worked out rather well. He went back upstairs. Must look after Di. That's what Thomas would have wanted.

Di had righted the chair, and was sitting in it, with her head rested on her arms on the desk, making little snuffling sounds, almost like snoring. The back of her head was matted with blood. Better get her cleaned up, see the nature of the damage.

Things to do, people to see. Now they could really get on. But first he took advantage, and leaned over her to see what she had written.

Your mother Christina is behind that door in the cellar. That's where she drowned.

Oh, fuck.

CHAPTER NINETEEN

There was a picture in her mind. An abstract design of black stripes, with flames of red curling between them, like a vision of fire behind bars. She had woken, screaming that the house was on fire; a room was on fire and the cellar was in flood.

'Oh, Di,' Saul said. 'Why didn't you tell me?'

'You wouldn't have wanted to know.'

The morning after, and she was drowsing downstairs, sitting in Thomas's chair in the snug, the chair with the life of its own, although she thought it still smelled of him and that made it the best place to be. The delirium had passed into calm: she was feeling safe and at the same time unbearably sad, clutching at the arms of the chair, wanting to consult Madame de Belleroche and instead looking at the nude on the wall and the smudge of a painting to the other side.

'Was there a storm?' she asked. 'There should have been a storm.'

'No storm,' Saul said. 'No fire or flood either.'

Water and aspirin was what she swallowed, and aspirin

was good for the heart, she remembered that; good for maintaining the health of it and useless at mending a broken one. Saul had no heart, or maybe he did, but it lived in his eyes and sometimes in his fingers and Saul was ministering to her and it was such a strange sensation that she struggled not to resist it. There was nothing tactile about Saul, and yet the brusque deftness of his therapy was oddly moving and soothing, as if she was being stroked in the hairdresser's with the same effect, leaving her calm and unusually submissive.

'Titanium white,' she said. 'Without titanium. No strength. Why did we have to do it all over again, Thomas? Like being in a play,' she said. *As if last time it was a rehearsal. First it was Thomas, and then it was me. Shut up, shut up, shut up.*

'More like a farce than a play,' Saul said. 'You were hit with a phone and a rope. She didn't even have a knife, wouldn't have known what to do with a knife. Stupid bitch. She isn't as mad as her mother. Christina was more dangerous than that.'

'Yes. She was.'

Saul waited for her to move between silence and loquacity, the way she did. Her skin was raw with wounds, she was light headed and she was being soaked and sponged like an invalid, and this was wrong, too. It was she who was the nurse. *Snip, snip,* Saul was cutting off her hair, the better to bathe the scalp wound, the hair so thin already she really couldn't care and she thought irrelevantly of paintings of women in hats. Thomas loved hats.

'I'll get a hat,' she said.

Saul was so precise, *snip, snip, snip* with his scissors, careful with his applications of warm water, lavender, witch hazel, tiger balm; a panoply of benign disinfectants which he used with the care of a fastidious hypochondriac armed with his own arsenal of remedies. Saul was giving her the tender loving care she had given to Thomas, with the difference that he was administering it with the careful attention to detail of someone preserving a precious object without any personal attachment to it. So, first discover the extent of the damage by careful swabbing and wiping away; then retouch with care and if it was hardly the same as being loved, it served the same purpose for the moment. There was none of the anxiety in his touch as there had been in hers towards Thomas; none of the complications and clumsiness caused by fear of causing pain, although there was perhaps a small amount of genuine concern towards the canvas on which he was working. There was something liberating in that, if only she could stop gabbling, mimicking other people's voices.

'Christina was in here on the night of the storm,' Di said. 'She'd been here earlier, pleading for love and money and he'd told her, no. She was angry, she stormed off and then she came back after dark. She was going to set a fire in the cellar. It reeked of paraffin, I remember that. Thomas was upstairs, working, listening to music. She hit him and tied him to the chair and she was going to strangle him. She told him that if she couldn't have what he had, he had to die, and his damn collection with him. That's when I came in. I cut the rope on his hands.'

She began to weep.

'Don't do that,' Jones said.

'That you, Jones?'

'Who the fuck else?'

The picture of the bars and the flames faded away, leaving instead the sight of Jones's big worried face, and the comforting feel of the chair.

'Was it just like you wrote?' Jones said, coming in.

'Yes. Thomas told me to go. He didn't want anyone else going up in flames. And then you all went and left him. And she'd gone down to the cellar to hide, and she fell and then the water came in. You shouldn't have read what I wrote. You shouldn't.'

'I think I may have an alternative career as an embalmer,' Saul muttered. 'And, my dear, it would appear from what you wrote, that this woman in the near vicinity, Christina, could do with even more extreme cosmetic treatment than you. Her in the cellar, I mean, but it'll be too late for all that, she must be a skeleton by now. Oh, my dear Di, all these years you knew she was dead down there. I do apologise, but I did read what you typed, it was there, and you do write well, you know. Admirably well taught.'

'You shouldn't have read it,' she repeated, stubbornly.

'Oh yes, *we* should. Somebody had to. And when we write, dear, we write it for someone to read, ultimately. Writing's not secret. You wanted *someone* to know.'

'And maybe Thomas did, too,' Jones said.

Saul wanted her to go on, pressed the cotton wool against the wound on the back of her head, hard enough to prompt her. Be cruel to be kind; they needed to know, Jones and he.

'You don't know that Thomas didn't kill her,' Jones said.

Di's speech was slower, more painful and considered until she shifted in her seat where everything was uncomfortable again and she was squinting at the light through swollen eyes. Saw the nude, and smiled at it. Thomas loved that painting, as well as that smudge on the wall.

'Course not. I knew that because of what Thomas was like and because of what I remembered. I saw him hurt – sick, weak and hurt and telling me to go when he should have been screaming for help for himself. Then there was the cellar, when I came in. She was already upstairs, hitting him, taunting him about the fire, throttling him before she heard me come in and she ran. She'd piled up stuff to start the fire, poured paraffin; I remembered the paraffin smell as soon as I crawled through. I saw the kindling, smelt it. And then,' Di touched her own throat, felt the outline of her mouth as if to prove it was there, swallowed hard. 'And because I knew about that kind of storm. Because I'd been down that cellar when I was a kid, and I know, when you get the northeast wind and the freak high tide, they can flood so fast, you couldn't run from it. And she'd be hiding in a corner, and then . . . '

'It's like the sea coming in from beneath and the rain from above combine and make a geyser, and the drains explode,' Jones said. He spoke as if he could see it and feel it. 'Seconds, not minutes.If she panicked and ran to hide, and stumbled . . . You can drown in two inches of water. There would have been three feet of it. That quick.'

'Even if I hadn't seen, I knew Thomas didn't kill her.'

Di's voice was clear. Saul's voice was dulcet and persuasive, pressing on, still needing to know.

'After you freed him and the police took you, he was left alone. C'mon, Di, what might he have done? You don't know. You don't know what he might have done.'

'Nothing,' Jones muttered.

Di concentrated on the ceiling, spoke slower, talking solely to him.

'I know what he did. The last time you saw him that night, he was weaker than I am now. If last night was a farce, ten years ago, it was a tragedy. Thomas didn't *do* anger. Sorrow, yes, anger, no. He thought she'd got out and run, he didn't go down there until the morning, found her face down in sand.

He tidied her up; he made the coffin himself and laid her to rest. Then he built the wall; he got someone from outside town to help, there was a lot of rebuilding going on after the floods, no one noticed. It took a week. He left a door, because he always wanted someone to know. As long as it wasn't her children who knew.'

Jones was leaning over her. Such a big, stupid, kind face it was; as big as the moon.

'I've fucking got it, kid. Isn't that why you waited for two hours after he died? In case he might say it? Say where she was? Say she was still down there?'

Di closed her eyes; tired, so tired.

'Yes.' she said. 'Yes, yes, YES.' She paused. 'It weighed on his mind in the last weeks. Yes, I thought that if they revived him from the dead, he might have said something, because it was always on his mind, and if he had said something, well, he'd be famous for nothing else, would he? Not for being a good man, only for being a man who drowned his wife.'

Her head lolled.

'Do you get it? Thomas Porteous, pervert, who kept his wife in the cellar for a decade. Roll up, roll up, roll up. Bugger the pictures, bugger what he wanted to do. But I promise you, Jones, that wasn't the only reason why I waited, I wanted him to go with his dignity. And I wanted to sit in this chair with him for as long as I could.'

She touched her mouth again, then her forehead, all swollen. Made another image in her head to displace what she could see. *When was the time we painted the shells? We'll do them in ink, better than paint, more translucent. They'll look like jewels.* Jones's big, rough, kind face loomed above her, his heavy chin dark with stubble.

'Peg,' she said. 'Tell me about Peg.'

'Going to be OK, Di. Getting bail tomorrow. Sleep now.'

'Peg likes maps,' she said.

There were noises off. She could remember the geese flying overhead and the painting of the shells.

'As for your dad, Di,' Jones said to her dreaming form and her ugly grazed face, 'Monica might have been right. Maybe he did just want to help.'

The men went upstairs.

'If it was you shopped Peg, Saul, I'll knock your block off,' Jones said.

'More likely a friend of yours, isn't it?'

Jones nodded.

'Women,' he said. 'Fucking women.'

They began to tidy up the mess of the gallery room.

'Those daughters were entitled to the paintings,' Jones said. 'They earned them fair and square. Fucking lousy thieves, that's all. Ever heard of *agent provocateur*? They were fucking set up, that's what they were. Tricked into crime by being given bait. Can't expect them not to do it, can you? Shouldn't have hit her, though, fucking out of order.'

'And thus they learn what they are,' Saul said, smoothly. 'Thieves. They'll still be quids in for something if they keep their heads. All perfectly honourable, better than they deserve. And Gayle caught on camera, beating up her father's little wife while her husband vandalises. They can't claim now. We've got them.'

'I got to tell you something,' Jones said, heavily. 'Half the cameras didn't work.'

'So? They don't know that, do they?'

*

Di touched the back of her head and felt damp, short hair and a crusted lump and the dull ache that was nothing to do with headache pain and more to do with the heart which aspirin could not cure. Saul would never understand about the cellar. She could not count how many people had found refuge in it over the years of her residence, let alone the years before. The wall was built for shelter as much as subterfuge. The cellar was always safe. A picture came to mind: that beautiful woman in the blowing pink skirt, trying to keep her hat on in a brisk breeze on the beach. Thought of how to keep the cellar open and yet keep it closed, thought of Peg and Patrick, thought ahead and thought of her father coming into the room.

I only want to help.

Maybe she could bury Thomas now.

Thomas, my love: Did I really know you? I feel a hundred years old.

The collection matters more than anything, doesn't it? Gayle must let Patrick come back. Gayle deserved better. Gayle was the child you loved best, the oldest, the one who remembered most. Gayle was the one who lost the most because her mother lied.

Let me sleep.

Jones and Paul paced the gallery room, tidying up. A pink sky loomed through the windows. They were drunk with fatigue, and for all that, it was thin Saul who led the way, with Jones plodding behind him, prodding him with comments. They were armed with black bin liners and sprays, cleaners to the manner born, dividing the tasks without argument. Saul did the wiping down, Jones the collection.

'And another thing,' Jones said. 'We're destroying evidence. Look at it.'

Saul looked at a piece of bloodied rope. 'My, my,' he said admiringly. 'Fancy her chewing her way through that. Put it in the big bag, will you? You know Di wants the evidence destroyed. She'd never have anyone put on trial, but they won't know that.'

The room was tidy and almost normal. The screen was clean. The bloodstained carpet was rolled against the wall.

'The difference is that no one else came in, this time,' Jones said.

Saul hesitated.

'When I was standing on the pier,' he said, 'Watching the front door and realising something was wrong, I thought I saw a man, framed in the light. He waited a little while, and then he went away. That's all I saw.'

Jones nodded. Saul touched the rope and winced at the feel of it, vicious and ineffectual, like the woman who wielded it. He was wondering at the same time, how long or short it would be before Di started defending her.

The pink light through the windows sank and turned grey and winter day unrolled. They worked on, yawning.

Saul leant against the desk. Soon it would be as if no one had been here at all, the room back to its former glory.

'Why did you get me to stick a camera in this room? When they were never going to come into the house?'

'For posterity,' Saul said, airily. 'Precaution, just in case.'

'Bollocks,' Jones said. 'You're a fucking bastard, Saul.'

'Bones,' Saul said, suddenly. 'Old bones, we have to get rid of old bones. I do want to use that space, potentially magnificent. So we've got to knock down the wall and get rid of the bones.'

Jones considered. 'I know of a man,' he said, slowly. 'But he's the last we could ask.'

'Fed to the fishes, in whole or in part? Burial at sea? Any ideas?' Saul rattled on.

'What Di says, goes. It's Di's house,' Jones said. 'Don't you ever forget it. This is *her* house. Always has been.'

They went downstairs. Jones secured the front door by jamming it closed. It would not be open again before the spring. The gallery was pristine, the house restored.

'The man on the steps. The one I saw. Was it her father?'

'I don't know,' Jones said, truthfully.

And then Saul was off on another tangent, laughing loudly, braying, his voice breaking up and coughing as he pointed to the wall in the snug, towards that little smudge of painting that hung without a frame on a hook near the big nude and next to the shelves with the teapots. He reached for it, took it down and turned it round. There was another painting on the back.

'Dürer,' he murmured, reverentially as if saying a prayer. 'It's only Dürer, painting St Jerome on a piece of wood, and then when you turn the panel over, he has the sun in a black sky. How Thomas had it, I don't know. We've been researching it for years, Thomas and me. The National Gallery has the equivalent. This is really for them. The worth of this smudge? Not a million. Nearer five. And they missed it. They came into the house, walked straight by and missed it.'

'You mean it's worth that, and they passed it by and took two fucking frauds?'

'Not frauds, no,' Saul said, hurt. 'Genuine works of art.'

Jones looked at the tiny, dirty painting. Turned it over and saw the glowing sun in the dark sky.

'You could have taken it,' Jones said slowly. 'You could have taken it any time and run.'

Saul nodded.

'Yes, I might have done, but the fact of the matter is, I don't really love it.'

'What's love got to do with it?' Jones said.

'Everything,' said Saul.

The next day, Di wrote to Raymond Forrest.

Dear Raymond, I think, I think, I think, that due to certain events, we might be able to insist on getting Thomas out of the morgue.

Late afternoon, early evening. In his office, which was devoid of any decoration, Raymond Forrest was staring at a blank wall and having a surprising day. He had received extraordinary communications from Edward, to the effect that Edward and family were no longer wanting to contest the will of the late Thos P; no longer wanted the second post mortem and that his son Patrick was free to visit whenever he wished. Raymond tried to phone his client, to leave a message, thought again and sent an email, to which he got a stunning reply in the form of an image.

Picture. *A funeral cortege, with plumed horses, drawing a gun carriage, in which the body lies in a coffin, draped with a blue cloth rather than a flag, the carriage flanked by men in dinner suits and ladies in evening dress. Petals and confetti are thrown, as if at a wedding. A life is being celebrated. Possible fanciful reconstruction of the funeral of the Duke of Wellington, like a picture in the dormitory.*

That's how I'd like it to be, Di wrote.

Raymond wrote back.

No. Thomas wanted his ashes scattered at sea.
So he did, she wrote. *So he did.*

And now, Raymond thought, let us see. Perhaps now the real Diana Porteous will emerge.

Now she has it all.

EPILOGUE

May, the next year
Di's diary.

We have learned to fish on the pier and we learned about birds in the sanctuary on the far side of the bay. The hide's a wooden shed, reached by a concrete path, flanked by a couple of benches at each corner of the route which led around the edge of a high bank, covered with every variety of wild flowers and foliage; it's a riot of intense colour at the best time of the year. The hide has nothing else in it but a bench and a narrow slit of a window, facing on the hidden lake, with the graceful reeds surrounding it, swaying in the breeze that made ripples in the calm water, and we watched, through the long window, peering through the slit.

    The plover's so small, you can scarcely see it without binoculars even from twenty-five yards, unless you had spectacular eyesight, like Patrick has. The bird's a mere fifteen centimetres; a tiny little wader with a furtive, hunched attitude that has nothing to do with confidence, often seen alone, feeds singly; has rapid, graceful movement. The plumage changes with the season, so that it's always disguised. It loves to eat spiders and other insects, is partial to very small, marine snails invisible to the eye. It's a dowdy little tough, with a limited voice, that either goes wit, wit wit, *or makes a dry* prr, prr, prr; *Thomas could mimic it, so can I. I taught him, I'm teaching Patrick.*

Then I said, My, it's close in here. Look out, look, over there. It's an egret, has legs like a pair of wands.

And then beyond that on the far bank of the hidden lake, there was a figure coming over the near horizon, wearing a cap and carrying either a stick or a gun. The illusion of him shimmered.

Then I looked again.

It was only Jones, coming to find us.

And Gayle is coming to fetch Patrick tomorrow.

On a day like this, Thomas, I really think I've got it all.
Better than gold.

ACKNOWLEDGEMENTS

With profound thanks to Angus Neil, for the ideas, the passion for painting, and the generous imparting of knowledge, some of which I've retained.

You have enriched my life and sharpened my eyes.

All mistakes are my own.